IMPEA...
OFFENSE

IMPEACHABLE
OFFENSE

BASED ON THE BEST-SELLING
LEFT BEHIND® SERIES

NEESA HART

TYNDALE HOUSE PUBLISHERS, INC.   WHEATON, ILLINOIS

Visit Tyndale's exciting Web site at www.tyndale.com

Discover the latest about the Left Behind series at www.leftbehind.com

Written and developed in association with Tekno Books, Green Bay, Wisconsin.

Designed by Alyssa Force

Edited by James Cain

Published in association with the literary agency of Alive Communications, Inc., 7680 Goddard Street, Suite 200, Colorado Springs, CO 80920.

Published in association with the literary agency of Sterling Lord Literistic, New York, NY.

Library of Congress Cataloging-in-Publication Data

Hart, Neesa.
    Impeachable offense : based on the best-selling Left behind series / Neesa Hart.
        p. cm.
    ISBN 1-4143-0036-0 (sc)
        1. Rapture (Christian eschatology)—Fiction.   2. Church and state—Fiction.
I. LaHaye, Tim F. Left behind series.   II. Title.
    PS3558.A68357147 2004
    813'.6—dc22   2004009721

Printed in the United States of America

07   06   05   04
5   4   3   2   1

What People Are Saying
about the Left Behind Series

"This is the most successful Christian-fiction series ever."
Publishers Weekly

"Tim LaHaye and Jerry B. Jenkins . . . are doing for Christian fiction what John Grisham did for courtroom thrillers."
TIME

"The authors' style continues to be thoroughly captivating and keeps the reader glued to the book, wondering what will happen next. And it leaves the reader hungry for more."
Christian Retailing

"Combines Tom Clancy–like suspense with touches of romance, high-tech flash and Biblical references."
The New York Times

"It's not your mama's Christian fiction anymore."
The Dallas Morning News

"Wildly popular—and highly controversial."
USA Today

"Christian thriller. Prophecy-based fiction. Juiced-up morality tale. Call it what you like, the Left Behind series . . . now has a label its creators could never have predicted: blockbuster success."
Entertainment Weekly

1

Rumor had it that White House Chief of Staff Brad Benton was a hard man to kill. And after the second failed attempt on his life in the last three days, even Brad wasn't going to dispute the rumor.

He was learning to be very, very careful.

As he gingerly pushed open the door of the Shiloh Baptist Church in northwest Washington, D.C., he wondered how he'd reached a point in his political career where someone—anyone—wanted him dead so badly.

For that matter, he wondered how he could have lived through the events of the past few days. He'd survived the Rapture, which had claimed his wife and three children as well as nearly a third of the world's population. Then he had surrendered his life at last to Christ, only to land in a minefield of death and danger. He'd seen evidence that pointed to the murder of the former White House press secretary. He'd witnessed the horrifying rise to power of a man whom he believed to be the biblically foretold Antichrist. And then the assassination attempts: a shooter had missed him and wounded his closest aide instead. And tonight an explosion had blasted his Alexandria apartment to bits less than an hour ago.

By the grace of God, he was still alive. He had a few cuts and bruises, though nothing major. He was lucky. That explosion had been meant to kill him.

Brad looked around the building but saw nothing out of place. He drew a weary breath. From where he stood in the foyer, he could see a light on in the back of the church, but the sanctuary seemed to be deserted.

"Hello?" Brad's fear began to mount as he surveyed the empty church. Marcus, at least, had promised to meet him here. Maybe Brad wasn't the only person in trouble right now. Brad had lost too many friends already. He began praying silently.

Brad entered the sanctuary. The only source of light in the room came from the platform area, where a warm glow emanated from the baptistery, which was mounted high in the front wall. The room was peaceful, in stark contrast to the chaos he'd left behind at his Alexandria apartment.

During the cab ride he'd realized just what could have happened to him. The tremors in his hands had spread to his entire body as shock began to set in. After the initial adrenaline rush from being on the edge of the explosion had faded, he'd felt weak and shaken.

But now the adrenaline came surging back.

"Mr. Benton?"

Brad turned to find an elderly black man watching him. He wore jeans and a work shirt with the name *Solomon* embroidered over the left pocket. He was leaning on the handle of a push broom. Brad wondered why he hadn't seen him at first.

"Yes?" Brad's eyes dropped to the embroidered pocket. "Were you expecting me, Solomon?"

"Yes, sir." The man grinned. One of his front teeth was

missing. "That's me. Solomon Grady." He patted the pocket that featured his name. "I used to work as a mechanic for the Metro system before I retired. I just never got out of the habit of wearing my name on my shirt."

"Brad Benton," he said, holding out his hand. Even in emergencies, Brad's long-ingrained political manners held sway. "Thank you for letting me in tonight. Do you know where Marcus is? Is he all right?"

"The reverend told me to expect you," Solomon said. "He's on his way. He's fine."

Brad swayed slightly with relief and exhaustion. "Good. Great, in fact. I'll wait here."

Solomon frowned. His face crumpled into a mass of wrinkles while he surveyed Brad. "I think maybe you'd better sit down, son. Looks like you've been through a lot tonight."

"Marcus told you?"

"Yes." He walked toward Brad, his steps stuttering on the wood floor as he moved in the rhythm of the very old. But Solomon's hand was steady and warm on Brad's shoulder as it eased him into a pew. "Why don't you sit, boy? After runnin' from everybody who's after you, you've got to be tired."

"Yeah." Brad knew he should say something more, but his mind was still reeling. He couldn't think of anything else to say that wouldn't take more explaining than he was capable of right now.

Solomon didn't seem to mind. "You just rest a minute, Mr. Benton, and I'll get you a cup of coffee. I put on a fresh pot when the reverend called."

Solomon shuffled away, leaving Brad alone in the sanctuary's semidarkness. If there had ever been a time in his life that needed prayer, this was it. Brad braced his forearms on the pew in front of him and dropped his head.

"Dear God," he whispered. The events of the last hours began to replay through his mind. "Thank You for saving my life." Had Brad not gotten that urge to check his mail tonight, he'd have been a dead man. Brad was pretty sure where that urge had come from.

That thought made him remember his daughter's letter. It was what he'd gone to the mailbox to look for. He slipped a hand inside the coat and retrieved the envelope from his pocket. Gently, he ran his finger over the elegant curves of his daughter's handwriting. Megan, his beautiful, artistic daughter who had been so much wiser than he. She was gone now, taken in the Rapture, but she'd told him last Thursday night that she'd mailed him a letter. Was it possible that so few days had passed since then? It seemed like a lifetime.

Brad carefully slit the seal on the envelope. This was the last tangible communication he would receive in this lifetime from his family. Grief and wonder washed over him as he prepared to read his daughter's words.

> *Dearest Daddy—*
>
> *Don't know why I felt like writing. E-mail is easier, but I was talking to a friend today about 1 and 2 Timothy, and how intimate and personal Paul is in those two letters.*
>
> *I realized that I hadn't told you how much we miss you. I know you're doing important work in D.C., but I really wish you'd come home.*
>
> *It's selfish, I know, and I promise not to whine. Everyone's doing okay. Mom's having a hard time with you gone, but we're helping. Even Brad's not being too much of a pain, though he's taking this 'man of the house' stuff way too seriously. You never should have told him that.*

My recital went well. Wish you could have been there. That stupid Middle East peace conference! Mom said she got the tape for you.

I miss you so much, and I want you to know that I pray for you every day. I pray that God will use you to do great and mighty things for Him. Stay strong, Dad. I know it's really hard. Mom tries not to tell us too much, but she lets things slip sometimes. It's got to be the pits being surrounded by people who are hostile every day. I can't even imagine what you must go through. Just know that we love you very much and can't wait until you're home.

By the way, I'm not sure if Mom told you, but I'm auditioning for a summer concert orchestra that tours the U.S. One of their stops is in D.C. If I make it, I'll be able to see you—and maybe you can catch the concert!

Love you tons,
Megan

A rush of tears filled his eyes. One slipped past his lashes and rolled down his cheek as he rubbed the pad of his thumb over her signature. How precious his life had been, how wonderful his family had been, and—fool that he was—he hadn't even known it. He'd taken for granted that his loved ones would always be there for him, that his political successes and ambitions were important enough to spend the last year away from Christine and his three teenage children. Had he been the Christian man they had thought he was, the man he had professed to be, then he wouldn't be sitting here now—alone, tired, and on the run. He'd be with them, gone from this world, safe in God's hands.

Behind him, he heard the door creak open. He turned so fast that the letter in his hands floated to the floor.

But it was Marcus, not some new death threat. "Good. You're here."

Brad reached down and picked up the letter, waiting for his heart to stop racing and his breath to return before he could say anything. He folded the paper carefully, put it in his pocket, and looked up at his friend.

The preacher was carrying a grocery bag and a black duffel. Clad in a sweatshirt and jeans, the normally dapper Marcus looked disheveled, as if he'd barely taken the time to pull his clothes on before rushing out the door. He set down his burden on the back pew and hurried toward Brad. "How are you? Are you all right?"

Brad considered the questions. "Define *all right*," he said at last.

"Let's stick with healthy."

"I'm in one piece," Brad said. "It's more than I deserve."

Marcus looked him up and down. "You're sure you weren't hurt?"

"I'm sure. I think I'm falling apart mentally, but I'm fine physically."

"How far were you from the explosion when you called me?"

"Half a block or so."

"I don't imagine you were thinking clearly."

"I wasn't. But I was thinking. I'm rattled but fine."

"Thank God." Marcus dropped into the pew behind Brad. "I've been praying since you called me. Did you have any trouble getting here?

"I don't think so. I had the cab do some evasive maneuvers. Somebody might have been tailing me, but if so, I lost him. I got out a few blocks ago and walked the last bit. I didn't see anyone."

"Good," Marcus said. "I stopped to pick up some things I thought you might need. Sorry I'm late."

Brad marveled at the deep sense of kinship and brother-hood he felt with this man. Just as it was hard to believe that so much had happened in the past few days, so he found it incomprehensible that he'd known Marcus only a short time. Of course, Brad had met Marcus Dumont, a prominent black evangelist, several times at political rallies and events over the past few years, but it had taken the extraordinary event of the Rapture and the global terror that had ensued to bring the two of them together as friends and new Christian brothers.

Despite his profession and his reputation as one of the D.C. area's finest preachers, Marcus had never accepted his own need for Jesus and the grace of God. Only after the Rapture, only after he'd been forced to admit his rebellion against God, had the dynamic minister humbled himself to ask for God's mercy. Only then had he felt the peace that came from surrendering his life to Christ.

Brad understood. Despite their differences, he saw a lot of himself in his new friend.

"You look exhausted," Marcus told him.

"Yeah." Brad remembered being tired before the evening had blown up in his face. A flight across town later, he felt like he'd been hit by a truck. "I think the shock is setting in." He looked over his shoulder. "Solomon went to get coffee. He was waiting when I got here."

Marcus leaned back in the pew. "He's a good man. He's hurting right now. He lost his wife, his son, and his three grandchildren."

"Oh no." Brad scrubbed a hand over his face. A day's worth of whiskers chafed the inside of his palm. "That poor man. Sometimes I forget I'm not the only one suffering. There's so much grief out there now. You've told me that it's going to get worse. It's tough to believe that it can. I can't imagine what the next seven years are going to be like.

I'm trying to brace myself for the battle, but I have to tell you—" he gave Marcus a look—"that I almost wish I'd been killed in that explosion. At least my suffering would be over."

"But not your mission." Marcus's smile was wry. "God's not finished with you yet. Sorry."

"Good point." Brad shook his head. "My mission. Did you ever wish God had picked someone else?"

"Sure," Marcus said. "And not just me. It's a bit of a paraphrase, but in his second letter to Timothy, Paul reminds his friend that not every person in God's service is designed for the same use. Some are set apart and refined for special purposes. Some are bronze, some are silver, some are gold, and some are just wood and clay." He chuckled. "There have been times when I was perfectly satisfied to be inferior workmanship—God's wood and clay. I never asked to be bronze or silver or gold. Nor did I want to be."

"I guess I'm not alone, then," Brad said. "Does thinking that make me a bad Christian?"

Marcus laughed. The sound was a balm to Brad's raw nerves. If Marcus could still find a reason to laugh right now, then surely everything was not as bleak as it seemed.

"Are you kidding?" Marcus asked. "Do you know how many men and women in the Bible tried to tell God to look somewhere else? Most of the great ones said it at least once. Moses, Gideon, Samson, Rachel, Paul. All of them wanted out of the bargain at one time or another."

A silence settled between the two men.

When Brad didn't respond to his comment, Marcus sighed. "I know it's hard, brother. I guess the real question is: If you'd known this was coming before you accepted Christ, would you still have done it?"

Brad thought that over. He considered the way his new-found faith had sustained and encouraged him, the way he'd found hope in the belief that he would see his family again. He was sure his loved ones were safe in the arms of Jesus. He thought about the deep bond he felt with his new Christian friends, about the courage he'd found over the past few days in the knowledge that God was protecting him and that God was with him always. Solemnly, Brad nodded. "Yeah. I would have."

"Then wanting to get out of the line of fire doesn't make you a bad Christian. It makes you normal." Marcus leaned forward and braced his arms on the pew. "Tell me exactly what happened tonight."

Brad paused for a second to gather his thoughts. Finally, he recounted how he'd driven his government-issue vehicle home, parked on his street in Alexandria, then unlocked the door of his apartment. As he prepared to go inside, he'd belatedly remembered that he was expecting a letter from his daughter, so he'd propped his briefcase in the door so he wouldn't have to fiddle with the locks again and headed back to check the mail. "I was pulling the mail out of my box when the apartment blew. I was out of the blast zone, sheltered by the foyer's enclosing wall and the building's elevator and staircase. If I'd been inside my apartment—"

"Hmm. It was meant for you then, not a blast meant to destroy something they thought might be in your place. Must have been on a timer triggered by the front door."

"That's what I figured, too."

"Did anyone see you on the street after the explosion?"

"Yes, but it was pretty chaotic. People were running out into the street to see what was going on. One man spoke to me at the mailbox, but I didn't recognize him."

"What did you say to him?" Marcus asked.

"That I was in the neighborhood visiting someone."

"Did you recognize him?"

"I think he lives three doors down."

"Good. If he hasn't seen you before, he probably believed you. If he's a neighbor, it doesn't matter. If whoever planted the bomb sent him to be sure the building blew with you in it, he clearly didn't recognize you. If so, that might buy you some time."

"That's doubtful," Brad said. "Whoever tried to kill me is going to know I escaped as soon as the police can't produce a body."

"I know, but the fire won't be out for most of the night, and the investigation won't start until tomorrow. Your briefcase was in the apartment and your car was parked in the street. For tonight, at least, I bet they'll assume you were there. I think it'll be at least a day or two before they start looking for you."

"Unless they had someone watching the house or keeping tabs on me."

"If they'd been watching the house for you, I doubt you'd have made it here alive. I think they believe that you were in that apartment when it went up."

"Probably true," Brad agreed. His head had begun to throb.

"If you don't go back there for a while—"

"I can't stay away," Brad said. "I have to get the briefcase back."

Marcus's eyebrows rose. "You think it could have survived?"

"Sure. It's fireproof," Brad explained. "And it's supposed to be bombproof. White House issue. They give them to all the staff in case we have to transport classified materials."

"What's so important that you need to risk your life for it?"

"Christine's Bible," Brad said. "I need it back."

"Oh." Marcus sighed. "I'm sorry, Brad."

"Once the fire is out, I'll look for it. If I can, anyway. I'm sure they'll have the place roped off as a crime scene, at least until they finish the arson investigation."

"I'm still not sure how wise it would be for you to go back there," Marcus said. "Until we can figure out who's behind this, I think the best thing for you to do is stay out of sight."

"I'm getting that Bible," Brad insisted. "And some other things from my apartment, too, if they survived. I had a suitcase with the clothes Christine and the kids were wearing when they disappeared and a few other personal items. I brought those things back from California. The bag was in the back bedroom, so there might have been enough of the structure between it and the explosion to keep the suitcase out of the worst of the blast. The walls were soundproofed. It was one of the reasons I chose the building."

Brad frowned slightly as he remembered unpacking those clothes the night after he'd raced back to Washington for Senator Max Arnold's Capitol Hill hearings. Less than a day had passed before he'd felt the need to put the items back in the suitcase. He'd been unable to bear the thought of them lying in the half-filled drawers of his rented furniture. Christine had been the family-heirloom type. The cold sterility of his Alexandria apartment had bothered her, and though he'd resisted most of her attempts to personalize it for him, there had been a few pictures and mementos she'd insisted he have there to warm up the space.

Still, he had known, somehow, that she would never have been comfortable there. That thought had driven him to repack the clothes. In the back of his mind had been the idea that he should probably look into moving them somewhere more personal. It looked like his instincts had been more accurate than he could have ever guessed. "Those clothes and Christine's Bible—they're the only things in that whole place that really matter to me."

"I can understand that. We'll figure out a way to get in and search for them," Marcus assured him. "I'll ask Mariette in the morning. If there's a person alive who would have a better idea of how to access and search through a disaster area, it would be the assistant director of FEMA."

"You didn't call them when you heard about the explosion, did you? I'd hate to think they were grieving over me." Mariette Arnold and her college-aged son, Randal, were the other two members of Brad's new Christian circle. Both were now believers like him, and along with Marcus they had formed a tight bond since the events of the Rapture. Brad considered them his new family.

"No," Marcus told him. "I called Solomon to ask him to unlock the place for you, but I wanted to talk to you before I told anyone else what had happened and that you were fine."

"I can understand that, but I think we should call them now. Even though it's late, I'd hate for them to see something on the news and assume the worst."

"You've got a point. Besides, we'll need their help. I'm sure Mariette's got connections with the Alexandria police, and I'm equally sure that she's done her share of fire investigation and recovery."

"Okay, then." Brad closed his eyes and dropped his head to his forearm. "Randal's going to expect me at work tomorrow. We need to think about what to tell him. Not to mention what we should tell the White House." Having Mariette's son as his driver had been an answer to prayer— for both Mariette and Brad. Mariette appreciated the influence Brad had on Randal. Randal reminded Brad of his own son. Though new to his faith, Randal had the same zeal and fire that Brad Jr. had possessed. Randal would be outraged, Brad knew, that the bombing had happened. Unless he was properly briefed, he would probably be ready to brandish his spiritual sword in warfare for his friend Brad. And if he did, what would happen to him? To his mother?

"I can call now—," Marcus began.

"No," Brad said, lifting his head. "On second thought, we shouldn't call them from here. I've probably already put you at risk by being here. I don't want to endanger them, too."

Marcus tapped his fingers on the back of the pew. "What's your gut tell you about who's after you?"

Brad glanced over his shoulder. Though they were alone in the sanctuary—Solomon still had not returned—he felt the need to lower his voice. "There's only one possibility I can think of."

"You think it's related to the sniper in the parking garage?"

A few days ago, in a widely publicized incident, a sniper had breached White House security and fired at Brad in the parking garage. But Brad had moved at the critical instant, wholly by chance, and his longtime assistant, Emma Pettit, had been shot in his place. She was recovering now in a Washington hospital. At the time, Brad had wanted to believe the attack was a random act of terrorism, but tonight's events had convinced him he really had been the target.

"It has to be," he said. "And I think I know why. I've seen evidence that proves there's a murder cover-up going on among the president's closest advisors. I don't know who's behind George Ramiro's disappearance, but I do know that whoever killed him doesn't like the questions I'm asking. And it has to be a White House insider behind it. To get access to the garage the way he did, the shooter either had to be an insider or had to have a connection deep inside the White House."

"And you think the same person is behind the bomb?"

"It's unlikely that two sets of people are trying to kill me," Brad said. "So, yes, that's my guess."

Marcus nodded. "We might have to consider another possibility, Brad."

"What possibility?"

"That maybe there *are* two sets of people who want you dead. Sure, you've been pushing hard to find out what happened to George Ramiro. But remember what happened today when you and the rest of President Fitzhugh's staff watched Carpathia's little stunt at the UN? Have you considered the fact that you were apparently the only person in that room in the White House—and if the evening news is to be believed, maybe the only person in the world—who saw what happened and remembers that Nicolae Carpathia murdered those two men at the United Nations? If Carpathia's powerful enough to persuade everyone who saw it except you to overlook the horror of that, then don't you think he's powerful enough to know you weren't fooled?"

Brad's eyes widened. That afternoon, he'd watched from the White House conference room as Nicolae Carpathia—the charismatic Romanian former president and new secretary-general of the UN—murdered two of his supporters.

Given the way Carpathia appeared to fulfill certain biblical prophecies about the end times, Brad and his friends were convinced that he was not a mere man—or would not remain one for long. They believed he was the Antichrist, the biblically foretold deadly enemy of all things Christian, the harbinger of the end of days.

Brad had watched Carpathia's mesmerizing performance, understanding why people were so easily deceived by the good-looking, intelligent Romanian. And then the unspeakable had happened. Carpathia had calmly taken a firearm from one of the security guards, ordered his friend and financial backer, Jonathan Stonagal, to his knees in front of Joshua Todd-Cothran, the former head of the London Exchange, and had summarily murdered them both. Carpathia had then turned to the observers in the room and on camera and expressed his sorrow and grief at witnessing the murder-suicide of his good friends. One by one, the occupants of the room had concurred that they'd seen Jonathan Stonagal wrestle the gun from the security guard, then kill himself and Todd-Cothran. Even the watchers in the White House had nodded at that assessment. Except for Brad.

Brad had immediately turned to his friends for advice. They had met, prayed together, and discussed the future facing them. Brad had finally left the meeting to drive home, where he'd triggered the bomb that had nearly taken his life. But not until just this instant, under Marcus's prodding, had it occurred to him that there might be personal ramifications because he'd witnessed the crime and, apparently, was the sole person to retain the memory of the murders.

"Do you think it's possible?"

"Marcus, you don't think—"

"I know it sounds incredible, but hear me out. That sniper attack might have had nothing to do with Ramiro's death. Didn't you say that the attack happened the same day you asked Emma to begin digging up information for you on Carpathia?" Marcus asked.

Brad blinked away the memory of Emma crumpling to the floor of the garage, shot in the torso and bleeding heavily. "Yes."

"And now this bomb thing." Marcus shook his head. "It may seem unbelievable, but I think that you have to at least consider the idea—"

"—that the enemy of God is after me? Unbelievable . . . you could say that."

"All I'm saying is, we can't rule it out."

The idea made Brad shudder. He was a government servant, a behind-the-scenes guy not even well liked by President Fitzhugh and his people. He'd been given the job because it was politically expedient for Fitzhugh, but he'd been shut out of real power early on. In Brad's opinion, he wasn't important enough to be targeted by the Antichrist.

"I just can't believe that, Marcus. I'm not in a position to threaten him. Besides, if Nicolae Carpathia is after me and he's powerful enough to know I wasn't deceived, then I have to believe that he wouldn't have missed . . . twice."

"That's probably true," Marcus conceded.

"So if for no other reason than to retain my own sanity, I have to believe this is about George." He rubbed a hand over his face. "I'll lose my mind if I dwell on the other possibility."

"You really believe that someone would want to murder you simply because you're asking questions about Ramiro?"

"Someone murdered *him*," Brad pointed out. "If whatever's at stake was worth killing for once, it's got to be worth killing for again." He shook his head. "Admittedly, they have the worst timing in history. I'm sure that whoever killed George didn't plan on having the Rapture happen the same night. If the killers had known that they'd have a convenient excuse to cover up George's loss. They never would have issued the statement that he'd resigned. They just would have let people think he had disappeared in the Rapture along with everyone else."

"And no one would have gone looking."

"Exactly. But the resignation story—that was suspicious. Not calling to try to find George when the president needed him to deal with the media after the Rapture was even more suspicious. It meant that they knew he was gone."

"Then why—?"

"Because it was too late. They'd let the news out before the Rapture, and they couldn't take it back. After all, explanations had to be made right away about where George was, once he wasn't where he was supposed to be. Then, after the disappearances, we were all in the Sit Room. No one knew what had happened, but the story about George's resignation had already begun to circulate. Once the cover-up had begun, it was too risky to change stories midstream. By the time we knew what was happening, it was too late to just point to the Rapture and say, 'A pity about poor old George.'"

"I can see that," Marcus said. "But that still raises the question of why someone wanted George dead. Why do you think they had him killed?"

"I'm not sure. But I have my suspicions about that," Brad told him. "And I have a reporter friend looking into it."

"Then he could be in danger, too."

"She," Brad said with a frown as he thought of Liza Cannley, the young reporter for the *Los Angeles Times* he'd tipped about the potential story. "I've thought about that, but I didn't take it seriously until tonight."

"You'll have to warn her."

"She's in California. I'll call her as soon as I can get to a secure phone. I don't think I should use my cell phone right now, not even my private one."

"That's probably wise," Marcus assured him. "You know, if you flew out to California tomorrow, you could tell her in person."

Brad heard the distinct sound of Solomon's feet shuffling as he approached. Brad wondered where the man had been all this time. And he wondered what he should do next. He didn't want to leave D.C. How could he make Marcus understand that he wasn't the type to run? He felt like a fugitive, and he hated it. Not only that, but Brad felt like God wanted him to be in D.C. for the long term. It was, as Marcus had said, Brad's mission to be here. But Solomon spoke before Brad had a chance to express that to Marcus.

"Reverend," Solomon said.

"Hello, Solomon. Thank you for coming in tonight."

"Oh, no problem. No problem." He handed Brad a mug of steaming coffee. "Sorry it took me so long. I went ahead and made up your room."

Brad glanced at Marcus, his eyebrows raised in inquiry. "Room?"

"We have a small apartment in the back," Marcus explained. "It's left over from the building's former life as a Presbyterian church. We bought the property several years ago."

"We converted the rectory to Sunday school space," Solomon added, "but we decided to leave the parson's apartment intact."

"For times like this," Marcus said.

Brad took a sip of the coffee. No cream, no sugar, and strong enough to melt a spoon. Solomon must have thought Brad needed fortification.

Marcus stood and reached for the bags he'd placed on the back pew. He tossed the duffel bag to Brad. "I brought you some clothes. I think we're close enough in size for me to guess right."

Brad picked up the duffel bag as he forced himself to stand. His legs ached, and his head was pounding. "Thanks. I hadn't even thought that far ahead."

Marcus picked up the grocery sack. "I got you some basics, too, enough food to get you through the night. Tomorrow, we can talk about what you ought to do."

"You're sure it's okay for me to stay here?"

Solomon's laugh was genuine and warm. "Lord, son, what kind of stewards of God's house would we be if we refused shelter to one of His neediest children in a time like this? Come on. I'll show you to your room."

Carrying the bags, as well as mental burdens far heavier, Brad followed Solomon into safety for the night.

2

For what seemed like the tenth time in the last few days, Mariette Arnold was awakened by a shocking phone call.

"Someone tried to kill Brad *again?*" She gripped the receiver as she sank to the side of her bed. A weak shaft of early morning sunlight glinted through the blinds on her Silver Spring house's window. Her mind reeled with the shock of Marcus's news. "Is he all right?"

"He's fine," Marcus told her.

She shot a glance at the clock on her nightstand. It was just after six in the morning. "Where is he? If his home was blown up, where did he stay last night?"

"I thought about bringing him here to my house," Marcus said, "but we both decided that might be too risky. Someone might be watching me. He'd managed to shake any pursuers before he came to the church. We wanted to keep it that way."

Mariette tucked her feet beneath her as a sudden chill seemed to pervade the room. Since the night of the sniper attack, she knew Brad had suspected someone might be after him. Last night's bomb confirmed it. For her, as well as him. "You think he's under surveillance, then?"

"I'm not sure. But if he is, then I probably am, too. We've been tied together in so many ways the last few days."

And with me, as well, Mariette thought. She reached for a pillow and pulled it to her chest. The idea of being watched left her feeling vulnerable and exposed. "So where did Brad go?"

"I knew a place I thought was safe, at least for last night."

But not for long, she thought. Not if Brad was being watched and followed. Not if someone was determined to do him in. "What's he going to do?" Mariette's mind was racing in a thousand directions as she considered the implications of these events. Someone was trying to murder her brother in Christ. More upsetting, Brad was her son's boss. If Brad was standing in the bull's-eye of the target, then Randal would be right there beside him. Mariette's heart started to pound.

Had the world not been in the grip of its biggest crisis in history, with the national and global infrastructure and economy teetering on the precipice of disaster in the wake of the Rapture, this would be the biggest story of the year. Brad and Randal would be surrounded by federal agents determined to protect them.

Instead, it seemed only Brad's closest circle of friends was even aware of the peril. Mariette began to pray. They would all need God's hand over them.

"I advised Brad to get out of town for a couple of days, out of the city," Marcus said.

"What about his job?" she said.

"He called in late last night from a pay phone." Marcus sounded both distressed and amused. "He told an aide that he had a few personal matters to attend to. Since no one knew about the bombing there yet, they gave it to him without comment."

"Personal matters, huh? That's an understatement," Mariette said. She mulled the situation over for a moment. A trip far away might help. Brad could go home to California and see to his personal business. His last trip home, taken after his family had disappeared, had been cut short by the Senate hearings Mariette's ex-husband, Senator Max Arnold, had used to inconvenience nearly everyone on the eastern seaboard.

At the hearings, Brad had confided to her that he still felt the need to spend some time back home, remembering his family and saying good-bye to them. Had it been only a few days ago? It seemed impossible to believe.

If Brad went back to California, it would certainly make it clear whether he was being stalked or if he was merely a convenient target here in D.C., one who was less protected than Fitz and most of his staff. Whoever was watching him would surely be more visible. Maybe he'd even shake his stalker entirely for a bit.

"That's probably a good idea," she said.

"I'm not sure his problems won't follow him, but it will at least give him a chance to see if they're really there. It might bring them out into the open. Maybe the trip will also help him figure out what he should do next."

"Does he think this is about the press secretary's death?"

"Yes." Marcus paused. "Mariette, I don't want to say too much on the phone. I'm not sure how secure the line is."

She shuddered at the thought that Brad's enemies might know him well enough in so short a time to have tapped her line or Marcus's, but she'd lived in this town too long not to accept the possibility.

She also had to address the possibility that her son, as

Brad's driver, might be at risk. "What are we going to do about Randal?"

"That's another reason Brad's thinking about taking some time off. He doesn't want Randal caught in the middle if someone's got him in the crosshairs."

"Randal will be outraged," she said, knowing her son would immediately want to do something—fight back, launch an investigation, expose the killers. His youthful sense of justice would have him demanding action, however inappropriate that action was for an unseasoned college boy.

"I'm sure he will," Marcus said. "Brad feels that if he's out of the way for a while, Randal will not only be safer, but maybe he'll also be in a position to hear things." He paused. "The drivers talk."

"That's what Randal says." Despite her discomfort at the idea that her son was caught up in this intrigue, she'd felt God telling her that she needed to surrender Randal to Him. It was a hard lesson to learn, and she wondered if this was God's way of testing her. Maybe it was. Some lessons were just too hard. "Think about what you're saying, Marcus. I can't believe this."

"I know. But it's real, and we have to deal with it."

At that comment, her training and professional expertise kicked in. She focused on the potential needs of Brad's situation. "Does he need food, clothes, anything?"

"Actually, there is something you can do. Brad wants a little assistance recovering some belongings back at his apartment."

Mariette listened while Marcus explained, mentally developing a strategy as she heard about Brad's desire to recover his briefcase and suitcase from the charred house.

"I thought you might know someone who could help," Marcus said.

"We'd have to get access," she mused. "I'm sure the police and the arson squad are already on the scene."

"No doubt."

"If we don't want to draw suspicion, we'll have to send someone in who'd have an official reason to be there."

"That's what I thought. One of us would draw attention."

"And I guess we'd better get on this before the White House sends someone over. Especially if we think—" She stopped short of mentioning George Ramiro again. Marcus was right—someone really could be listening. She wouldn't bet on it, but neither did she think taking precautions was a bad thing.

"Yes," Marcus agreed. "Exactly."

Mariette thought for a moment, then realized the answer was obvious, if not particularly palatable to her. "I think I can swing it. Let me make a phone call."

"Brad's desperate for that Bible," Marcus said.

"I understand." She knew how she and Randal both had taken to poring over her mother's Bible, both for the content and for the tangible link it provided to the past and the person they'd loved and lost. As much as Brad was struggling with the guilt and grief of losing his wife in the Rapture she'd had every reason to believe he'd experience along with her, losing Christine's Bible would devastate him. "I'll call you back in a few minutes. Have you talked to Brad? Is he going? If so, when's he leaving?"

"Later this morning. I'd like to be able to tell him we're taking care of getting his things from the apartment, if it's possible. You'll tell Randal about last night's excitement? Tell him to play dumb?"

"I will. Thanks for the heads-up, Marcus."

Mariette stared at the receiver a moment, her thoughts in turmoil. Could this really be happening? Could she really be involved in something like this? Despite her ex-husband's high-profile political career, Mariette never dreamed that she could be pulled into the political intrigue that permeated the Washington culture. Her divorce a few years back from Senator Max Arnold, presidential candidate and unfaithful husband, had been messy and widely publicized, souring her on politicians and their games forever. She'd somehow managed to distance herself from the political arena despite her position at FEMA.

But she realized she'd built a career and a reputation on her ability to overcome tremendous odds in bringing relief to strangers. Just in the past few days she'd organized, with the help of her office, enough food aid to keep most of the country from starving in these turbulent times. Even now, she was spearheading a joint operation with the New York mayor's office to continue providing goods and services into that city despite the near collapse of its infrastructure. If she could do that for strangers, then surely she could do something for a man who was her Christian brother and rapidly becoming a mentor and a father figure to her son.

Determinedly, she dialed the phone.

"This better be important," said a sleepy and irritated voice on the other end.

"It is," Mariette told her ex-husband. "I need a favor."

★   ★   ★

Just after 8:00 a.m., Brad slipped into Emma's room at George Washington Hospital. She was resting quietly. The steady hum and beep of the monitors reassured him that his assistant and close friend was still on the road to recovery.

Early this morning, Marcus had finally persuaded him to leave town for a few days. Brad had resisted because leaving town now felt a little too much like running to him. No one, he knew, was going to believe he'd died in that fire when his body didn't turn up. By tomorrow morning, if not now, whoever was after him would know that he'd escaped alive if they compared the time of the explosion and the time of his call for a few days off. And he was sure they'd do that.

He also wasn't comfortable with the idea of leaving the fate of Christine's Bible in someone else's hands, but Marcus had insisted that Mariette was in the best position to handle it.

Brad still wasn't convinced he should go until he'd remembered Liza Cannley. If his suspicions were correct, and if whoever murdered George Ramiro was now trying to silence him as well, then his journalist friend who'd been asking questions at his request was also in danger. Brad owed her a warning and an explanation. Calling her on the phone might actually increase that danger. He'd put her in the path of danger, so he owed her a personal warning to get her out of it.

And Marcus was right about the rest of it, too. A trip to California would give him time to tend to the business he'd left unfinished when he'd been so precipitously called back to Washington for Max Arnold's hearings. Brad had lost his family in the Rapture. He had to come to terms with it.

Though reluctant to leave, Brad had finally agreed. He'd booked a flight out of Reagan National for later that morning, a round trip. He wasn't ceding the field in Washington to his enemies for very long. Just long enough to get his life straightened out a little bit. He was glad he'd had time to stop by and visit with Emma before he had to go to the airport. She was regaining strength every day. Knowing her like he did, it wouldn't surprise him if she insisted on going back to work as soon as she was halfway healed.

Brad studied his old friend for a few moments, wishing he knew the status of her soul. Brad had been afraid to witness to her right after his conversion. He'd been terrified that not only had he gotten her killed but that his reluctance to talk to her about Jesus had caused her to face eternal damnation. Emma had asked him about his newfound faith in the short time before the paramedics had arrived. Later, he'd talked to her about God's grace and his new relationship with Jesus as he'd sat next to her hospital bed, but she had been unable to respond.

He hated leaving her now. He wanted to know that she'd heard him. If the last few days had taught him anything, he'd learned that life was short and unpredictable. He would never again make the mistake of not seizing every moment and every opportunity to do what God wanted him to do.

With a slight sigh, Brad slipped an envelope beneath Emma's hand where it lay on top of the blanket. Her sister would be here soon, so he knew he wasn't leaving her alone for long, but he had been unable to bear the thought of leaving town without telling her why. Emma had been with him a long time. She was, in many ways, the last member of his family still here with him.

"God," he whispered, "please continue to watch over Emma. Protect her from harm and heal her. Please."

And then he slipped from the room.

★ ★ ★

Randal Arnold was sitting in the hot seat.

He forced himself not to squirm under the close scrutiny of Harmon Drake, head of the U.S. Secret Service, and Charley Swelder, President Fitzhugh's top policy advisor. His mother had told him that morning about Brad's near miss the night before. Outraged, Randal had wanted to go to work and demand that the White House security detail call in the FBI to see who was targeting his boss. Surely Brad had enough clout that someone would take this seriously.

But his mother had talked him out of that. Brad had decided to exercise caution, and, she'd argued, so should they.

Randal hadn't liked it, but he had finally yielded when Mariette told him about her conversation with Marcus and their mutual agreement that with Brad out of town Randal would be able to move freely among the drivers and support staff at the White House. He would be in the best position to overhear potentially valuable information, especially if he managed to persuade the staff that he was oblivious to Brad's suspicions of foul play.

The plan had seemed easy enough—until he reported to the motor pool. From there he was summoned to Drake's office. Randal had entered the director's office to find Charley Swelder and Drake faced off across Drake's desk, apparently in the middle of a heated exchange. Both men turned to stare at Randal like he was some kind of alien.

"I can . . . um . . . come back," he'd offered.

Drake had given Swelder a quelling glance, then looked at Randal. "No. No, that's not necessary. I've been waiting for you. Sit down."

Looking nervously at the furious Swelder, Randal had taken the other seat across from Drake's desk. Both men had pinned him with the kind of close scrutiny that reminded him of the time his father caught him stealing money from his wallet.

But Randal was pretty sure that even an upset Max Arnold would have quailed before the angry men staring at him right now.

"Mr. Arnold," Harmon Drake said. "I assume you are

aware of what happened at Mr. Benton's apartment last night."

"I heard about it on the news," Randal said. "I'm really worried. I was hoping I'd find out more here." He glanced at each man in turn. He didn't want them to know what he knew. "Do you have any idea what caused the explosion? Is Mr. Benton dead?"

"No," Charley said. His voice sounded like he'd been chewing on glass for most of the night. "As for Brad, we have reason to believe he survived the attack. And we don't know who's behind it. At least not yet. The Alexandria police haven't told us if they've found anything of interest in the apartment. All they'll say is that the arson investigators are looking into things."

"Arson?" Randal looked at them, wide-eyed. "You mean, they think it might not have been an accident?"

Drake shot Swelder a look. "All fires require an arson investigation," he said vaguely.

"Oh." Randal leaned back in his chair. "'Cause I was thinking it could have been a gas leak or something. I mean, ever since those manhole covers in Georgetown started blowing off, they've known something was wrong with the gas lines around here. You hear about this kind of thing every now and then, you know. Somebody's house blowing up and all."

"Could be," Drake said. "We'll know for certain when we see the report."

"How long does a report like that usually take?"

Drake's expression turned wry. "With the Alexandria police, always too long." He made a dismissive gesture with his hand. "I'll have jurisdiction over the scene within the hour. I've already got agents there to assist with the investigation."

Or take it over, Randal thought. Mariette had told him

about Brad's briefcase. She'd been on her way to meet Max when Randal left for work. He had no idea what contacts his father might have that would allow him access to a site that, evidently, even the Secret Service had not been able to penetrate, but he knew that Max Arnold was a master at getting his own way. If anyone could get it done, he could.

"Does the Service know a lot about arson?" Randal asked. "I thought you guys just did counterfeit money and bank fraud and stuff." He couldn't resist that gibe.

Charley Swelder, Randal noted, looked positively gleeful, while the storm clouds gathering in Drake's eyes told him he'd scored a direct hit.

"We're in the business of protecting the first family and the leaders of the administration," Drake said, his voice hard. "Arson or not, Mr. Benton's security has been compromised."

"Compromised? Is that what you call having Mr. Benton's apartment blown to bits?" Randal said.

Drake made a noise like a steam engine about to explode.

Time to back off, Randal thought. "I can see why you'd want agents working the site. I mean, there might be clues or something about who did this that an arson investigator could miss."

Randal suspected, however, that they weren't alone in their desire to get their hands on Brad's apartment. If Brad was right and if whoever killed George was really after him, then plenty of people were going to want access to that apartment and its contents. Brad had told Randal about the photos of George Ramiro's corpse. No one else knew that Brad had sent them to his reporter friend in California. If Brad's would-be assailant suspected Brad still had those pictures, he'd want them back. Still plaguing Randal was the fact that Brad had no idea who had sent the pictures and why. The entire thing smacked of foul play, and Randal wondered just what he should tell Harmon Drake.

He decided to err on the side of caution. Fully aware that Charley Swelder and the rest of the White House believed that the only reason Brad had hired him was because his father was Max Arnold, Randal covered himself with the guise of an inexperienced politician's son who was impressed to simply be in the corridors of power. At the moment, it seemed to Randal that no one was trustworthy outside his small circle of family and friends. He wouldn't trust these men with his lunch money at the best of times. These certainly weren't the best of times.

Drake was still watching him closely. "You can understand why I need to ask you a few questions, Mr. Arnold."

"Sure," Randal said. "I'll do anything to help you and Mr. Benton." He could feel Charley Swelder's gaze boring into him, searching for some indication that Randal knew more than he was saying.

Drake steepled his fingers beneath his chin. In the dim morning light, his face looked ominous. The semi-shadowed interior of his office gave the whole scene an intimidating atmosphere that Randal was sure Drake used to his advantage. "You weren't there at Brad's residence at the time of the explosion. Is that right?"

"Yes, sir."

Swelder looked surprised. "You didn't drive Mr. Benton home?"

"No, sir. Mr. Benton decided to drive himself home. He asked me to meet him here in the morning."

Drake's eyes narrowed. "Does Mr. Benton usually drive himself home?"

"I've only worked for him for a few days," Randal answered, "so I'm not sure. But he's been so busy I don't know what his regular habits are. Sometimes I park my car in the reserved lot at his apartment so I can drive him into the city, but if he's got a real early appointment or something, I catch the Metro in. My mom lives in Silver Spring. It's convenient." He glanced from one man to the other. Both seemed to be irritated by his apparent sincerity. He'd had no idea until now that he had such a knack for acting. "The car stays at Mr. Benton's house," he assured them, "or I bring it back here." He hesitated. "That's regulations."

Drake grunted in response. "Did Benton mention anything to you about the previous attempt on his life?"

"The sniper?" Randal asked. "Sure. He told me that's why he needed a driver. His car is impounded, and you guys didn't think it was safe for him to be driving himself around in a regular car—you know, one without the bulletproof glass." He looked at Charley Swelder. "I think Mr. Swelder told him to get a driver."

"It was a mutual decision," Drake said. "We felt we could better protect him that way."

Swelder seemed to be losing patience with this give-and-take. "Did Benton say anything about who he thought was responsible for that attack?"

"He said you guys were looking into that," Randal hedged. He gave them a deliberately innocent look. "Still no suspects?"

Several seconds of silence ticked by while Drake appeared to weigh the truthfulness of his answer. Randal could feel his pulse racing as he tried to sit motionless beneath the probing stare. His palms felt damp, and he had to resist the urge to wipe them on his khakis.

Finally, Drake broke the silence. "We're still pursuing several leads. We don't know anything definitive yet."

Randal felt air begin to fill his lungs again. He hadn't even realized he'd stopped breathing. "Oh," was all he could manage.

"You haven't seen or heard anything suspicious since you've been driving Benton?" Drake pressed.

"Not that I recall," Randal said, "but I gotta admit, I wasn't really looking. I mean, I didn't think it was still a problem now that you guys were taking care of it and everything." He drummed his fingers lightly on the arm of his chair. "I'll be paying attention now, though. You can believe that."

Drake held Randal's gaze a few seconds longer, then dismissed him with a wave of his hand, apparently feeling he'd gleaned all he could from him. "Don't worry about that. You've told us what we need to know."

Randal stood, hoping they wouldn't notice the slight wobble in his knees. "I . . . uh . . . guess I should just go back to the motor pool. I mean, until we hear about Mr. Benton."

"Yes," Swelder told him. "That's the best place for you."

"Okay. Hey, if I think of anything else, you want me to tell you?"

Drake reached in his top drawer and pulled out a business card. "That's the number for the agent I have handling this case. You can talk to him."

Randal took the card. "Great. I'll try to think about it today—you know, see if I can come up with something."

"Don't worry about it, Mr. Arnold," Drake told him. "I assure you we have the matter under control."

Randal turned to go but was halted by Charley Swelder. "Arnold."

"Yes, sir?"

"Do call me if you hear from Benton."

"Oh. Yes, sir. Sure."

"And I think it would be best," Drake added, "if you talked to Mr. Swelder first. If Mr. Benton is hiding somewhere, I'm certain he wouldn't want news of that getting around."

"You can count on me," Randal said. He wondered if he sounded as ridiculous as he felt.

"Good. Good." Charley Swelder looked him over. "You know, I was hesitant when Benton said he wanted to hire you. I wasn't sure how Max Arnold's son was going to fit in around here."

"Well, my dad might not agree with the president's politics, but he'd be the first to tell you that no one has the right to violate the security of the office."

Drake nodded. "True enough. I don't like these kinds of things happening in my house."

"I'm sure you'll find whoever did this, sir," Randal said. "I just hope you find him before it's too late."

"Count on it," Drake retorted, and something in his tone made Randal shudder.

"Is that all?"

Swelder nodded. "Get back to work, Arnold. We'll let you know if we need anything else."

"Yes, sir," Randal said and fled the room.

3

Later that afternoon, Brad cast a furtive glance over his shoulder as he headed toward the rental car lot at Los Angeles International Airport. He hated living like this—hated feeling trapped and on the run. Hated being unable to do his job or see his friends. His instincts had told him to show up at the White House that morning as if nothing had happened. He figured he had mere hours before whoever was after him knew he was still alive. If it was someone at the White House, they'd known since last night when he'd called in to request time off. He'd bought the plane ticket in his own name with a credit card, and if his suspicions were correct, either act—the call or the ticket purchase—would verify to his assailants that they'd failed to kill him once again.

Marcus and Mariette both, however, had urged him to make this trip despite the fact that his enemies would certainly know he'd survived the explosion. He needed to see to his house, which now stood empty. He needed clothes and whatever other personal items he could find there to replace the ones ruined in the explosion, and he needed time in the empty space to fully realize the loss of Christine and the kids.

And then there was Liza Cannley. Marcus was right. If, indeed, George Ramiro's murderers were the people after Brad, then Liza wouldn't be safe either. Brad took another look around at the congested traffic of Los Angeles. The Rapture had caused havoc here as planes had fallen from the sky and cars with no drivers had careened into barriers and other vehicles. The massive airport was still operating, but at an extremely limited capacity, with only two runways open and many of the parking garages still impassable.

He noticed the crumpled shell of a parking shuttle when he sprinted across the lot. Would anything, he wondered, ever feel normal again? At least he had the comfort of knowing that Mariette was retrieving Christine's Bible from his bombed-out apartment. If his briefcase was still intact and still there amid the charred rubble, she'd find it. He trusted Mariette, Marcus, and Randal with his life and knew that they'd all understand the importance of the Bible to him. Mariette would fight hard to make sure she got it for him.

He rented a nondescript midsized car with a cell phone and navigated his way to the interstate before he tried dialing Liza Cannley's mobile number. When she answered on the second ring, Brad breathed a sigh of relief. "Good, you're there. This is Brad Benton."

"Where did you think I'd be?"

Dead, he thought, *or on the run.* "Never mind. I'm in town. I need to meet you somewhere so we can talk."

"Funny you should mention that," she said with an edge to her voice. "I was planning to call you today. I was looking at some—"

"Liza," he said, "if you don't mind, I'd rather not talk about this over the phone."

She seemed taken aback. "Okay, you may have a point. Where do you want to meet?"

"I'm leaving the airport now." He briefly considered his options. "You remember the bench where I talked to you last time?"

"Yes."

"Meet me there in two hours."

★ ★ ★

Mariette entered the Pennsylvania Avenue coffee shop just below the Hill and stopped to shake the rain off her umbrella. In typical spring fashion, Washington had turned rainy and wet. She'd found something ironic in the fact that nature, at least, seemed to be tramping on completely unaffected by the approaching demise of human life on earth.

She spotted Max near the back of the crowded restaurant and headed his way. He looked older, she thought, even though she'd seen him less than a week before at the hearings. "Hi," she said as she took the other seat at his table.

Without comment, Max reached under his chair and produced a badly scarred briefcase. He looked at her a moment before sliding it over to her. "I don't know what's in that, but it's popular."

"What do you mean?" Mariette's fingers closed around the handle of the case in an instinctive need to protect the precious contents.

"The Secret Service was already demanding access to the site when my people got there."

"I know better than to ask you how you managed this, then."

Max tapped his fingers on the table. "Lucky for you, the police aren't friendly with the Secret Service. A few more minutes, and a congressional order would have gotten them in the door." His gaze dropped to the case. "I'm sure they would have wanted that."

"There's nothing official in it, Max. The only thing in here that Brad wants is his wife's Bible. I wouldn't have involved you if there had been anything classified."

"Your conscience wouldn't let you ask me to break any laws." He shook his head. "I know. That's one of the reasons you weren't a very good political wife."

She ignored that. "What about the suitcase? Were you able to retrieve it, too?"

"Yes. It's in my office," he said.

Mariette breathed a sigh of relief. "Thank God." Now the only things in that apartment that had mattered to Brad were in safe hands. "I'll come by and get it later today."

Max shrugged. "Whenever. No one knows it's there, so I think it's safe. I would have brought it here, but I didn't want to look too conspicuous dragging it down the street. That wreck of a briefcase was bad enough." He paused to take a sip of his coffee. "Goes against my image, you know."

The slight gleam revealed the playful side of Max she'd always loved—and hadn't seen in far too long. Mariette gave him a grateful look. "Thank you, Max. This means more to me than you can imagine."

He inclined his head slightly. "Gave me a thrill, actually. Just the idea that I might be depriving Charley Swelder of something he wanted—" Max's smile was slightly sardonic—"was almost worth getting up at 6 a.m."

Mariette's heart rate, which had been running at accelerated levels since Marcus's phone call earlier, finally began to return to normal. "Still, I know this wasn't easy for you to pull off, no matter how good your connections are with the police. You didn't have to help me."

"I figured I owed you at least that much," he said softly. Mariette's eyes widened. That was as close as Max had ever come to apologizing to her for the humiliation and hurt he'd caused her during their marriage and divorce. "However," he continued, "there *is* something you can do for me if you'd like to return the favor."

So much for an apology, she thought wryly. Washington was a town built on deals and trade-offs, and Max was a master of the game. She knew him well enough to know that his presidential ambitions had been ignited by the apparent chaos inside the Fitzhugh White House. If someone was trying to kill the chief of staff, then there was a story in that, a story Max could easily exploit for his own political gain. "I don't know anything about who's after Brad Benton, if that's what you want to know. So don't ask me—"

Max held up his hand. "Hold it. Hold it. Who said anything about Benton?"

"You didn't have to say anything about him," Mariette said. "Someone's apparently trying to kill the White House chief of staff, and given your very public enmity toward Fitzhugh, I know you're dying to know what's going on."

"Sure. Me and everyone else in this town who knows about it."

That took her back. Brad believed that only a handful of people in the White House even knew that the sniper attack had been directed at him. "Who else knows?"

Max looked amused. "Come on, Mariette. Didn't you learn anything while you were married to me?"

Plenty, she thought. She'd learned that she was too trusting, too naive, and too vulnerable. "I learned how to be suspicious."

Max didn't take the bait. "You ought to know that this town is built on two things: power and rumors about power. Everyone who's got power wants to keep it, and everyone who doesn't have it wants to get it. It's the way things work."

"And there are rumors about Brad?" she guessed.

"Talk," he assured her. "There are some people who believe the shooting in the White House garage was random."

"The explosion in Brad's apartment will certainly confirm it for them."

"Yeah. You can imagine how this has my campaign manager practically salivating."

"Well, I don't know anything," Mariette told him. "All I know is that Brad asked me to get the Bible back for him."

"And even if you did know, you wouldn't tell me," he said. "This is why I know better than to ask."

"Thanks."

"Don't worry, Mariette. I'll find out about Benton my own way." He gave her a speculative look. "How did you say you know him?"

"Musselman," she said, deliberately noncommittal.

That made Max laugh. He knew Bernie Musselman, Mariette's boss and the director of FEMA. The two men had a long history of political hostility. "Bernie still has you doing his job for him?"

"He's tight with the White House staff."

"While you're the one out slogging through floods and digging people out of earthquakes. Mariette, when are you going to realize that the world is beyond redemption? You can't save it, and neither can anyone else."

How ironic, she thought. Before she'd come to know Christ, she would have agreed with him and shot back some adage about trying to save at least her corner of the world. Now, however, she recognized that all she could do was surrender herself to be God's servant. The rest was up to Him. "I like what I do, Max."

"I know. I don't know why, but I know." He began to carefully arrange the ends of his tie in a telltale sign she'd long ago learned to recognize as his stalling tactic when he was calculating his next move. It had driven her crazy for years, but now she waited patiently as he painstakingly aligned the points and gave them a sharp tug. She braced herself for whatever Max was going to throw at her. When he looked at her again, though, she saw a surprising lack of guile in his expression. "How is Randal?"

She stared at him for a moment, speechless. She hadn't heard Max sound so vulnerable since the days just after Randal's birth. She could clearly see lines of fatigue around Max's eyes. She knew he'd been incredibly busy. The congressional hearings he was conducting about the disappearances were ongoing, and Max was a frequent guest on Washington's countless news and talk shows. He and his entire campaign machine were scrambling, Mariette was sure, to figure out how to turn the Rapture to their advantage. This was a midterm election year, and as one of the highest-ranking members of the Senate, Max had more to lose than almost anyone if his party failed to retain control. With so much at stake, she wasn't surprised that he was running himself ragged. But she wouldn't have expected him to ask her about Randal.

"Randal?" Max prompted, with that same uncanny shrewdness that always made her feel like he was reading her mind.

"He's fine," she said. "Why do you ask?"

"Because he's my son, too, Mariette."

"I didn't mean that," she explained with a twinge of guilt. Max had paid hugely for his infidelity during their marriage, both personally and in the media. Randal had never forgiven his father when the details of Max's extra-marital adventures had become lurid tabloid headlines. "I just mean . . . well, you haven't really shown much interest . . ." She trailed off, a little embarrassed. "Randal's fine. He's good, actually."

"Is he safe?" Max prodded.

"Safe?" She concealed her surprise, barely. Not only had Max shown a decided lack of interest in Randal since the divorce, but aside from one comment the first day of the hearings, he'd never sounded remotely concerned about their son's well-being. "Max, where's this burst of pater-nal—?"

"Is he *safe?*" Max insisted, his tone turning hard.

She hesitated, stung. "I didn't mean to—"

"I'm sorry," he muttered. "I didn't mean to snap. I'm just worried about him."

She remembered the sheer terror she had felt in the first few days after the Rapture, waiting alone for news from Randal. But Max hadn't called. Still, if Max had experienced even a tenth of the anxiety she'd felt, she pitied him. She carefully considered what she should tell him. To say that her son was completely out of harm's way would not be true, but Max wouldn't understand if she tried to explain that she'd surrendered Randal into God's keeping. She drew a calming breath. "Randal is as safe as anyone could be right now."

The familiar signs of a brewing storm of anger drifted across his hard expression. "What's that supposed to mean?"

"These are dangerous times, Max."

"And my son, according to my sources," Max said, slamming his palm down on the table, "is the driver for a man with a target painted on his back." When he drew several stares from the other patrons, he cursed and wearily rubbed his eyes with his thumb and forefinger.

"Max—"

"Don't you think Randal's at extreme risk?" he asked, quietly this time.

"No," she answered. "Frankly, he's too high profile to be at risk. Whoever's after Brad isn't going to let Randal get caught in the cross fire, not when they know the media would have a feeding frenzy over your son getting injured while working for the White House."

"He could have been in that apartment, Mariette." His tone had changed to an echo of remembered agony. "You didn't see it."

Her heart went out to him. Poor Max was not accustomed to the clutch of fear and anxiety that most parents knew so well. He'd never stayed up nights monitoring a kid's high fever or gotten all those stricken phone calls from school nurses. He hadn't been around when Randal had learned to drive or begun dating. He'd missed all the opportunities to stay up late and pace the floor.

"No," she responded. "There was no chance he'd be in the house. Whoever planted that bomb would have known that. If Randal had driven Brad home, he'd have been on the clock and in communication with the dispatcher about returning the car to the motor pool. Brad can take it home at night. Randal can't. He's not allowed to leave the vehicle unattended. It's considered a security risk."

"I know. I know." Max pressed his lips together in a thin line—another sign she knew too well. He was furious, and he was determined that someone was going to pay for putting him through this unexpected agony. "I'm not going to tolerate having him in danger."

"The heat's off Randal. Brad's out of town for a few days, so that danger isn't an issue right now. Randal is just another driver in the motor pool until Brad returns. When he does get back, Randal and I will figure out what to do about it."

"You trust Brad to make sure Randal's all right?"

"I do." *Along with Marcus, more than anyone else on earth.*

He hesitated but finally nodded. "Then I'll take your word for it. You're the most cautious woman I know. You wouldn't say that if you weren't absolutely sure."

"I'm sure." She tipped her head to study him in the dim café lighting. "You said there was something you wanted from me. A favor?"

"Yes." He looked uncomfortable.

She wasn't surprised. Already he'd revealed more than he'd probably planned. Letting her see him as a concerned parent had not been easy for him, and neither was having to ask for her help. He wasn't used to asking for things. He took what he wanted and intimidated his way into whatever he couldn't steal. "I'll do it if I can."

"I want to talk to Randal," Max said.

Mariette's breath caught. Would he ever stop surprising her today? "Oh."

"You sound shocked."

"No." She shook her head. "Well, maybe. I mean, it just wasn't what I was expecting. Like I said, you haven't shown that much of an interest in him in the past."

He shrugged. "A third of the world's population never disappeared before. Now they have, and I find it more than a little unsettling. I *am* capable of some human emotion, you know."

"I know. I always knew." She gave him a quizzical look. "Everyone else you had duped. But I don't know if I can help you. It's not completely my choice."

"I know you can't make him see me, Mariette. He's not a little boy anymore."

And if Max had spent more time with him when he was younger, she mused, Randal might feel differently toward him. It was an old battle, one she'd long ago stopped fighting. Max had made his choices, and though they'd hurt Randal deeply, her son had found other people to fill the void in his life. Even now he had men like Brad Benton and Marcus Dumont to provide a paternal influence. Max was the one paying the price for his actions. "He's stubborn," she told Max. "Like you."

"And he resents me."

"It was very hard on him when the details of the divorce hit the papers—the affairs."

"No matter what you think, Mariette, I did not leak that to the press," Max said, his voice pained.

"I know that now. I probably knew it then, but I was angry and bitter and you were a convenient target." She shook her head. "I've tried to get Randal to let it go, but he's not ready yet."

"I appreciate the fact that you never tried to turn him against me." At her surprised look, Max nodded. "I know you never thought I did, but I know you. You were far too good for me, Mariette." He exhaled slowly. "You still are. All I ask is that you talk to him. Tell him I'd like to see him. I'll meet him on his terms. Wherever and whenever he wants."

"And if it happens to coincide with a strategic vote on the Senate floor?" She couldn't resist the remark. Randal had paid too often for Max's other priorities.

"I'll miss the vote. In fact, I'd miss my own swearing-in for a chance to really talk to him."

Mariette was staring at him in amazement when the buzz of her cell phone broke the spell. She pulled it from her trench-coat pocket and flipped it open. The display showed David Liu's private line. She was pretty sure it couldn't be an emergency. She'd talked to him several times already today. After all the disasters of the last few days, David needed a lot of hand-holding. She understood the feeling. She hit the mute button and slipped it back in her pocket. The call—and David—would keep for a few minutes. Still looking at Max, she clutched the handle of Brad's briefcase as she stood. "I'll try. That's the only thing I can promise you."

Max stood with her. "That's all I can ask." He jammed his hands into the pockets of his raincoat. "Did you drive or take a cab?"

"I drove. I dropped Randal at work."

"I'll walk you to your car then."

4

"Okay, David," Mariette told her assistant when she arrived at FEMA headquarters later that morning. "What's on deck today?" She set Brad's briefcase next to her desk.

David gave the charred leather case a curious look. He whistled softly. "Hey, Mariette, what happened to that thing?"

"It's a long story." She'd contemplated leaving the brief-case in the car, but with Max's information that the Secret Service had already been casing Brad's apartment fresh in her mind, she was unwilling to let it out of her sight. "I'm just glad I wasn't there when it happened. Sorry I couldn't take your call earlier. I was tied up."

"No problem." David rustled through a stack of folders. "Mayor Berger's called twice."

Mariette took the folder. "I'm not surprised. I spoke with him a couple of days ago about the problems New York is having moving goods into the city. All that publicity at the UN isn't helping."

David groaned softly and sank into the chair across from Mariette's desk. "We can't take on anything else,

Mariette. Not without extra help. We're barely keeping our heads above water as it is."

"I've talked to Musselman about coordinating with some other agencies," she said. "He's looking into it."

"Which means he's not doing a thing. When are you going to learn that the only things that man cares about are his White House connections and his name in the papers?"

"I know, but that's the system we have. We have to work within it."

"Yeah, well, whoever designed the system hadn't planned on a disaster of this size. Wouldn't you say?"

Mariette gave him a speculative look. "David—"

He rushed on. "We can barely get the phones answered for new calls coming in. The Midwest is running out of water because of chemical and fuel spills in the Mississippi. The West Coast can't get food and durable goods because the highways are still practically shut down. In the South, we've got toxic air and pollution from the chemical industry. And the Northeast is almost paralyzed. There's no end to it, and we can't help."

Mariette took a deep breath. "Okay, David." She held out a hand to him. "I hear you."

"But the only thing you're going to do about it is talk to Musselman."

Experience told her his stress level, not his organizational talent, was talking, and the best thing she could do was let him vent the steam. "I didn't say that."

"Isn't it getting to you?" he shot back.

"Yeah." Mariette carefully set the New York folder aside. "Sure it is. It's very stressful. There are too many bases to cover and not enough players on the field—if you'll excuse the cliché. But panicking only adds to the problem. You know, I'm not going to tell you I know how you feel, but I am worried about you."

He dropped his gaze and picked an invisible speck of lint from the thigh of his pants. "I'm all right."

Mariette shook her head. "I don't think so."

He looked at her again. "No, I am." He sighed. "I'm sorry I snapped. I'm just a little overwhelmed today, that's all."

"I understand that, but—"

"I wasn't expecting Berger to call so soon," he continued. "I haven't put together those reports you wanted on the rail system yet. I've been so swamped dealing with Southeast; I don't know when I'll have time to get to it."

"I'm not talking about the workload," Mariette insisted quietly. "I'm talking about you." She paused to let that sink in. "You're showing signs of post-traumatic stress, David."

He laughed. "Don't be ridiculous. How many of these crises have we been through together?"

"More than I can count. Which is why I know you're not looking at this objectively."

"That's absurd."

"Really? When was the last time you went home?"

"Yesterday afternoon," he said.

"And before that?" When he hesitated, Mariette said, "Before that, you hadn't been home since this started."

"That's not—"

"I know you've been sleeping in the infirmary, David."

"There's a lot to do."

"And you're not going to be very helpful if you fall apart. You know that."

"I haven't cracked up yet, have I?"

"No. And I don't want you to." She studied him for a moment. The fluorescent lights hid little. His skin looked pale, his eyes bleary. He seemed tense and agitated, two common symptoms of PTSD. Mariette thought about argu-

ing with him, then made a quick decision. "I want you to
see one of the stress counselors today."

His expression turned angry. "No. No way."

"Look, it can't hurt. It might even help. You're not in a
position to look at this objectively. They can give you perspective."

"It's a waste of time. We've got work to do."

"I'm not giving you an option," she said, reaching into
her desk for the requisite referral form. "Just give them an
hour. That's all."

"And what? You'll put a report in my file saying that
when things got really dicey I couldn't hack it?"

"No," she said carefully, signing the form. "I'm not even
going to ask for the summary. I just think you could stand
to get a few things off your chest."

David's expression remained belligerent. "If I refuse?"

"I'll put you on temporary leave."

"You can't do that!"

"I will if I have to." She gave him a close look. "I need
you, David. This office needs you. I have to know you're all
right."

"Seeing some stress counselor isn't going to help." He
uttered a disgusted oath. "The whole thing's ridiculous."

"Then humor me. Go for an hour. If it doesn't do any
good, I won't make you go back."

That seemed to mollify him a little, but he still looked
angry. "I wish you wouldn't do this."

Mariette handed the form across the desk. "Sorry. I'm
still in charge, and this is the way it's going to be. Either you
go, or I'm sending you home."

He hesitated but took the referral. "Fine. I'm telling you,
though, it's pointless."

"Good," she said. "You can take the hour break, then get
on those rail reports I need." At his sour expression, she of-

fered him an apologetic smile. "I'm sorry, David. I know you're angry about this."

"We've been friends a long time, Mariette."

"That's why I'm doing it." She indicated the New York folder on her desk. "Chances are, I'll have to go to New York tomorrow—which means I'm leaving you in charge of the office again. What kind of friend would I be if I ignored the fact that the stress might be getting to you?" When he didn't answer, she added, "You'd do the same for me."

"Maybe. Can I at least finish my summation on the Southeast before I get my head shrunk?"

"Sure," she agreed, then waved at the form. "But take care of it this morning. I don't want to see you back in here until you've had a session."

He mumbled something as he stood to leave. "Are you going to try to catch the morning shuttle to New York?"

"Depends on my conversation with Berger." She picked up the folder again. "I'll let you know." She watched him leave, frowning slightly at the stiff set of his shoulders. She'd known David for years, and she'd learned to depend on his usually calm nature and excellent stress-management skills. In their work, situations could often become overwhelming. When they had too many people in need and not enough financial or personal resources to meet those needs, it was always easy to lose perspective among the clamoring voices of urgency.

David's strength came in managing the office and overseeing the monstrous task of coordinating local and federal relief efforts, while she excelled in the fieldwork. He could analyze a problem and see clear solutions, but he had difficulty coping with the human factor. Too many suffering people tilted his emotional balance. The relief and recovery efforts they had cooperated on had been minimal compared to the herculean task FEMA now faced in the wake of the Rapture. She hoped David could handle the strain.

She sensed that David was struggling with the enormous emotional burden of a crisis that apparently had no end—and she doubted that an hour with a stress counselor was going to help much. She sent up a silent prayer for wisdom. *He needs You so much, Lord. Please show me how to reach him.*

The intercom on her desk buzzed, startling her. With a slight shake of her head, Mariette reached for the phone. "Yes?"

"Randal is on line two, Mariette," the receptionist told her.

"Thanks, Becky." Randal had promised to call if he learned anything about the attempts on Brad's life. Mariette punched the line and leaned back in her chair. "Hi."

"It's me."

Mariette cringed at the still-terse tone of his voice. They'd argued that morning—about Max, about the risks Randal was taking while working for Brad. He accused her of being overly protective. She'd accused him of being rash and immature. They'd parted angry. She felt rotten. "About this morning—"

"I was calling to see if you got what you wanted from Dad," he said. By unspoken consent, neither mentioned the briefcase or Brad by name.

She stifled a sigh. For as long as Randal had been able to speak, he'd been like this. He'd talk when he determined it was time and not a minute sooner. "Yes. I want to apologize."

"Accepted. Are you going to call and tell our friend?"

She closed her eyes and mentally reached for her patience. Randal had gotten that stubborn streak from his father. She was always the first to cave in a conflict with the people she loved, but not those two. Max could bear a grudge for life, and Randal ran him a close second. "Honey—"

"Look, I really can't talk about this right now. I just wanted to know if you got the stuff."

She let it go—for now. "It's taken care of. And, yes, I'll call him."

"Good."

"Everything okay there?" she pressed, hoping he wouldn't think she was prying.

"Yeah. A few questions about the car and where I was. That sort of thing. The Secret Service is looking into it."

"So I hear," she said.

"You heard . . . oh." He apparently made the connection. "Dad."

"Yes. He's holding something for me. I plan to pick it up today or tomorrow." Mariette paused. "You want to go?"

Randal snorted.

"He wants to see you."

"Yeah, well, he didn't especially want to see me before. Why's he so hot to get to know me now?"

She sighed. "Things are different, Randal. The Rapture— well, he just seemed concerned. I think he's worried about you."

"Then the two of you finally have something in common again. I'm not a six-year-old, you know."

Mariette rubbed her temples with her thumb and middle finger. How could she make him understand that parental concern was a lifetime commitment? "He wants to talk to you."

"I don't want to talk to him," Randal countered.

"Just promise you'll think about it."

"Sure. Yeah. I'll think about it."

With a sigh of resignation, she shook her head. Sooner or later, her son was going to have to come to terms with his bitterness toward his father. As strongly as she'd believed that before becoming a Christian, she was now utterly convinced of it. Randal needed to forgive Max as much for his own peace of mind as for his father's. Their relationship was long overdue for healing. So instead of pursuing the matter, she pushed her maternal instinct aside and changed the subject. "I've got to run. New York is demanding my attention."

"Still?" he asked.

"Yes. It's a mess up there. I've got to talk to the mayor today to see what we can work out. Their entire transportation network is running at less than 30 percent capacity."

He let out a low whistle. "I imagine the chaos at the UN isn't helping matters any."

"It's not. The city's swarming with media, protestors, and curious tourists. And, not surprisingly, they all want food and water and clean flush toilets."

"Yeah, well, from what I hear around here, things are only going to get worse, not better."

"How?" she asked.

"Remember when Marcus was telling us about one of the events of the Tribulation being the seven years of peace in Israel?"

"Yes."

"Evidently, Carpathia's got it all worked out. He's negotiated some treaty with the Israelis that's going to guarantee them enough time and money to rebuild the temple in Jerusalem."

Mariette closed her eyes as a chill ran down her spine. "You just heard that?"

"This morning. I was sitting outside the policy director's

office and overheard them talking about it." He paused. "It's kind of weird—seeing all this stuff happen."

"Yes. It is."

"I just thought you'd want to know. Look, I gotta go, too. I have to drive some ambassador guy back to his embassy. Good luck with New York, okay?"

"Thanks." She paused. "Please be careful, Randal."

"I *am*, Mom," he responded, his tone impatient.

Mariette ended the call reluctantly. She was trying to remember that she had to turn her son over to God now. He was in God's hands and in God's protection. She couldn't shelter him any longer, nor could she treat him like a child. He was an adult. He had a keen mind, a strong sense of honor, integrity, courage, and determination.

He was also a child of God—which meant the Lord now had responsibility for his welfare—but which didn't mean, she thought with a weary smile, that she was going to stop worrying about him.

★ ★ ★

"Thanks for doing this, Joe." Brad pushed the door of Joe Shaker's office shut. He'd first met Joe at a political party several years ago. They'd developed a good friendship, and Brad had often relied on the seasoned forensic scientist for inside information on potentially volatile cases. During his flight, Brad had made the decision to talk to Joe about the pictures of George Ramiro's body. After meeting Liza, he'd asked her where the pictures were. She said she had stored them in a safe-deposit box near the offices of the *Los Angeles Times*. Brad had called Joe Shaker to make an appointment, then stopped with Liza at the bank to pick up the pictures on the way to the medical examiner's office in Lincoln Heights.

"This is Liza Cannley," he told Joe. "She's been helping me research this."

"It's a murder, you think?" Joe inquired.

"I think," Brad said. "I also think someone's trying to pass it off as a suicide."

"Let me see what you've got," Joe said.

Liza handed Joe the manila envelope. "These are the pictures."

As Joe took the envelope, Brad reached out to keep him from opening it. "I feel like I have to warn you that I think someone's trying to kill me because of what's in that envelope."

Brad had briefed Liza on the events of the past several days on the way to Joe's office. She'd confirmed his worst fears by explaining that she had encountered several roadblocks in her efforts to gain information about George. Twice she'd been told the information that should have been available for public access had been sealed. Too many documents and records had been lost, and too many people had developed conveniently hazy memories not to have raised her suspicions that someone, somewhere, was trying to cover up what really happened to George Ramiro.

Joe loosened the clasp on the envelope with a slight nod. "Duly noted. Like I said on the phone, I'm not sure how much I'm going to be able to tell you from just looking at the pictures."

"Anything would be helpful," Brad said.

Joe indicated the two battered chairs across from his desk. "Shove whatever you have to out of the way and have a seat." He pulled the stack of photos from the envelope as he rounded his desk. He took a moment to clear a space on the laminate desktop, then began to spread the pictures, one by one, across the surface.

Brad hadn't seen the pictures since he'd sent them to

Liza. One of the things that was bothering him, in fact, was that he still had no idea who'd delivered them to him at the White House and why. He and Liza watched as Joe painstakingly rearranged the photos to his liking. Once he had them aligned in three neat rows, he reached in his desk for a loupe, then switched on his halogen desk lamp. As he examined the photos, the only sounds in the office were the monotonous drone of the air-conditioning system and the ticking of the wall clock. Only when his fingers began to ache did Brad realize he was gripping the arms of the old chair.

Finally, Joe looked up and dropped the loupe in his hand. "You have no idea who sent you these?" Limned by the afternoon light, his expression was difficult to read.

Brad shook his head. "None. They came in an unmarked envelope."

"Hmm." Joe picked up a close-up shot of George's head and looked at it again, his mouth slightly puckered, his face a mask of concentration. "Well, whoever sent them to you wanted you to know Ramiro was murdered. This wasn't a suicide, and they didn't make much of an effort to make it look like one."

"So the pistol in his hand is just set dressing?" Brad asked.

Joe nodded. "Look here." He extended the picture so Brad and Liza could examine it.

"No gunshot residue," Liza said.

Joe shot her a slight grin. "Everybody's a forensic expert these days. Too much television."

Liza looked at him in surprise. "I thought that was the absolute indicator of how close a firearm was to the victim when fired."

"It's one piece of evidence," Joe agreed, "like blood spatter, but it's only conclusive in the movies. Criminals watch

TV, too, you know. They're getting smarter about forensics and how to cover their tracks." He pointed to the picture again. "There's no way I could really tell from this picture whether or not there's gunshot residue. I'd have to examine the body."

"So how do you know it wasn't suicide?" Liza pressed.

"Two things," Joe said. He traced the outer edges of the entry wound with his index finger. "See the size of the depression here in his skull?"

Brad nodded.

"For a bullet to build up that wide an angle of force at entry, it would have to be fired from some distance." Joe flipped the picture so he could study it again. He tilted it toward the light, searching it intently. "I can't tell what caliber weapon was used, but I can tell you it had to be fired from at least ten feet away."

Liza had pulled out a notepad and was furiously scribbling. "You're sure of that?"

"I've got twenty-two years of looking at gunshots," Joe told her. "I'm sure."

"Anything else?" Liza asked.

Joe picked up another picture. This one showed George's body splayed across a leaf-strewn surface. The hand clutching the pistol was outstretched beside him. "Look at the blood pattern." He indicated the large dark stain on the leaves. "And look at his tie." The end of George's tie was flipped up. "This body's lying on an incline. His head is lower than his feet." He pointed at the entry wound. "If he'd shot himself here, then, given the average arm length, the exit point should have been close to the top of his head."

Liza leaned forward to take a closer look at the photo. "The blood's spread around his shoulders."

"Yes," Joe agreed. "Ever cut your face or your head?"

"In college," Brad said. "Football accident."

"There was a lot of blood, wasn't there?" Joe asked.

"Yeah. I thought it would never stop."

Joe gestured to the picture. "If this man were bleeding from the back of his head and considering the incline, the pool of blood should be up here." He traced the area above George's head with his index finger. "The fact that it's around his shoulders says he's bleeding from the base of the skull."

Brad frowned. "So he was shot from above?"

Joe shook his head. "Not exactly." He picked up another photo. This one had been taken from an angle. "Look here." Joe pointed to George's knees. "What do you see?"

Brad frowned and took the picture. He leaned toward the halogen lamp and looked closely at the detail. The fabric at the knees of George's trousers looked different. Though the photo was grainy, there was still a noticeable difference. "The knees look wrinkled."

"Or snagged," Joe said. "Wrinkles around the thigh area are normal. Comes from sitting. But you know anybody who gets wrinkles and snags in the knees of their pants?"

"Only if they're kneeling," Liza said.

"Right," Joe agreed. "It's a little hard to tell in that photo. The resolution's not the best, but my guess is whoever killed him made him kneel, then shot him through the forehead."

Brad's mouth had gone dry. The graphic evidence of the pictures was confirming his worst fears. "Like an execution."

"There's something else, too." Joe picked up the close-up again. "See the angle? Your killer was probably left-handed. Even accounting for the distance of the shot and for the bullet to enter at this angle, he'd have to have fired the weapon with his left hand or held it at an unnatural angle with his right."

Liza looked at the picture, then continued to jot down notes in her notebook. "Is there anything else you can tell us, Mr. Shaker?"

"One more thing. This body was wrapped in something and moved after he was injured. He might have died lying in this pile of leaves, but he was put there after he'd been shot."

Brad frowned. "How can you tell?"

"These could be mud stains on his suit coat and trousers," Joe said, "but my guess is they're blood smears. Either way, he wouldn't have gotten mud or blood on the front of his jacket if he'd shot himself and landed on his back." He scooped up the photos and stacked them neatly. "I'd have to see the body to give you anything else."

"You told me exactly what I needed to know," Brad said, taking the pictures. "And I don't think I have to tell you—"

"We never had this conversation? Brad who?"

"I'm sorry." Brad wiped a hand over his face. "It's just better for you that way."

"I understand. Believe me, this isn't the first time I've had a politically sensitive conversation in this office."

Brad looked at Liza. "Any more questions?"

She scanned her notes. "I don't think so. I wish you could tell us more about those stains—" She stopped abruptly when Brad's cell phone rang.

It was his new private phone. Only Mariette, Marcus, and Randal had the number. He reached for it, hoping it was news about his briefcase and Christine's Bible. The call came from the White House. Randal, he figured. "Hello?"

"Brad. Good to hear your voice."

Brad didn't recognize the voice. "Who is this?"

"Harmon Drake. Where in the world are you?"

Brad stepped into the corridor outside Joe's office. "Didn't Charley Swelder tell you? I decided to take a few days off. I've got some business I need to take care of at home."

"Sure, sure. I imagine you do. I just figured that after what happened at your place last night, you'd consult with me first. I need to put a detail on you."

"I don't need a detail."

"It's not up for debate, sir," Drake said. "President's orders."

Brad frowned. "When?"

"Fifteen minutes ago. I briefed him on the progress of our investigation then."

"Is there any?"

"Progress? Not yet. But you might be interested to know that the Senate Armed Services Committee had someone at your place early this morning. The guy was looking for something. Any idea what that might be?"

"Beats me," he said. Then it hit him. *Max Arnold. That's how Mariette got the briefcase out of there.* "Maybe they thought there might be a national-security issue at stake when a White House staffer gets his house blown up?"

Mariette must have called Max to get his help retrieving his briefcase—and it was a wise move on her part. In addition to Max's very public and powerful chairmanship of the Armed Services Committee, he also chaired the Senate Appropriations Subcommittee on Transportation with oversight of federal highway dollars. With the D.C. area's legendary traffic problems and both Virginia and Maryland always asking for major funding from the committee, Max's clout with local and state officials was unparalleled. There was no way Max would talk nicely to anyone in this administration. Nor would they go begging him for answers. Brilliant. "I bet they're worried some senator could be next."

"Maybe," Drake said. "My men told me the committee representative removed two items from the site. We tried to secure the place, but the Alexandria police—" He delivered a blistering condemnation of the locality's law-enforcement procedures. "All I know is that the investigation has been compromised by their general incompetence."

"I'm sure you're doing the best you can." Brad glanced down the dimly lit hallway. Except for the occasional employee navigating the tile-and-concrete passage, he was alone.

"Yeah. Well, in the meantime, I'll get a detail to your location."

"I really don't—"

"Mr. Benton," Drake said, "you've got no choice. The president ordered a detail, and we're going to provide it. We can do it the easy way or the hard way."

Brad sighed. "Fine. But for the record, I don't like this."

"So noted. Tell me where you are, and I'll let the L.A. office know."

Tell me where you are. The request should have seemed simple enough, but it felt ominous. Brad wasn't about to tell Drake or anyone else at the White House that he was at the medical examiner's office sharing pictures of George Ramiro's corpse with a forensic scientist.

"It'll be easier on everybody," he hedged, "if I hook up with them somewhere. I'm between spots right now."

Drake paused but finally seemed to relent. "Give me an address."

Mariette hit the security button on her car. The alarm didn't bleep off like it was supposed to. She frowned and hit it again. No response. Dead battery, she figured.

She gave her watch a glance as she hurried across the FEMA parking lot. She had just enough time to make it across town to Max's office to retrieve Brad's suitcase before she had to meet Musselman at the Old Executive Office Building for a briefing. With any luck, the traffic wouldn't—

She stopped short when she saw the gleam of broken glass under her car. It was probably nothing, a broken taillight from an earlier fender bender perhaps, but after Max's warning, she wasn't willing to take chances. She clutched the handle of Brad's briefcase with one hand and slid the other into her pocket to retrieve her cell phone. She prepared to push the emergency 9 key.

A look around confirmed that she was alone in the garage.

Mariette cautiously approached her car while she glanced back and forth between the vehicle and the elevator nearby. She was five steps away from the car when she realized the passenger-side window had been shattered.

The broken window could easily have been random vandalism. It wasn't unusual in this part of town. There'd been a rash of robberies lately, too. She looked inside the car and noted that her high-end CD player was untouched. Not robbery then. When she tested the handle of the driver's-side door, she found it unlocked. Her fingers tightened on the handle of the briefcase. Had someone wanted it badly enough to break into her car?

Reaching down beside the driver's seat, she pulled the switch to release the trunk. Inside, she found what she feared. Her trunk had obviously been searched. And the searcher had made no effort to cover his tracks. The carpet cover for the spare tire was pulled aside, and her box of emergency supplies had been dumped. Mariette slammed the trunk and hurried back into her vehicle.

What to do? If she reported the incident to the police, they would ask questions. She didn't want to answer questions. Not now. Unwilling to tell another soul that she had possession of Brad's briefcase, she fastened her seat belt and jammed her key into the ignition. Hands and legs shaking, she started the car and backed out of her space.

One thing was now clear: Somebody knew she had the briefcase. And they weren't going to be deterred by good manners and law-abiding behavior in their quest to get it. She only hoped she was such an unimportant cog in the machine that they weren't considering murder. But how could she keep them from getting Brad's bag? Then there was the matter of the suitcase waiting in Max's office. Brad wanted them both so badly—as connections to his life before the Rapture. So no matter what the danger was, her only choice was to take Brad's suitcase from Max, then place both items in the safest possible place where nobody would think to look for them until Brad returned to Washington to retrieve them.

As she negotiated her way through the afternoon traffic, she punched Brad's number into her cell phone.

He answered on the first ring. Mariette quickly told him about the briefcase, about her car, and about her suspicions.

"Is there anything in the case they could be after?" she asked.

"Yeah. The photographs of George's body. I bet they think I have the photographs in there."

Mariette jammed her foot on the brake to avoid hitting a jaywalking tourist.

"I'm sorry I dragged you into this," Brad was saying.

"I've got it under control," Mariette said. "I think I know where I can stash both cases until you get back to Washington. The only thing I need to know is the security code for the locks on your briefcase."

"542 on the left and 859 on the right. Why?"

"I'm going to remove Christine's Bible. I don't care how safe I think it is, I'm not letting it out of my sight."

"Thank you, Mariette," Brad said quietly. "I had no idea this was going to put you at risk."

"Well, somebody's after those photos; that's certain enough. And if they broke into my car," she said as she sped through the dogleg in Pennsylvania Avenue and headed toward the Senate office buildings, "I don't think they're going to stop until they get them."

"Don't take any chances."

"Same goes for you." The Russell Senate Office Building loomed ahead of her. "I gotta go. Take care of yourself."

"I will."

★   ★   ★

Randal hurried to pull open the passenger door as two im-
posing-looking men exited the White House at the front
portico. He was glad for the diversion. With Brad out of
town, he'd been assigned to general duty. Except for his
meeting that morning with Harmon Drake, he'd been
bored most of the day. Despite what his mother seemed to
think, he was hardly dodging bullets and neck deep in intrigue. He'd worked three crosswords in major metropoli-
tan newspapers already that day.

So when another driver had told Randal that he'd
picked up these two men at the airport earlier for a meeting
with Charley Swelder, Randal had persuaded the driver to
let him take them back to the airport in the afternoon. Relieved to avoid the always tedious afternoon rush-hour
traffic, the driver had readily agreed.

The two men ducked into the car, their expressions
grim.

Randal got in the vehicle and slipped behind the wheel.
"Where to, sirs?" he asked.

Already deep in conversation, the older of the two
looked at Randal in surprise. "You're not the same driver
who picked us up."

"No, sir. That was another general duty driver."

"Oh. Airport," the man said. "Quick as you can."

"Yes, sir."

Randal eased the car down the long driveway through
the security entrance and out into the traffic. He could see
the men reflected in the windshield. Though their voices
were low, they were talking intently. "Do you mind if I listen to the radio?" he asked them.

The younger man waved dismissively. "Just raise the
glass."

Randal pushed the button to raise the dividing glass between the front and back seats. There was a trick to the White House fleet that he'd learned from one of the drivers, and with Brad's life in danger, he didn't hesitate to use it. By inserting an earbud and tuning the radio to the appropriate station, he could listen to the conversation in the backseat.

Cautiously, he adjusted the radio first, scanning several channels to avoid rousing suspicion. He pulled the earbud from his pocket and plugged it into the jack to dampen the sound. Palming the bud in his left hand, he pretended to scratch his ear while he slipped the tiny device into place. The signal was clear as a bell.

"Something doesn't add up here, Bill," the younger man said. "I've known George Ramiro for years, and I just can't believe—"

"Greed makes a man do strange things."

"Ramiro would not have sold out the president. I don't care how lucrative the book deal was."

"Well, it's beside the point now, isn't it? He disappeared along with everyone else. So unless he actually put anything in the hands of that agent . . ."

"Charley seemed to think he hadn't met with the man yet."

"Then good thing he disappeared before he was supposed to go to New York. That's just what we needed: Conrad Dishun handling a tell-all book about the administration by one of Fitz's insiders."

"George certainly knew where all the bodies were buried."

"Too many bodies. And if he'd started talking, Boston would have blown up in our faces." The older man cursed baldly. "I can't believe Tuttle would have stayed silent for that."

The name made Randal frown. Though he'd deliber-

ately distanced himself from Washington, politics, and his
father, some habits had died hard. He'd always stayed informed about who was who and what was what in the political arena. Edward Tuttle was the former chief of staff at
the White House—the man Brad replaced when Tuttle was
forced to resign under the cloud of a brewing sex scandal.

"He took the fall for that incident with the Foley girl,"
the younger man agreed, "but I think you're right. He's not
going to let Fitzhugh and Swelder send him to jail—no
matter how much dirt they have on him. He might have
been Rudd's man at one time, but he's not that loyal."

"Who can blame him? Victor knew what was going to
happen to Tuttle when he sent him to Washington. As soon
as the scandal broke, Rudd, Fitzhugh, and Swelder planned
to set Tuttle up as the fall guy."

Randal navigated around a minor accident, drumming
his fingers on the steering wheel. Victor Rudd—quite possibly the most powerful nonelected official in the president's
political machine. Reportedly, Rudd had given millions in
soft money contributions through party channels and political action committees to ensure that Fitzhugh's election
was secure. Though plenty of rumors surrounded Rudd's
corporate business affairs, to date there had been nothing
solid to suggest that his vast wealth had been acquired ille-
gally. Still, there was enough smoke to keep the media nip-
ping at his heels.

The most recent rumors, Randal remembered, had to do
with Rudd's dealings with the Federal Reserve Bank in New
York City and the gold market. With more of the nation's
gold reserve than all of Fort Knox, the New York Fed had
acted quickly to quell any reports that the reserve may have
been compromised and that Rudd might have been involved in a possible international barter of the bullion. But
there were two congressional committees looking into the

matter, and had the Rapture not captured center stage, the story might have been bigger.

"Let's just hope it's all behind us," the older man was saying. "If Swelder's right and Ramiro hadn't talked yet, we're safe."

"I hope so. The polls haven't looked as good as I would have liked lately. We gained some after the disappearances, but things are still precarious."

"Carpathia's visit should fix that. Everyone loves the guy. What could be better for polls and fund-raising than him shaking Fitz's hand on the podium?"

"A personal endorsement?"

The older man's laugh was short and unpleasant. "You get that, Ryan, and I'll personally ensure you get Benton's job after the election."

Their conversation shifted to the pending congressional elections, and Randal took a deep breath as he exited onto the George Washington Parkway. Delivering his two riders to the airport now took on a new urgency. As soon as possible, he needed to use a phone.

★　★　★

"We've been subpoenaed," Isack Moore told Marcus as he dropped an envelope on Marcus's desk.

Marcus raised an eyebrow while he opened the envelope to inspect the legal document. "Who has? By who?"

"All of us. By Theo Carter." As New Covenant Evangelical Ministries' communications and media director, Isack was one of the few members of Marcus's widespread organization who had been left behind in the wake of the Rapture. His wife and three children, his parents, his wife's parents, and most of his extended family had all been swept away. It had left Isack angry, grief stricken, and devastated. "We need a lawyer."

The subpoena was for a deposition in the class-action lawsuit Marcus's former attorney had filed with the federal court. "When did you get this?" Marcus probed.

"Today." Isack's eyes narrowed. "And since nobody else wanted to talk to you about it, I am." He crossed his arms over his chest and gave Marcus a belligerent look. "Have you done anything at all about hiring a lawyer—or are you still waiting for a message from God?"

Despite Isack's condemning tone, Marcus didn't flinch. The night of the Rapture, a bitter Isack had hurled accusations and angry words at him. Marcus had been in no position to argue. "Yes, actually I have made a couple of phone calls."

"But have you hired anyone?"

"Not yet." Marcus's heart grieved as he saw the stubborn set of the younger man's jaw. Of the handful of employees and contributors who'd been left behind, only Isack had spurned Marcus's apology. He was angry at God and Marcus, and despite the prayers and efforts of those around him, he seemed determined to stay that way. Marcus remembered too well a time in his own life when he'd felt the same way. Patience and persistence and an utter reliance on God's ability to pierce even the hardest heart were the only tools he had now to try and reach Isack.

"Carter's going to take you down," Isack warned. "You knew when we hired him out of Harvard that he could fight dirty."

Marcus calmly slid the subpoena back in the envelope, then met Isack's condemning gaze. "I'm aware of that. I'm looking into it."

Isack stared at him a moment, then dropped into the chair across from his desk. "I'm sorry, Marcus, but I don't see a lot of evidence here that you're even concerned. You're so wrapped up in all this—" he waved his hand over the books on Marcus's desk—"Rapture stuff, you don't even seem to be mentally here anymore."

Marcus sent up a quick prayer for wisdom and discernment. "I'm sorry you feel that way. I'm also sorry if you feel I haven't kept you fully informed about this lawsuit, but I promise you, I *am* seeking a new lawyer, and I *am* taking this seriously."

Isack frowned. "You're seeking a Christian lawyer, you mean?"

"Preferably. Yes."

"That wasn't such a priority when you hired Theo. Was it?"

"Things are different now," Marcus said quietly.

Isack muttered something under his breath. "In case you haven't noticed, there aren't a lot of Christians running around these days. By the time you find a lawyer, Theo will have sued this entire organization out from under you. Did you even read the report I gave you yesterday?"

"Last night." Marcus pulled the red folder from his in-box and flipped it open. Isack had put together a detailed list of the ministry's contributors—those among the missing and those they'd been able to locate. He'd also compiled a list of pending estate, insurance, and annuity settlements. The numbers had shocked Marcus. Though he'd suspected that the ministry stood to gain a healthy financial settlement, he'd had no idea that his contributors had willed the organization such a mind-boggling amount of money.

Marcus ran his finger down the column, scanning the familiar names, his heart heavy. These people had had such faith in him and his ministry, they'd given sacrificially in life and in death. And though he'd confessed it to no one,

Theo Carter's lawsuit had come as a partial relief from the
overwhelming guilt Marcus felt about the way he'd deliberately cultivated these donors. Though he'd prayed earnestly
about it for the past few days, he had not yet made peace
with the idea of accepting the money. "Did you have any
idea that the list would be this long?"

"Not really."

"Me either." Marcus's mind reeled as he continued to
scan the numbers. He'd been halfway through the report
last night when Brad had called to describe the explosion at
his apartment.

"Marcus?"

He glanced up. "Hmm?"

Isack pointed at the report. "That money could solve a
lot of the problems we're facing."

That was true enough. With his contributor base deci-
mated, donations had slowed to a trickle. But Theo Carter,
who had called Marcus the night of the Rapture and told
him he could no longer work for the ministry, was now the
head attorney for a massive civil suit filed by the left-be-
hind families of Marcus's contributors. The suit alleged that
the donors had been defrauded, believing they were leaving their money to an organization headed by a Christian
minister committed to the principles of the gospel. Since
Marcus had publicly admitted he was not a believer prior to
the Rapture, the suit contended that the monies were not
owed to his organization.

Marcus nodded. "I'm aware of that."

"And now that it looks like the courts are actually going
to release it . . ." Isack trailed off.

"Any new developments on that?"

"The Sixth District court ruled yesterday afternoon that
since the official position of the United States is that we've

been attacked, the insurance companies can't hide behind the acts of God clause."

That came as no surprise. Political and public pressure had practically demanded the verdict. Following the Rapture, as the courts had begun to rule on insurance settlements and estate distribution, the pendulum had gradually swung against the insurance companies who'd argued that the Rapture certainly fell under the acts of God clauses in their policies. Standing to lose billions of dollars, the insurance industry had flatly refused settlement on life-insurance policies.

"The only thing the courts allowed the insurance industry," Isack continued, "was exclusion if their policies contained terrorism clauses."

"Which most don't," Marcus said. After the terrorist attacks on America in 2001, public outcry over the insurance industry's refusal to settle life-insurance claims had caused sweeping congressional and industry reforms.

"You didn't catch the morning news today?" Isack asked.

He'd been busy helping Brad get out of town. "No. I was tied up."

"The Fed chairman was on CBS. They've agreed to guarantee the banks' liabilities. People should begin receiving settlements within the week."

Now Marcus set the report down and looked at Isack. The same belligerent set of his jaw marred the features of his otherwise handsome face. "That's one of the reasons why I've been waiting. Depending on the court's ruling, the whole thing might become moot."

"But it's not." Isack leaned forward. "And if you don't make a decision soon, you could lose what's left of this place."

Marcus steepled his fingers beneath his chin. "We have enough cash reserves to see us through about six months."

"And the settlement money would give us security for the next twenty years." He gave Marcus a look. "Since you're the one telling us we've only got seven years to go until the end of the earth, I'd think you'd be eager to take the cash."

Marcus exhaled a weary breath and reached for his patience as he reminded himself that Isack's accusations were the product of grief and disillusionment. "I just don't have a clear sense of direction yet."

"Well, while you've been waiting for God to talk to you, I've been talking to the media." Isack shook his head. "The only thing you've got going for you right now is that everyone's in love with Carpathia and he's *the* hot news story. The media's not too interested in you. Otherwise, we'd have a feeding frenzy on our hands."

"Nicolae Carpathia," Marcus said, inwardly shuddering. "Given the circumstances, I can't say I'm grateful he's diverting all the attention."

Isack started to say something, then seemed to think better of it.

"What is it?" Marcus asked. When Isack hesitated, he said, "Go ahead, Isack. Tell me what's on your mind."

He relented. "I know how you feel about Carpathia. But I have to tell you, Marcus. I just don't see it."

Marcus wasn't surprised. Most of the world, it seemed, was unable to look beyond Carpathia's polish and veneer to see the evil lurking at the core. "You're not alone."

"If anything, I'd think you'd have embraced the guy. For the first time, some politician is finally doing something about world peace and hunger and poverty. The nuclear disarmament plan—" Isack shook his head. "It just seems like he's all about the things you've been advocating for so long."

"There was a time," Marcus said carefully, "when you would have been right. I would have seen the apparent good he's doing and welcomed it. Frankly, I would have also been eager to jump on his media bandwagon. That used to be very important to me."

Isack's expression turned speculative. "You know he's pushing for a summit of world religious leaders?"

"I've heard."

"Personally, I think that single world religion concept is a load of—well, he's a fool if he thinks he can get Jews and Muslims to agree to quit killing one another."

Marcus didn't bother to point out that the Bible prophesied just that. "It's a monumental task."

"I know you don't exactly agree with the man's politics, but if you were to get yourself invited to that council meeting—"

"Isack, there is no way I'm going to—"

"I don't see why not," Isack protested.

Marcus knew he could never explain that he had no interest in being associated with anything that contributed to Carpathia's growing base of power. "I'm just not."

"It would take pressure off us for this lawsuit. If we put you back in the public eye in a positive light—"

"It's not open for discussion," Marcus said. "Period."

"I think that's shortsighted. You can rest assured that Theo Carter is playing every media angle he can get. A little positive publicity would go a long way toward taking the wind out of his sails."

Marcus struggled with his frustration as he reminded himself that he had trained Isack to be this aggressive and self-serving. He was responsible for the young man's outlook and attitude about self-promotion and glorification.

"I can appreciate what you're saying. And six weeks ago—six *days* ago—I would have agreed. But I've told you before, things are different now."

"I know. I know," Isack said. "You've seen the light—or so you've said. I just don't understand why you're determined to take us all down with you."

"I'm going to do whatever I feel God calling me to do. Regardless of the consequences. One day, I hope you will understand that."

Isack crossed his arms and gave Marcus a hard look. "Since you're so sure Carpathia's wrong and you're right, tell me how you know God's not calling you to be the one to go to that council meeting where you could argue your point."

The words had a ring of truth that made Marcus shudder. Hadn't he made a similar statement to Brad last night as they discussed the future? Hadn't he been the one to say that God often called His followers to tasks that seemed insurmountable and unachievable? From the moment he'd heard about the ecumenical council meeting, he'd known the impact it would have. The Bible clearly said that a global religion based on lies and godlessness was one of the key events of the Tribulation. The inevitability of what would come from that council meeting was one of the many reasons the idea repulsed him. Yet Isack's words hit a nerve. Who else, his conscience had plagued him, was going to speak the truth in that forum?

The cost, he knew, could be high. His reputation. His ministry. His life. But echoing in the back of his mind was the verse he'd meditated on that morning: "For you have been given not only the privilege of trusting in Christ but also the privilege of suffering for him." Could he really count it a privilege? Marcus wondered. Was he willing to make that much of a sacrifice? His heart told him yes even as his mind screamed at the folly of it all.

Isack was still watching him closely. "How can you claim that God is telling you to speak the truth now, after all these years, but that you're only supposed to speak the truth here in Washington?"

Or to a tightly knit group of hurting, receptive people? Marcus's eyes drifted shut for a second as he accepted the sting of conviction. When he looked at Isack again, the man's eyes were probing, searching. "You could be right." At Isack's surprised expression, he added, "I'm willing to consider it."

That seemed to assuage some of Isack's frustration. "Can I make some calls at least? Just to put out some feelers about how we'd get an invitation."

"No." Marcus tapped his fingers on his desk. "If it's God's will, it'll come to us."

"We never sat and waited for God's will before."

"Like I told you," he said with a sad smile, "things are different now."

Isack hesitated but finally shook his head. "Fine." He levered out of his chair. "But faith doesn't feed people. Money does."

"And God still provides manna when His people are starving."

"I'm of the opinion right now that God is a cosmic bully who likes to play games with our lives," Isack admitted. "Why else would we be in this mess?"

Marcus's heart twisted. How well he remembered hurling those same accusations at the heavens when his wife had died after a long battle with cancer. He, too, had shaken his fist in defiance and demanded that God explain Himself. Lacking an answer, he'd turned his back on grace.

And look where it got me, he wanted to scream at Isack.

"All I can tell you," he said instead, "is that I know what you're going through. I know what it's like to lose everyone you love."

Isack stared at him a moment, and Marcus sensed the war in the man's soul. He was wrestling with God, and at the moment his anger and bitterness were keeping him from seeing the truth. "Just do something about a lawyer, Marcus. We're all involved now. You owe us protection." He turned to go. As he strode across the thick carpet, Marcus could see the barely suppressed rage and disappointment in his purposeful strides and squarely set shoulders.

"Isack?"

Isack stopped, his hand on the door handle. He turned to look at Marcus. "Yes?"

"I know this hasn't been easy for you, staying on. I appreciate it."

"To be perfectly honest, if I had somewhere else to go, I would. This may come as a surprise to you, but there aren't a lot of job openings at the moment for someone who's been the communications director for an admitted con man."

Marcus didn't flinch, though the angry words hit a nerve. "You have a job with us as long as you want it."

"If you don't do something about Theo Carter, you won't be in a position to keep that promise."

Isack left through the heavy glass door, and Marcus watched it glide silently shut behind him.

Weary and defeated, Marcus walked to the large plate-glass window that overlooked a breathtaking view of Washington, D.C. The city still showed the scars of the Rapture. Airplane wreckage littered the banks of the Potomac. Several buildings bore huge black craters where fires had ripped through the neoclassic structures.

Had it really been just over a week since he'd watched at this window as God had taken his faithful and covered the earth in a blanket of righteous judgment? It was hard to fathom. It seemed as though the world had turned upside down since then. In desperation and fear, people had turned to anyone who looked capable of providing leadership and promising relief. Carpathia's agenda of a global religion, unilateral disarmament, a global currency, and a single world power would have been ignored or ridiculed just a few weeks ago.

Yet the Bible had foretold all those things for centuries. Arrogant men, learned men, men like Marcus, had discounted it all as allegory and myth. Only now did he see the truth in it. Only now—when God had literally driven him to his knees and humbled him to the point where he'd lain prostrate on this very carpet and poured out his soul in a desperate cry for mercy—did he understand the terrible truth of it all. God was raining down His judgment on the earth.

The more Marcus studied and prayed, the more he'd begun to develop a vision for what he believed God was calling him to do. Having failed God in the past, Marcus was committed to living out His will now, no matter what the consequences. But thus far, he'd only had the courage to share that vision with Brad. They'd agreed to pray about it independently, then discuss it again in a week. And there was simply no way for Marcus to deny that carrying out that vision would have enormous personal and financial costs.

So he'd wrestled with the conundrum. The settlement money felt like ill-gotten gain, but hadn't it been left to his ministry as a means of carrying on God's work? Though he'd solicited it under false pretenses, would it now be wrong to use it for the kingdom?

Marcus rubbed his neck as he studied the view. He'd

been asking the questions for days. God had not yet answered. Or had He? He glanced at his desk where Isack had left the subpoena. Was God giving him a not-too-subtle push to take action? And what of Isack's convincing words about the religious council? Could that also be the voice of God?

He managed a brief smile as he remembered a minister friend from South America. Though lacking formal education, Paco Mendez was a very wise and very learned man. He now sat in the presence of God, and oh, how Marcus envied him. In his broken English, Paco used to refer to the way Gideon had tested God's promises as "fleecing the Lord." Marcus had never been able to explain the nuances of the idiom.

Jesus Himself had said, "Don't be troubled. You trust God, now trust in Me." It was past time, Marcus thought while he crossed to his desk, that he quit relying on his own power and begin living what he believed and taught. "Lord, I believe," he said quietly. "Help my unbelief."

Marcus pulled open his top drawer and found the business card Brad had given him. He punched the number on his phone.

It was answered on the second ring. "Office of the White House Counsel. How may I direct your call?"

Marcus glanced at the card. "Sanura Kyle, please."

"May I tell her who's calling?"

"I'm a friend of Brad Benton's."

★   ★   ★

"Hi, it's me," Randal told Brad when he finally reached him on his cell phone. He'd dropped off his two passengers at the airline terminal, then stopped to make the call from an airport pay phone. He had already decided that he wanted to replace his cell phone before using one again for any conversation of importance. His conversation with Drake and Swelder that morning had left him feeling a little paranoid.

"How nice to hear a friendly voice," Brad said. "I just got a call from Harmon Drake."

"Hmm. That guy gets around. He had me on the carpet earlier this morning." Randal rested his hand on top of the pay phone. "Wait a minute—isn't this your top secret, dedicated line?"

"Yeah." Brad sounded worried.

"Then how did he get your number?"

"I don't know. I didn't ask. I'm assuming it wasn't by calling directory assistance, though."

"Did he say anything about what's going on here?"

"He said your father's people removed something from my apartment this morning."

"He did. Mom has it. Drake was probably chafed about it, huh?"

"I'd say so. He's assigning me a security detail."

"You're going to let them follow you?"

"No choice. Fitzhugh gave the order." Brad paused, and Randal could hear the buzz of traffic on the other end of the phone. "How are things there?"

"Like I said, Drake and Swelder hauled me in this morning to ask me a couple of questions. I played dumb."

"How hard was that?"

Randal grinned. "Piece of cake. I learned it hanging around political campaigns."

Brad laughed, and Randal was glad to hear it. Despite the age difference, he felt close to Brad and considered him both a mentor and friend.

"I can imagine," Brad said. "Anything else happen besides your meeting with Drake and Swelder?"

"Oh yeah." Randal told him about the conversation he'd overheard in the car, making sure to carefully relate sketchy details he overheard about Victor Rudd. "I'm not sure if that makes any sense to you or not. But if Rudd had anything to do with Ramiro's disappearance, well, let's just say you're not going to be able to hide from him long. Not even in California."

"Victor Rudd," Brad mused. "You're sure?"

"Completely."

"Hmm."

At Brad's noncommittal response, Randal frowned. Was Brad protecting him, too? Like Randal's mother, did Brad think he was too young to have a role in all this? "What are you thinking?"

"Do you know your way around the FEC?" Brad asked.

"Sure." Around Randal's twelfth birthday, Max had started sending him to the Federal Election Commission headquarters to pull quarterly reports on his opponents' contribution records.

"Then see what you can find in the last three or four years for a guy named Constantine Kostankis."

Randal pulled a pen from his breast pocket and quickly scrawled the name on his dispatch ledger. "Who is he?"

"His name surfaced a couple of months ago in a meeting in the Oval. I especially want to know if the guy's connected to Rudd and what kind of PACs he might have contributed to. Check out Rudd as well. Might as well see what we're up against."

"Okay. Anything else?"

"I want to know if Rudd has any international holdings in Crete."

"Is that where this Constantine guy fits in?"

"Maybe. He's an international financier based in the Greek Isles. The Select Committee on Homeland Security is

looking into Kostankis's possible ties to several antiterror-
ist militant groups in the Middle East. Kostankis might
have been the middleman if a deal was made to transfer reserves through South Range. When we discussed this in the
Oval, Fitzhugh and Swelder both seemed anxious to put
the lid on the speculation. I didn't think much of it at the
time, but now it seems to fit together. They're clearly worrying about something surfacing. That might be it."

"I'll see what I can get." Randal pocketed his pen. "What
about Carpathia's visit to Washington? You going to try to
get back for that?" The news that Nicolae Carpathia was
coming to Washington had shaken Randal. Until now,
he'd been able to mentally distance himself from the
thought of the Antichrist.

"I don't know if I can make it. Any idea when it's scheduled?"

"No, but it's soon." Though he believed what Marcus
had told him and the rational part of his brain accepted
that Carpathia appeared to be the man who was using the
forces of evil to set the events of the Tribulation into motion, he hadn't felt personally threatened until he'd learned
that Carpathia was scheduled to pay a visit to the White
House.

"Did it sound like a done deal?" Brad asked. "Or just
something Fitzhugh was bragging about?"

"Done. They were talking about using footage from the
visit for the campaign."

"Do you know who your passengers were?"

"No. It would normally be on the manifest, but I didn't
do the pickup this morning. I agreed to take them to the airport as a favor to another driver. He'll have the paperwork."
Randal thought about it. "An older man named Bill. He
called the younger one Ryan. I don't know if that's his first
name or last name."

"Doesn't ring a bell. Any chance you can get your hands on the manifest?"

"Sure. I just gotta flirt with the dispatcher a little. She'll tell me."

"Okay. Do that when you can, but don't take any chances."

Randal frowned slightly. "You don't have to protect me, you know."

"It's a matter of saving my own skin. Your mother will kill me if I don't send you home in one piece."

Randal stifled his irritation. Mariette had everyone convinced of his general naïveté and vulnerability. "All I'm going to do is ask questions. I'll make sure I don't rouse any suspicions."

Brad hesitated but finally agreed. "Just keep your head down."

"I will."

"And no matter how normal things seem, don't trust anyone at the White House. Not even Drake."

"Don't worry. My dad taught me everything I'll ever need to know about not trusting politicians." Randal glanced over his shoulder. Traffic continued to whiz by on the George Washington Parkway. "Look, I gotta go. They're going to start wondering where I am if I don't have the car back soon."

"I understand."

"You coming back soon?"

"Maybe tomorrow. I got what I needed here."

"I'll get that information for you as soon as I can."

"Just be careful, Randal. Very, very careful."

6

"Amen," Marcus said, and Randal and Mariette echoed it in unison. It was just after 8:30 p.m., and they'd met at Shiloh Baptist Church tonight to pray for Brad's safety and to talk about the future. Marcus normally would have invited them to his home, but given Brad's suspicions about surveillance, the church seemed slightly safer—at least for now. Though it had been just under twenty-four hours, it seemed like a lifetime had passed since the bomb exploded in Brad's apartment.

Marcus noted the obvious tension between mother and son but refrained from comment.

Randal seemed eager enough to fill the strained silence. "All right," he said, rubbing his hands together, "let's get down to business. Brad mentioned he might be back here as early as tomorrow." He'd already told them both about what he'd heard in the car and his conversation with Brad. "I checked on some information for him today, but I've got a lot to go through." He glanced at his mother. "FEC reports."

Mariette winced. "My sympathies."

Marcus watched the exchange with a sense of relief. Whatever was causing strife between the pair, they still maintained a common ground.

Randal leaned back in the pew and stretched his arms across the back. "I forgot to ask him if he found the reporter."

"He did," Marcus confirmed. He'd called Brad to discuss his conversation with Sanura Kyle.

Mariette nodded. "They were on their way to the coroner's office when I called him about the Bible."

Marcus smiled slightly. "I'm sure he enjoyed having us all check in today."

"What I want to know is how Harmon Drake got Brad's private cell number," Randal said.

"Secret Service," Mariette said dismissively. "They're like the FBI. They know everything. And what they don't know, they can find out."

"Maybe," Randal said. "I still don't like it. I'm not thrilled about Drake's security detail on Brad."

"I'm sure Brad's unhappy about it, too," Marcus concurred. "But I'll bet he can lose them if he has to. I'm sure he learned how to handle himself during his Navy Special Ops training."

"You think?" Randal said. "I don't think it's going to be that easy."

"I have faith in Brad and in God for providing us all with opportunities when we need to do His work. Brad'll handle it. Right now, he's going where they want him to go. I'm sure he wants to be back here for Carpathia's visit." Marcus rubbed a hand over his face. Like Randal, he had felt shocked and somehow violated to think of Carpathia in such close proximity to him. And Mariette was headed to New York tomorrow, where she would be exposed to the man and his media circus. Marcus deliberately derailed the thought. God was big enough and powerful enough to handle that matter. He didn't need Marcus's help or advice.

"Did Brad learn anything from his reporter friend?" Randal asked.

"All he said is that he'd gotten what he needed," Marcus replied.

"Okay, then. I don't know anything else to report except what I already told you about this Kostankis guy Brad wants me to research."

"Marcus," Mariette probed, "you said you had something else you wanted to talk about tonight. Something you'd discussed with Brad."

"Yes." He had hoped to wait until Brad returned, but with Mariette leaving, he now felt a sense of urgency to talk about Theo Carter's lawsuit. "I talked to a lawyer today about the lawsuit, someone Brad recommended from the White House."

"Oh." Mariette propped her chin on her hand. "I thought about you this morning when I caught the court's ruling on the insurance issue."

"I heard that on the radio," Randal added. "The insurance industry is screaming that paying off the claims for the vanished is going to bankrupt them."

"It might." Marcus braced his forearms on the back of a pew and pressed his fingertips together. "I didn't actually even know how much of it New Covenant stood to gain until last night. A member of my staff put together some figures for me. It's an enormous amount of money."

"More than you thought?" Mariette guessed.

Marcus had estimated the amount would be a couple million dollars. "About ten times more."

Randal let out a low whistle. "*Ten* times?"

Marcus nodded. "I had no idea we'd been that successful with fund-raising. It makes the dilemma a little tougher."

Mariette drummed her fingers on the back of a pew. "What did the lawyer say were your chances of actually getting the money?"

"She felt good about it from what I described. She's coming to get the paperwork from me tomorrow."

Comprehension dawned on Randal's face. "That's got to be Sanura Kyle."

Surprised, Marcus raised an eyebrow. "You know her?"

"Not until today. She came down to the motor pool to ask if anybody knew the Crystal City area. She said she didn't have the address with her, but she was going to need some directions tomorrow. I told her I could help." He laughed slightly. "Man, I didn't know it was your office. I'd have told her I could find the place in my sleep."

"She's not a believer, but Brad says she's a top-rate litigator," Marcus told them.

Randal jabbed Marcus's arm. "That's not all. Wait until you meet her." His eyes twinkled. "That is one fine woman, if you know what I mean. Smart, assertive, and drop-dead gorgeous."

"I'll keep that in mind," Marcus said dryly.

"It's tough not to," Randal said. "You'll see. Call me after you meet her and see if you're still so calm."

"I'm sure Marcus can handle meeting an attractive woman." Mariette turned to Marcus. "Did you tell her you're undecided about taking the money?"

There it was, Marcus thought, the same question that had kept him up nights and on his knees seeking an answer. Mariette and Randal understood the guilt he was feeling when he considered accepting the money. He knew how much good he could accomplish with the windfall, how many people he could help, how many souls he could reach with the gospel. On the other hand, it felt a little like dirty money. In desperation, he'd finally tossed out a fleece. "I think I went down an inevitable path today by contacting her. If we win this case, then I have to believe it's God's will that we use the money for ministry. If we lose, then my problem is solved."

"That makes sense," Randal mused. "I know you could do a lot with that much money."

"That's what I wanted to talk to you both about." Marcus linked his fingers behind his head and studied the stained-glass window above the baptistery on the front wall. It depicted Jesus carrying a lamb over His shoulders. Marcus realized he'd never really looked at the window before, but now the allusion to Christ as the shepherd watching over and caring for His flock felt validating. "I believe God has given me a vision." He looked closely at the two of them. "When I discussed this with Brad, I told him I wanted him to pray about it and see what answer he got. I'm asking the same thing of both of you."

"Sure." Randal leaned forward, his expression intense. "What are you thinking?"

"In Revelation, the Bible clearly states that the Great Tribulation is going to test all of us. It'll bring horrors we've never dreamed of."

"That scares me," Mariette confessed. "My dreams are pretty horrific."

"I imagine you've seen some awful things through your work," Marcus said.

"I have. And if it's going to be worse than those catastrophes, it's hard for me to imagine."

"God will protect us," Randal said, his voice full of youthful confidence. "For as long as He has work for us to do."

Marcus didn't bother to point out that the prophecies

also talked about martyrdom for many of the so-called tribulation saints. None of them had any guarantees that they would make it to the end. They might not even see tomorrow, Marcus knew. But now wasn't the time to address that.

Instead, he focused on the issue at hand. "Lately I've been studying a lot about the persecution of the saints and the remnant of Israel that God promises to save from the destruction. I think there is a major disaster coming. It wouldn't even surprise me if somebody launched a nuclear attack. We've already seen nuclear weapons used on Israel, even before the disappearances. God interceded in that attack, but another could happen again at any time. The world's very unstable since the Rapture."

Randal's eyes widened. "Nuclear attack . . . like a bomb?"

"Yes. And the Bible speaks of terrible natural disasters as well. I have felt more and more led to talk to both of you and to Brad, about the need for a shelter of some sort, a place we could go to ride out the disasters."

"I can't picture living the rest of my life in some fortified hole, Marcus," Mariette said.

Marcus held up a hand. "I'm not talking about staying down there permanently. What I see is that we could make plans and prepare the place in case we need it for a while. Other believers are going to need shelter, too."

"This sounds kind of cold warish to me," Randal said. "I still remember reading all kinds of 'nuclear winter' fiction when I was in school. I think the teachers wanted to give us the same nightmares they heard about as kids."

"This is going to be a war," Marcus concurred. "Probably a worse war than any cold war theorists could have imagined. But I don't feel any of us would want to sit back and let it happen around us without doing whatever we can for the cause of Christ." He glanced at Mariette. "I don't think we're wired that way."

"Maybe not," she said. "But if we go to the shelter to avoid the blast—or the fires or floods or famines or whatever might be coming—then what do we do after the dust settles?"

"The Scriptures clearly state that when the Antichrist is fully in control, he'll begin persecuting the believers. Everyone left alive will be required to take a mark—an identifier of some type—and anyone who refuses the mark will be put to death. But God has promised to protect a remnant of believers. The Bible says He'll gather them from around the world and shield them from the disasters." Marcus paused to let that sink in. "And I feel led to play a part in helping that remnant escape and survive."

"What do you mean by escape?" Randal asked.

"I believe people will have to flee from persecution the same way the Jews had to flee the Nazis to survive during World War II. Christians will need money, false identities, transportation, and gathering places. I think if we take on this project and build the shelter correctly, we can become one of the stops for shelter along the way to safety."

"Like the Underground Railroad." Randal's eyes gleamed. "That's incredible."

"Look, I do disaster relief for a living." Mariette frowned. "Do you really think we're equipped for that? We're talking about a global mission that will require massive amounts of stockpiled goods."

"I think that if God is truly calling us to this mission, He'll send us whatever resources we need, human or otherwise."

"We'd need killer computer systems. And some kind of secret transportation." Randal's mind was clearly racing with the possibilities. "And a Web presence with a multi-location server."

"Hold on," Marcus said. "I think you're getting ahead of yourself here. I want both of you to be aware of the risks involved and give this some serious thought."

"I don't have to think about it," Randal assured him. "It's been driving me crazy just sitting around waiting for Carpathia to do something. I've been begging God to give me a mission, something that matters." He looked at his mother. "I know you're worried about me, but I couldn't live with myself if I didn't do everything I can to bring about God's will on this earth. If I've only got seven years of my life left—or less—I want them to count."

Marcus said a silent prayer, thanking God for sending this passionate young man to him. In Randal's youthful enthusiasm, Marcus found energy and hope for the future. Mariette, however, looked unconvinced. "Mariette?"

"I can't tell you right now," she said. "This is very ambitious. I'm going to have to pray about it first."

Marcus nodded. "I completely understand."

She tucked a strand of hair behind her ear. "But I do know that if things go the way I expect them to in New York tomorrow, I'm going to be in and out of there a lot. I've established a decent rapport with the mayor, but the city has some pretty major problems dealing with all this. It's probably one of our biggest challenges right now as far as relief efforts are concerned."

"New York," Randal said. "Gateway to the world. Can't you see it, Mom? Can't you see what those contacts could do if we had to smuggle someone out of the country?"

"We don't have to make any decisions tonight," Marcus told them. "We just need to see what God wants from us."

"What did Brad say about your idea?" Mariette asked. "I'm assuming you told him about it."

"I did, and I don't know yet. He's praying about it, too. That's all I'm asking both of you to do. But I think this financial windfall might very well be a sign that we're supposed to do something major. Maybe we'll have some answers tomorrow after I talk to the lawyer."

★   ★   ★

"It's not safe, Liza," Brad said into his cell phone. After they'd left the medical examiner's office, he'd dropped Liza at her car so he could head home.

He strode to the window of his suburban Los Angeles home and eased back the curtain. Parked across the street from his house was the beige sedan of his security detail. They'd been waiting for him when he turned onto his street. At least they were punctual and fairly discreet. The tinted glass made it difficult for neighbors to tell there were two men inside keeping a constant watch on his house and his movements.

The call from Drake, coupled with Randal's information about Victor Rudd, had given Brad a clear look at his situation. For the first time, he genuinely feared for the lives of the people he'd involved. Brad had told Liza that as far as he was concerned, he wanted her to drop the story. He'd warned her that her life was probably in danger.

Evidently, she hadn't listened. She had just told him she finally reached an associate of Ramiro's who was willing to talk. Frustrated, Brad paced the living-room floor. "I told you to drop it."

"Yeah. I'm going to drop what could be one of the biggest stories of the year."

"If you don't, you're probably going to get killed."

"I'll take my chances. That's what reporters do. This guy I found, he works for a PR firm in L.A. He worked with Ramiro before he went to Washington with the president. He talked to Ramiro a couple of weeks ago, and he has a pretty good idea of what the guy was working on. He didn't want to talk to me on the phone, so I'm going to meet him."

"Are you out of your mind?" Brad felt like he was talking

to one of his daughters. "Did I mention that someone has tried to kill me twice already because of this?"

"I'm only going alone if you don't go with me."

"Like that's an improvement. I'm a walking assassin magnet lately." Brad ground his teeth. "Do you understand what you're dealing with here? This isn't a game, Liza. These people have the power to make you disappear."

"Just like they did George Ramiro and tried to do to you. For that matter, who knows how many others they've made disappear. Aren't you curious about what he's got to say? You're not dropping this, are you?"

"No," he admitted. He wouldn't be able to live with himself if he turned like a coward and ran.

"Then I'm not either. You made me your partner in this when you sent me those photos. You probably wish you'd picked a journalist with more clout. . . ."

"No. I gave you the story because you've always been fair. I valued that fairness when I was on the gubernatorial campaign, and I still do."

"Then are you coming with me to meet this source or not?"

"I can't talk you out of it altogether?"

"No chance."

"Then I'm coming." He closed his eyes in resignation. "Tell me where to meet you. I've got a security detail to lose."

★   ★   ★

"I should have warned you not to wear your good shoes," Liza said three hours later as she and Brad picked their way through the muddy, debris-filled Union Pacific rail yard. "Don't you know informants always want to meet some place dirty and dark?"

"I haven't met a lot of informants." Brad slid his hands

into the pockets of his Windbreaker. A stiff breeze put a chill into the otherwise mild evening.

Liza laughed. "Yeah, well, a couple of things I can tell you. There are two kinds of informants. There are the ones who want fame. They're usually pretty useless. Then there are the ones who are scared to death they're going to get caught but can't live with themselves if they don't talk. I think this guy is the second kind." She stepped over one of the rails so she could walk down the center of the tracks.

"How did you find him?"

"Fluke. I started doing background research on Ramiro by doing a Lexis-Nexis search on his name. You can understand how the White House press secretary's name is going to appear in thousands of articles."

" 'According to White House Press Secretary George Ramiro—,' " Brad recited.

"Yep. That showed up a lot. It took me a few days to cull articles that weren't specifically about Ramiro, but I finally got it manageable." She leaped over a puddle of grimy-looking water. "This guy wrote an article about Ramiro while they were both grad students at Stanford. I wouldn't have thought much about it, except for a comment he wrote about Ramiro's sister. It sounded really personal— you know, like he knew it because he'd met her, not because he was researching an article."

"That had to be twenty years ago."

"Nearly. It was a long shot, but I was running out of leads. I talked to surviving members of George's family, and as far as I could tell, they didn't know anything. Evidently, George's relationship with the rest of the family had been strained for years, and they hadn't talked to him since he'd called home at Christmas." They reached a junction in the tracks, and Liza stopped and scanned the dimly lit yard. "He said freight terminal six. You see anything?"

Brad searched the darkness. Except for a group of indigents huddled around the dull glow of a trash-can fire, he saw no signs of life. If someone wanted to commit murder, he thought, this was as good a place as any to do it. To his left, he heard a sudden thud and a loud rattle.

Liza gave him a sharp look. "What was that?"

Brad narrowed his eyes as he strained to see in the shadows. With a screech, a mangy tabby cat leaped down from a barrel and bounded across their path. "Morris, the killer cat."

"Man, oh, man." She looked down the tracks again. "I feel like Woodward and Bernstein tracking Deep Throat. I'm so nervous my knees feel wobbly."

And not without reason, Brad thought. With two close escapes under his belt, he'd become fairly paranoid in the last few days. "You're sure this isn't a setup?"

Liza continued walking down the tracks. "Pretty sure. The guy sounded scared enough on the phone. And I contacted him; he didn't come to me. Reporters are mostly baited into setups."

Brad fell into step beside her. "You didn't finish telling me how he knew George."

"Oh. Turns out the *Stanford Daily's* writers have their own alumni organization. The Stanford Daily Publishing Corporation owns the paper, and Ramiro was on the board of directors. My source says he talked to George three days before he disappeared about some issue the board was considering."

Before Brad could respond, he saw movement about twenty yards down the track. A figure stepped from the shadow of a freight car and started toward them. "Is that him?"

Liza pulled her press credentials from her pocket. "Either him or railroad security. Come on." She hurried toward the approaching figure. They were six feet away when the man tipped his head to the left and led them over a junction in the tracks to a loading bay. The massive cranes used to transfer sea/land containers between flatbed cars loomed over them like a giant web of steel.

"Let me see your ID," the man said.

Liza handed it to him, and Brad examined the man's appearance—neat and well groomed, with a jacket that looked like designer leather. He looked like what he claimed to be: an innocent bystander whose conscience wouldn't let him sit on information.

The man handed Liza's ID back and looked at Brad. "This the guy?"

"Yes," Liza said. "I told you I might bring someone with me."

The man searched Brad's face. "You really the chief of staff at the White House?"

"I've got a business card, if you want it."

"No, it's okay." The man glanced over his shoulder. "The only people stupid enough to dig this up would be reporters, cops, or politicians." He looked around them and then to the right and left. "Let's make this quick, okay? My wife's waiting at home scared to death."

Liza pulled a microcassette recorder from her pocket. "Is it all right if I tape this?"

The man gave her a wary look. "You said no names."

"I'm not going to use your name. I'm not even going to directly reference this conversation. I just want to be able to make sure I get it all accurately. It's easier if I tape it."

He hesitated. "I don't think—"

"I'll protect you as a source."

"You've got a good reputation for that. I checked." He studied Liza's face. "All right."

She nodded as she hit the record button. "I already told

Mr. Benton about your connection with Ramiro. Tell us what you two talked about the last time you called him."

"We had a board meeting coming up. We talked about a policy amendment for a few minutes; then we asked the usual questions about each other's family. You know, how are the kids, how's the job—that kind of thing." He glanced over his shoulder again. "Nothing out of the ordinary."

"So how do you know George didn't kill himself?" Brad pressed.

The man ran a hand through his hair and looked at him. "Because when I asked him how he was enjoying Washington, he told me he'd just put down a big deposit on a house in McLean, and he was planning to permanently relocate his family to the D.C. region. Why would somebody suicidal do something like that?"

Liza shifted her recorder to her other hand. "Could have been debt. If the house put him in a bind—"

"He also told me he was taking a vacation, going to the Virgin Islands for about a week before the board meeting. He said he had an appointment for a big meeting in New York that Monday, and then he was going out of town."

Brad faced Liza. "The appointment." He'd told her on their way to the rail yard about his telephone call from Randal. "Anything else?" Down the tracks, a loud buzz and the grind of a junction switch signaled a train's approach.

The man shrank deeper into the shadows. "Well, yeah. Actually, I wouldn't have thought anything about it except that George just disappeared along with everyone else. But three days ago, I got an anonymous letter saying George was gone because he couldn't keep his mouth shut, and if the White House press secretary could disappear without a trace, so could an advertising executive and his wife." He turned to Brad. "Was George really murdered?"

"We think so. Was there a postmark on the letter?"

"Local. That's what bothered me. If it had come from Washington, I'd have felt a little safer. But someone's here, and they know where I live, where I work, that I'm married, and that I was a friend of George's."

"Who knew you'd talked to him?" Liza asked. She pulled up her jacket collar when a breeze swept along the concrete deck and wrapped them in its chill.

"I don't know. Some of the board members, my wife, maybe some friends. I have no idea who else I told. It wasn't any big secret."

"Did you bring the letter?" Brad asked.

He reached into his jacket pocket and produced a sealed plastic bag with an envelope inside. "It's here."

"May I have it?"

The man nodded. "Believe me, I'd feel better if somebody else had it."

Brad took the letter and slipped it into his pocket. In the distance, a dog barked as the train drew closer. The slow clatter of the wheels on the track indicated that the train was approaching slowly, probably pulling into the yard for its final stop of the night.

"Did you report this to the police?" Liza prompted.

"Are you kidding? I wasn't going to tell anyone. If it was just me, that's one thing. But my wife . . ."

"I understand," Brad assured him. "Why did you decide to talk to us?"

"I had no idea what had happened to George. As far as anyone knew, he'd resigned from the White House, then disappeared with everyone else. I wanted to believe that's what that letter meant, that if I'd just keep quiet, the whole thing would go away."

The train had grown louder. Down the tracks, Brad saw the headlights as the heavy locomotive entered the yards.

"Then you called me," the man continued. "When you

said George was dead and somebody was trying to cover it up—well, to be honest, I'd like to tell you I had a burst of conscience. But the truth is, it scared me to death. I don't know if my phones are bugged, or if my house is being watched. I can't sleep at night. I figured if you were digging into this, then somebody else probably was, too. I want you to find out who did it and stop them before they come after me and my wife. I think maybe you're my best hope of getting out of this in one piece."

The train had entered the yard and ground to a stop about thirty yards up the track.

The man glanced at the train, then back at them. "Look. I told you everything I know. I gotta get home now."

"Just one more thing," Brad said. "Did George mention any names when you talked to him, either about his trip to New York or his work at the White House?"

The man frowned. "No. Not that I remember. He did say something about some project he was working on. Southbridge. Southridge. Something like that."

The sound of voices calling out instructions drifted from the newly arrived locomotive.

"He didn't tell you anything about it?" Brad asked.

"No. Just that it was taking up a lot of his time, and he'd be glad when it was over." He looked back and forth between Brad and Liza. "I really have to go now."

Liza snapped off the recorder and stuffed it in her back pocket. "One more question. Off the record."

"What?"

"Did Ramiro tell you where he got the money for that deposit?"

"I asked about that. He just said he'd made a couple of really solid investments and gotten out while the market was still hot. He also said he was expecting a big payoff soon."

"Did he say that exactly?" Brad pressed. "A payoff?"

"No, he used another word. I can't remember exactly. Just that it was a big chunk of money." The man held up his hands. "I really can't tell you anything else. Please don't call me again."

"I promise," Liza told him. "Thanks."

The man turned and hurried into the shadows.

As they watched him go, Liza asked, "What do you think?"

"I think that if the money George was talking about getting was an advance, then I know why he was killed."

"Like a book advance?"

"He had that meeting scheduled in New York. He wouldn't be the first White House official to leave politics and write a tell-all book."

"But what kind of information did Ramiro have that got him killed?"

Brad shoved his hands into his pockets. "South Range," he said. He started down the tracks. "Let's get out of here. I'll explain in the car."

★   ★   ★

Randal shot a second look at his watch. The early-morning call from the dispatcher at the White House motor pool had told him to make this pickup at the Willard Hotel at 7 a.m. sharp. A major contributor to Fitzhugh's campaign needed a lift to the airport for an 8:20 flight. Bleary-eyed from a mostly sleepless night of thinking through the possibilities of Marcus's proposal, Randal had managed to drag himself from bed, take a quick shower, grab an apple while avoiding another potential confrontation with his overprotective mother, pick up one of the White House vehicles, and park in front of the Willard at 7:03.

Apparently, he hadn't needed to rush. It was almost eight, and his nameless passenger seemed in no hurry to make his flight. This, Randal thought wryly, was probably a good thing. The guy's chances of getting to the airport in time were slim . . . and slipping away by the minute. Randal waited in the lobby for ten minutes before calling up to the room number he'd been given.

Randal received instructions to go upstairs to room 1125, where the gentleman was wrapping up some last-minute business. The man acknowledged Randal's arrival with a brief nod, then returned his full attention to his phone call. A couple of aides busied themselves on laptop computers and cell phones, so Randal helped himself to a muffin from the overladen breakfast platters sitting around the suite before settling on the sofa to wait.

The television was tuned to CNN. Randal stretched out his long legs and idly watched the streaming information at the bottom of the screen while he waited for the man to complete his business.

Then one of the aides said, "Mr. Rudd?"

Randal nearly choked on his muffin. *Victor Rudd.*

Randal tuned out the sound from the TV and tried to listen in on Rudd's conversation. That's when he heard Rudd mention Brad's name. Randal shot a quick look at the other occupants of the room, found that nobody seemed to be paying attention to him, and shifted slightly on the sofa to turn one ear toward Victor Rudd. In the years before his parents' divorce, he'd mastered the art of subtle eavesdropping. He'd learned as a kid to sit without attracting attention, apparently absorbed in a television show or video game, listening to his parents exchange thinly veiled arguments and accusations. Their conversations had left him feeling guilty for listening and anxious about his future.

For the first time, he was thankful for the skill. He shook

his head in response to a report on the television about American military deaths near the Turkish-Syrian border while honing in on Victor Rudd's conversation. It took him a minute to tune out the other noises in the room—Victor's assistant still talked on a cell phone while another woman pecked away on a notebook computer.

Finally, Randal managed to isolate the low, controlled sound of Rudd's voice.

"I have been assured Benton is going to take responsibility for the South Range decision. We won't be implicated," Rudd said.

Randal frowned when Rudd paused to listen to his caller's response. He was fairly certain he'd never heard Brad mention South Range.

"Justice will probably receive the go-ahead to appoint an independent counsel next week," Rudd was saying. "Just make sure the heat stays on Benton. Understood?" He paused again, then nodded. "Excellent. I've got a plane to catch. I'll call you this afternoon."

Randal swallowed, then put on his game face. It was going to be an interesting ride.

7

"Ms. Arnold." Daniel Berger walked out of his office in New York's City Hall, hand extended, appearing relieved to see her. "Thanks for coming."

Though she'd seen him in the media plenty of times, Mariette found New York's dynamic new mayor even more impressive in person. This was one case where the reality looked better than the image, even up close and personal. She shook the man's hand. He had a firm grip.

"It's a pleasure to meet you," she said. "I have the full backing of the agency and the White House to see what we can do for you and your city, Mr. Mayor."

He flashed her a smile that made his brown eyes gleam. "Daniel, please."

As he led Mariette to his office, he shot a look at his receptionist. "Hold my calls, would you?" Without waiting for an answer, he pushed the door shut with his foot. "Come in. Please excuse the mess." Maps and charts were strewn across the floor; paper covered every conceivable surface; a large whiteboard in one corner held a chart of nearly indecipherable scribbles; and a three-inch stack of pink message slips threatened to overflow from his in-box. On a separate whiteboard, she saw Nicolae Carpathia's name scrawled in huge letters with a calendar of some sort taped underneath. "It's a little chaotic around here."

"You should see my place," Mariette joked, setting her briefcase down. She liked Daniel Berger, she decided, because his suit jacket was slung over the back of his chair and his shirtsleeves were rolled up. A man who rolled up his sleeves, in her experience, was a man who liked to solve problems, hands-on and personally.

He hurried to clear a space for her to sit in one of the chairs across from his desk. "Please, make yourself comfortable. Can I get you anything? You want coffee? water?"

"No. I'm fine." She stood while she watched him dump the stack of papers from the chair on his already overburdened desk.

Then he cleared the chair next to hers. He dropped into it with a slight groan and a dull thud. "Please," he said with a wave of his hand. "Please sit."

As she complied, she realized she was beginning to understand why New York had embraced this man so readily. Tall and distinguished-looking, he had just enough silver in his hair to make him look seasoned but not enough to make him look old. He was dynamic and unaffected and struck her as a politician with the rare and unusual drive to actually help the people who'd elected him. In the aftermath of the Rapture, when New York, like most major cities, had been thrown into panic, his administration had garnered rave reviews from citizens and public officials alike for his commitment to cutting red tape, supporting community efforts, and addressing the problems at hand.

"I've only got one city's worth of problems to solve, Ms.

Arnold," he was saying. "I can't even imagine what you're going through."

She reached for her briefcase. "It's a challenge, but we're managing. And if I have to call you Daniel, you have to call me Mariette."

"Good. I hate formalities."

With a slight smile, she snapped open the locks on her briefcase. "Then how'd you end up in politics?"

"Beats me," he said, his expression so genuine she laughed.

"I think that's the best politician's answer I've ever heard." She opened the briefcase to retrieve her hastily prepared folder on New York's infrastructure, challenges, and possible solutions. Christine Benton's well-worn Bible sat on top of the stack of reports, so she removed it and set it on the edge of the desk.

Daniel looked at the Bible, then at her, obviously surprised. "Is that yours?"

"It's a friend's, actually. I'm just taking care of it."

He leaned toward her. "Are you a Christian?"

She gave him a startled look. He was watching her with a keen interest that she found slightly unnerving. "Yes." Why would he want to know that? "Though I'm a fairly recent convert."

He watched her a moment longer, then collapsed back in his chair, his expression both awed and overjoyed as he looked to the ceiling of his spacious office. "Thank You, God."

Mariette could only stare at him.

When Daniel met her gaze again, she would have sworn his eyes were misty. "You can't begin to imagine what an answer to prayer that is."

"You're a believer?"

"Yes." He grinned. "New, naturally."

"But aren't you—?"

"Jewish? Yes. I was—am." He clearly saw her confusion. "Let's try that again, only clearer. I'm Jewish, but I have accepted Christ as my Messiah."

She felt slightly overwhelmed. Whatever she'd expected from Daniel Berger, it hadn't been this. "I see."

In a fluid motion, he stood and rounded his desk. He produced an equally well-worn Bible. "This belonged to a good friend of mine," he explained as he walked back to his seat. "A Christian friend. I'd known Josh for years. We played tennis together. We vacationed together. I was best man at his wedding. He was always telling me I had to get right with God, that being Jewish wasn't going to save my soul." Daniel sat down again and cradled the Bible in his hands. "And I was too stubborn to listen to him."

"My mother," Mariette said quietly, "tried to tell me. She was very devout. I didn't listen, either."

"This is probably why Shakespeare said, 'Pride goes before destruction and hautiness before a fall.'"

Mariette laughed. "Shakespeare didn't say that. It's in the Bible. Proverbs 16:18."

"See?" he pointed out. "At least you listened more than I did."

"My mother was a Baptist. We memorized Scripture almost as often as we ate. It didn't make me a Christian, just a well-read agnostic. I'm pretty stubborn. It took the Rapture to bring me to Jesus."

That made Daniel laugh. "Well, wherever that quote came from, it was pride and stubbornness that kept me from listening to Josh. And pride and stubbornness left me here while Josh went ahead." He looked at her closely. "Did you lose anyone?"

"Not really." She remembered the wrecked and empty

car in her neighbor's driveway. "Some acquaintances, but my son and ex-husband are still here."

"I'm not sure if that's a curse or a blessing."

"Both, I think. My son, Randal, is a new believer, too. He led me to the Lord, in fact. But I worry about what's coming and what could happen to him. It's hard for me to just turn him over to God."

Daniel shook his head. "I never had kids. I can't imagine what that fear must be like."

Mariette remembered that when Daniel Berger was elected the press had made an issue of his singleness. For a while, there had been ugly rumors about his private life, but he'd won the media battle by quietly insisting on dignity and not stooping to their level to confirm or deny whatever was thrown at him. Watching him now, she wasn't surprised. He seemed to be the kind of man who placed a high value on dignity and honor.

"Did you lose anyone?" she asked. "Besides your friend, I mean."

"Josh's family. His kids might as well have been my nieces and nephews. I was their godfather. I lost my parents when I was in college and Josh's family sort of took me in. His parents were raptured, too." Daniel paused, visibly struggling with emotion. "One of the hardest things has been knowing that my parents died as devout Jews who never knew that Jesus was our Messiah. It's hard for me to imagine—" He broke off with a slight shake of his head. "Other than Josh's family, I lost a few business associates, some political allies, but no one close. My career—and this job—have kept me from forming a lot of close relationships."

"I remember those days," she said sadly. "Max was on his way up and everything else got left behind."

He gave her a blank look; then comprehension dawned. "Max Arnold."

"My ex-husband."

"I didn't know that."

Mariette managed a slight laugh. "Believe me, there are times when I wish I didn't know it either."

Daniel set his friend's Bible on the desk. "The night of the Rapture, I went looking for Josh. I didn't know then what had happened, but when I got to his house, I found the clothes." His voice had turned husky. "I knew I needed to come in to the office. You can imagine the chaos."

"I was here last week with the emergency barges. Things were a mess."

"Still are. I'm sure you saw it on your way in from the airport. I knew I had to get here that night, but I couldn't make myself move. I just sat there for hours screaming at God for letting this happen to my friends."

Mariette's heart twisted as she pictured the scene. This, she knew, was what Brad had experienced. She'd seen first-hand how devastated he'd been. She couldn't imagine what Daniel Berger had gone through if he'd had no one to share his grief with. "How did you know? About what had happened, I mean. How did you know it was the Rapture?"

"When I couldn't put it off any longer, I made myself come down here. For the first twenty-four hours, everything was so crazy I just buried myself in work so I wouldn't have to think about any of it. It was sometime in the next couple of days when I finally had a chance to breathe that I remembered Josh giving me a key to a safety-deposit box after he survived a serious car accident. It changed him."

"I'm sure."

"He told me he'd put some stuff he wanted me to get if anything ever happened to him in that box. Papers, his will, some personal things. I always assumed they were life-insurance policies and things for his family."

"They weren't?"

"That was part of it. But there was a letter for me in there, too. He told me how he and his wife and his kids had been praying for my soul and how he knew I needed Christ. The letter said there were only two reasons I'd be reading it. Either he'd been killed and had gone on to heaven, or he'd been raptured along with the rest of his family. He gave me a list of Scriptures to read and begged me to get a Bible and get straight with God. Everything he'd ever said, every sermon I'd ever gotten from his parents about faith and sin and eternal life—it all started to make sense. So I drove out to Long Island that afternoon and got Josh's Bible from his house." Daniel took a deep breath. "I sat down on the deck outside and read until it got dark. And I met Jesus."

Mariette's eyes stung with unshed tears. "You had no one," she whispered. She couldn't imagine what this would have been like for her without the sheltering support of Randal and her two brothers in Christ.

Daniel looked at her intently. "I've *had* no one. I tried finding a church, but every one I went to was either closed because the bulk of their congregation was missing, or they had the same preacher they'd had before the Rapture, and he wasn't admitting that anything was wrong. I couldn't stomach that."

"I was lucky," she said. "I had Randal, and I have a very good friend—Marcus Dumont."

Daniel's eyes widened at the name. "The black evangelist. Is he still—?"

"Yes. He was left behind. But he came face-to-face with God as a result, and he's a great spiritual leader now."

"I'd like to talk to him." Daniel frowned. "I've been trying to read Revelation, just to get a feel for what things are going to be like. I have to confess; I'm lost."

"I would be too if it weren't for Marcus."

Daniel looked down at his Bible for a moment. "Has Dumont said anything about Nicolae Carpathia?"

Mariette's pulse tripped up a notch as she considered how to answer that. She had no idea what Daniel Berger thought of Carpathia, what his ties to him might be, and how he felt about having the man in his city. "We've been talking a lot about the current world picture." She leaned back in her chair, afraid he'd hear the way her heart was pounding. "Marcus is very knowledgeable about prophecy."

Daniel met her gaze again. "You know, some people think that Carpathia is some kind of messiah."

"His ideas are very popular."

"I think he's evil."

Mariette released the pent-up breath she hadn't even known she was holding. "So do we. Marcus saw it first." She dropped her voice to a near whisper. "Some people would think I'm crazy for this, but I think Marcus is right. He says Carpathia is the Antichrist."

"Whew, so it isn't just me." Daniel noticeably relaxed. "I think so, too. If he's not the Antichrist, he's definitely aligned with something—or someone—evil. You can't imagine what it's been like having him in the city."

"I'm sure the media presence is making a tough job more difficult," Mariette said.

"That's one problem. But the main problem for me is that I feel physically sick when I'm around him."

"How many times have you met with him?"

"Twice. Once when he first got here. I didn't know who he was then. He seemed charming enough, if a little smarmy. But when he was sworn in as secretary-general, we gave him the key to the city. It's a tradition in New York. It took everything I had just to stand on the platform with him."

Mariette remembered Brad's story about the day Marcus had led him to Christ. He'd physically felt the presence of evil, an oppression, as he'd neared his decision. Randal had reported the same thing. "Did it feel like something was clawing at you? Dragging at you physically?"

His eyes widened. "Yes."

Mariette nodded. "My son says the same thing happened to him the night he accepted Christ. Marcus says it's spiritual warfare. I know it sounds a little weird—"

"No, it doesn't."

"I've never experienced it myself, but I'm sure it's overwhelming."

"You can't imagine . . ." Daniel shook his head.

"You were protected because of your faith." Like Brad. She had a sudden thought. "Daniel, did you watch Carpathia's meeting with his new Security Council by any chance?"

"No. They wouldn't let media into the room. But I have to tell you, if there hadn't been a roomful of witnesses, I wouldn't have bought that story about Todd-Cothran and Stonagal. I know those men. Stonagal wasn't a killer. I don't care what anybody says. But there's no doubt in my mind that Carpathia is capable of killing."

"That he is. And he's also capable of brainwashing that same roomful of witnesses into believing the suicide story."

Daniel stared at her. "Are you serious?"

Lord, she prayed, *please let this be the right thing to do.* "If I tell you this, there's a chance I could be putting you in personal danger, in political danger."

"What do you know?" he asked.

She hesitated but felt a strong sense of peace at the

thought of telling him. She was learning daily to recognize God's presence and leadership in her life, and she had to trust it now. "The night Randal led me to the Lord, we were on our way back from that delivery in New York. We went to meet with Marcus Dumont. He was waiting for the White House chief of staff."

"Brad Benton."

"Yes. Brad's a new Christian, too. Since that night, the four of us have come together as a prayer team and a family. Brad lost his wife and three kids the night of the Rapture. He's gone through the same kind of grief you have. His whole family is gone."

With a frown, Daniel reached over to shuffle some of the papers on his desk. He produced the morning edition of the *New York Times*. He handed it to her. An article about the explosion in Brad's apartment appeared on the lower half of the front page. "This wasn't an accident, was it?"

"We don't think so."

"Is he all right? The paper says—"

"He's fine. He took the opportunity to go home to California for a few days." She set the paper aside. "That was the second attempt on his life in a week."

"Does he know why?"

"There are only two reasons we can think of. He's been investigating something inside the White House, something big. It's possible there's a cover-up and someone's trying to keep Brad from finding the truth." She gazed out the window where a tall tree was waving slightly in the breeze. One of its branches was tapping at the glass in a soothing rhythm, a stark contrast to the steady thrum of her heartbeat. "The other reason might have something to do with Carpathia."

Daniel looked shocked. "That's a powerful man to have as an enemy."

"Yes. The White House had a private satellite link to that meeting. Brad and a group of administration officials, including the president and several cabinet members, were watching the meeting from the conference room in the White House. Daniel—" she leaned forward—"Jonathan Stonagal didn't commit suicide. Nicolae Carpathia murdered him. And Brad saw it happen."

"But the witnesses—"

She told him what Brad had reported about Nicolae's systematic polling of the room's occupants. No one there remembered seeing Carpathia pull the trigger and neither—as far as Brad knew—did anyone at the White House.

Daniel sat in stunned silence for a long time. "Does Benton think Carpathia is after him because of it?"

"He's not sure. You got news up here about the sniper at the White House?"

"Yeah. Sure. Benton's assistant was shot, right?"

"Yes. That same day, Marcus and Brad had discussed Marcus's suspicions about Carpathia. Brad asked his assistant, Emma, to pull up some background information on the man. She'd chased him out to the parking garage to give it to him."

Daniel swore under his breath, then shot Mariette an apologetic look. "Sorry. Old habit."

"I have the same old habit."

"Surely Benton knows that if Carpathia's really after him, he can never outrun him in this country or any other."

"He knows that. He's out there closing up his house and doing some research on the other issue he's investigating."

"I've been in politics a long time, Mariette. It's not hard to believe that if Benton's hot on a story with potential political fallout, someone might want him dead."

"He knows that, too. He's actually pretty sure that's

who's after him. The other—" she shrugged—"I just don't think he can rule it out."

"No, I don't suppose he can." Daniel wiped a hand over his face, then looked at the ceiling. "What are we supposed to do?"

Remembering last night's conversation with Marcus, Mariette made a quick decision. She'd prayed last night and again this morning during her flight that if God was indeed calling her to be a part of Marcus's plans that He would give her a very real and explicit sign. The extraordinary revelation that Daniel Berger was a new believer, and the even more extraordinary revelation that he, too, shared their beliefs about Carpathia, seemed sign enough. What better contact could they have in smuggling persecuted Christians to safety than the mayor of New York City? With the enormous amount of international traffic leaving the city by air and sea, there was no easier port of entry or exit in the United States.

"I think I know the answer to that," she told Daniel. "I have to warn you though; it's risky and dangerous."

"Fighting evil usually is." His expression turned mournful. "I can't sit on my hands anymore, Mariette. I owe that to Josh. I owe that to God."

With a nod, she pulled from her briefcase the notepad she'd used that morning on the plane to jot down some thoughts about Marcus's plan. Setting the briefcase aside, she handed the notepad to Daniel. "Let me explain what this is."

★   ★   ★

Randal glanced over his shoulder before slipping into Emma Pettit's hospital room. He'd started working for Brad after Emma's accident and had never met the woman, but he'd seen the picture of her with Brad's wife and kids on Brad's desk. And he knew Brad trusted her implicitly. If anyone could shed light on the conversation he'd overheard that morning and Victor Rudd's references to South Range, it was Emma. He'd tried in vain to reach Brad on his cell phone and had finally decided he needed to ask Emma for some answers and advice.

An older woman sat by the bed reading a magazine. She glanced up when Randal entered. "May I help you?"

Randal looked at the bed. Emma appeared to be resting quietly. He was relieved to see she was no longer hooked up to the life-support systems Brad had described. "My name is Randal Arnold," he said quietly. "I work for Brad Benton."

Emma's eyes drifted open. "Brad?"

The older woman laid a comforting hand on Emma's arm. "It's all right, dear." She looked at Randal. "I'm not sure this is a good time."

Emma struggled slightly in the bed as she pushed herself up on the pillows. "Is Brad all right?" she asked Randal, her voice slightly hoarse. "He said he was on his way home to California."

"He is. I mean, he's there now." Randal ignored the chastising expression of the other woman and pulled a chair up to the bed. "I won't keep you long. I just need to ask you a couple of questions."

"I already told the police and the Secret Service everything I know about the shooting," Emma said.

"It's not about that." Randal braced his forearms on the side of the bed. "It's about a conversation I overheard this morning. Do you know who Victor Rudd is?"

Emma nodded. "Of course. He's one of the president's primary allies."

Randal tapped the security badge on his breast pocket.

"I'm Mr. Benton's driver, but when he's out of town, I report to the general motor pool. This morning I was asked to
pick up a passenger at the Willard and take him to Reagan
National for an early flight. It was Victor Rudd."

"What does this have to do with Emma?" the other
woman asked.

Emma smiled apologetically at Randal, then said softly,
"You'll have to forgive my sister. She's trying to protect
me."

"She needs her rest," the woman said.

"I understand," Randal assured her. "And I promise I
won't stay long."

"Victor Rudd," Emma said. "He said something about
Brad?"

"Yes. While I was waiting for him this morning, I overheard him on the phone. He said something about Brad
taking responsibility for the South Range decision, and he
mentioned that the Justice Department is about to appoint
an independent counsel to investigate it." He leaned closer.
"If someone's after Brad, could this South Range thing have
anything to do with it?"

"South Range," Emma said slowly. "You're sure that's
what he said?"

"Yes. Do you know what it is?"

"There's a Federal Reserve Bank transfer facility somewhere in New England called South Range. It's an underground facility, and the exact location is classified. When
gold bars are transferred between Fort Knox and the reserve
banks, they go to South Range first to be weighed and verified before they are distributed or vaulted. Just before Brad
went to work at the White House, a series of stories broke in
the *New York Times* reporting that transfer times had increased from a matter of days to as many as two or three
months. Armored vehicles would make deliveries to the

South Range facility, but no corresponding deposits were logged at the Federal Reserve or at Fort Knox until long after. In the past, the transfer time was as little as twenty-four hours and never more than a few days. That report sent the stock market into a tailspin."

"I vaguely remember the stock drop," Randal said, "but I don't remember hearing anything in the news about South Range."

"The story died quickly," Emma explained. "The reporter at the *Times* admitted he'd fabricated sources and distorted evidence. He was fired three weeks after the initial story appeared." She folded her weathered hands on top of the sheet. "Brad was briefed on the matter, and, as far as I know, once the Treasury Department and the Fed finished their investigation, the conclusion was reached that there had been some discrepancies and delays in the transfer rate, but not to the extent that the *Times* story had suggested. For a while, there was talk of congressional hearings, but the matter blew over. I haven't heard it mentioned since. I have no idea why it would come up now."

Randal rubbed a hand over his face. "Me either, but from what I heard this morning, the White House obviously hasn't let it drop. And I think they're planning on pinning it on Brad."

"You should be able to pull the *Times* article at the library," Emma suggested. "When you talk to Brad, tell him he might want to look up that reporter and ask some more questions."

"Good idea."

Emma reached for his hand. "Brad has a lot of enemies at the White House. A lot of people would like to see him out of there."

"I know." She didn't know the half of it, Randal thought, certain that Brad had not told her the extent of his troubles. Randal gave her hand an awkward pat. "That's why he needs you back at work. He needs you there to cover his back."

"As soon as I can," she assured him.

Randal left Emma to rest, and though she'd answered some of his questions, her information had prompted a dozen more. What interest did Victor Rudd have in South Range? And why was Brad implicated in whatever had happened there if, indeed, he hadn't even worked at the White House until just before the story broke? Could the *Times* reporter have been George Ramiro's contact in New York? And if so, how badly did the president, Victor Rudd, and whoever else had a stake in South Range want him silenced?

Enough to murder Ramiro? Enough to murder Brad?

Randal made his way quickly through the hospital to the parking garage where he'd left the White House car. He'd stopped by the hospital on his way to Capitol Hill for a pickup. If he hoped to avoid suspicion, he'd have to use a back route to miss most of the lunchtime and tourist traffic.

Twice today he was actually thankful for some of what he'd learned growing up in Max Arnold's house.

8

Marcus glanced across the conference table at Sanura Kyle. She had come to New Covenant's offices on her lunch hour to peruse the file on Theo Carter's lawsuit and discuss Marcus's possible options. Marcus knew exactly why Brad had recommended her. She was sharp, obviously capable, and, as she'd told Marcus when she met him, her father had been a black Baptist preacher in the Deep South. He'd died a couple of years ago, leaving Sanura, two sisters, and her mother behind. After the Rapture, Sanura was the only member of the family left.

And Randal was right, he thought. Much as she tried to disguise it with her wire-rimmed glasses, well-tailored suit, and classic hairstyle, she was simply gorgeous.

She finished reading and set the folder on the conference table. "He's very good. He's done his research."

"Theo knows the organization well—as well as I do, in fact. He was very high up the decision-making chain when he worked for us."

Sanura gave him a probing look. "I'm talking as your

attorney now, Reverend Dumont, so please mind what you're about to tell me."

"I don't have any secrets."

"It'll be privileged information, but you can understand how this could be delicate."

"Yes."

Sanura searched his expression, then pulled a yellow legal pad out of her briefcase. "All right." She produced a pen and wrote Marcus's name and the date at the top of the pad. "As I understand it, the basis of Mr. Carter's case is that the funds now held in probate were willed to you by supporters of New Covenant and that you and your fund-raising agents solicited those funds under false pretenses. Why don't you tell me your side of this?"

"What Mr. Carter claims is correct." She started to interrupt, but Marcus held up his hand. "I was not a Christian before all this, Ms. Kyle. I thought I was, of course. But if I had been, I wouldn't be here."

Sanura raised an eyebrow. "I'm not sure I understand."

"I'm not surprised," Marcus admitted. "I used New Covenant, the church, and the platform it gave me to advance my political career. I understood the message I was preaching. I even believed the message I was preaching. I just made a conscious decision not to surrender my own life to Christ. I knew of Him, but I didn't believe in Him."

"And Mr. Carter knew about your personal beliefs?"

"He did."

"Was anyone else aware of this?"

"My wife, I think," he said sadly, "though she never confessed it to me." He shook his head. "When I look back on it now—"

"You lost your wife in the disappearances?"

"Before. Cancer."

Sanura's expression registered sympathy. "I'm sorry."

"I am, and I'm not," Marcus told her. "She's with the Lord now. I'd rather her be there than still here to see how deeply I failed her and the people who believed in me."

Sanura nodded. "I understand. I know this is painful, Reverend—"

"No, it's all right. I understand why you have to ask." Marcus composed himself and continued. "Mr. Carter was correct when he said that I did not adhere in my own life to the basic principles of the Christian faith that I wrote about and preached and taught. In the eighties when postal regulations and changes in the tax code made raising nonprofit dollars considerably more difficult, we took the same steps many other organizations took. We began aggressively pursuing donors with significant estate and annuity potential by emphasizing the tax advantage and exploiting the inheritance-tax laws. Through our high-dollar development program, we encouraged our supporters to make us the beneficiary of insurance policies and trusts that would provide a shelter for their survivors and continue the work of a ministry they'd supported during their lifetime."

"The organization became the beneficiary," she probed. "Not you personally."

"No. I was ambitious, but I wasn't a criminal." Sanura kept writing, so Marcus went on. "To be perfectly honest, I had an entire staff who handled that aspect of our organization. Changes in the political and international landscape over the last couple of decades opened new opportunities for me to advance my own goals and public persona. I was too preoccupied with the demands of public appearances to be overly concerned about the development office. When we had exceptionally good news, they'd tell me, or when cash got tight, I was asked to make a personal appeal. Generally, our finances were in good shape. We were members of the Ecumenical Council for Fiscal

Accountability, so our books were independently audited every year. I knew we were paying our bills and expanding our operations. I knew we had been successful in cultivating some high-dollar donors. But I wasn't personally aware of the extent of that success."

Marcus reached across the table to shuffle through the file folder he'd given Sanura. When he found Isack's report, he pulled it out and showed it to her. "I had no idea the amount was this high until I saw this report."

She glanced at the report, then set her pen down. "The foundation of Mr. Carter's suit is that this money was designated under false promise, that these donors believed New Covenant's mission was what you publicly represented it to be, when, in fact, the mission of the organization was to promote your own career."

"Yes."

"So if you admit in court that New Covenant is a sham—"

"*Was* a sham," he said. "Actually, *I* was the sham. The ministry did everything it claimed to. We had worldwide evangelical crusades. We sent relief teams to several third-world countries. I preached the gospel on 157 radio stations and four television networks worldwide. In some parts of the globe, more people recognize my name than the president of the United States." He steadily met her gaze. "The only sham was me. I preached the Word, but I didn't believe it."

"Mr. Carter will argue that you and New Covenant are inseparable. That the two are one and the same."

"I'm sure he will."

Sanura picked up her pen and rolled it between her thumb and forefinger, her expression contemplative. "So my question to you is, if it's all just a fraud, why should I help you?"

"Because it's not a fraud anymore." Marcus used the next several minutes to tell Sanura the story of how he'd fallen to his face in repentance the night of the Rapture, how he'd finally seen that his arrogance and anger had kept him from admitting his need for God. He talked about the grief of losing his mother and family at a young age and later his wife to cancer. He explained how he had let all those things cloud his vision of God and separate him from grace.

"It took something as dramatic as the Rapture to break me," he told her quietly. "But I gave my life to Christ that night, and since then, I have committed myself and this ministry to making a difference in whatever time we have left."

Sanura didn't say anything for several seconds. When she finally spoke, her voice was slightly hoarse. "My daddy was a preacher."

"Brad told me," Marcus said.

"South Carolina, Aiken. Well, outside Aiken. We lived in the sticks, and Daddy was a real traditional pulpit pounder."

Marcus could practically see her reaching for words. He doubted she'd had this conversation many times since the Rapture. Brad knew about Sanura's background because he'd made it a point to check on the remaining members of the White House staff and learn their stories, but Sanura, he'd told Marcus, had submitted her answer to his inter-office memo in a curt e-mail message that discouraged any additional probing.

Sanura's gaze had dropped to the legal pad. She studied it with undue interest. "I resented him. It was tough enough growing up black in the South during that time."

"I remember," Marcus responded.

"And to make matters worse, Daddy was always talking

about turning the other cheek and passive resistance. I
wasn't interested in the politics of the whole thing. I just
wanted my life to be normal. I wanted to go to the prom
and the movies and the coffee shop without being jeered at
or threatened."

Marcus noted the tiny lines of stress that had appeared
next to her eyes. He'd been a bit surprised when she'd entered his office today. Something in the way Brad had described her had made him expect a woman closer to his
own age, but Sanura appeared to be in her thirties. She
would have been much too young to have witnessed the
civil rights movement but old enough to suffer some of its
backlash. Suddenly, the decade-plus years he had on her
seemed like an eternity.

"I think in some ways," he said, "your generation suffered the most. You weren't old enough to be politically involved in the fight for equality, but you had to pay the price
for the decisions the leaders of the civil rights movement
made."

She nodded. "My grandfather was an active supporter of
Dr. King. Even though there were times I heard him arguing
with my grandmother about the way Dr. King used the
church as a platform, Papa believed in him. But my sisters
and I weren't allowed the same freedoms as other kids we
knew. I can't remember how many times my daddy told me
that being in the world wasn't the same as being of the
world."

"No dancing, no smoking, no drinking, no cards," Marcus guessed.

A smile tipped the corners of her full mouth. "And no
television on Sundays."

Marcus laughed. "I like a man with high standards."

"It took me a long time to see him that way," she confessed. "Most of my life I remember thinking he was un-

reasonable and tyrannical and narrow-minded." When she looked at Marcus again, her eyes were misty. "My grandfather died when I was in law school. He never saw me graduate."

"He would have been very proud," Marcus assured her. "Not only that you were able to graduate from law school, but that you were able to go to law school in the first place."

"I know. And a part of me knew I got into law school because of the sacrifices men like my father made."

"The two-edged sword. You suffered the consequences through no fault of your own, but you reaped the benefits without paying the price."

"Yes." Sanura sighed and her expression softened. "I made my peace with my daddy long ago. I understood him better, understood his choices and his convictions. I had convinced myself that I had come to terms with the past until the disappearances. I lost my mother and both my sisters. My brother-in-law and three nieces and a nephew, too. Most of my cousins and aunts and uncles are gone. All the family I've got now is a couple of cousins in Chicago I've never met and an aunt in San Jose I haven't seen since my third birthday."

Marcus's heart twisted with compassion. She looked desolate and scared, and he had to resist the urge to beg her to open her heart and her eyes to the saving grace of Christ. That alone, he knew, would assuage the tremendous pain and anger she was experiencing. Nothing but the hope of eternal grace could bind her wounds and set her free. "I'm not going to tell you I understand what you're going through. That would sound flippant and insincere. I can't imagine your sense of grief."

She flicked a tear from her lower lashes with her finger. She had elegant hands, he noted, sophisticated hands. Hands that said she was a long way from the rural South

Carolina town where she'd grown up. "Thank you for that." The breath she drew sounded thready, as if she were still fighting a lump in her throat. "But I know you've had your share of grief." He must have looked surprised. Sanura nodded. "I did my homework."

"Sometimes I feel a lot older than forty-five," he admitted.

"And I also know that you preached regularly about the Rapture. I know you encouraged people to prepare for end times. My daddy did, too."

"I'm sure your father was a great man."

"Larger than life," she said. "But I could never bring myself to believe him. I figured that I was smart enough to make it in this world without leaning on religion. I could pick and choose what I wanted to believe from the Bible, live a good life, and that would be enough in the end."

"And now?" Marcus prompted.

"I don't know." She shook her head. "I know people who believe the Rapture has occurred and that we're in the last days of the earth."

"But not you?"

She hesitated. "It doesn't really matter what I believe. Daddy always said, 'God's going to have His way in this world whether I believe Him or not.' " She managed a smile. "I could never quite put together how the God my daddy claimed was loving and good would pour out this kind of terrible judgment on the earth He created and loved. I guess a part of me still doesn't want to believe it."

Marcus laid both his hands flat on the table. "The message of Revelation and the end times is one of hope, Sanura. Not judgment."

Her expression was sad. "You can say that when there's so much pain in the world? And I remember enough of my father's sermons to know that if he's right, then this is only the beginning."

"But the central message is that those who trust in the Lord for their salvation have hope. What we suffer now is only for a short time. It's a second chance for us to come to Jesus before it's too late."

"Maybe," she said dismissively, "but I'm not ready to put my trust in a God who seems like a great cosmic bully unleashing His fury on the earth." Before Marcus could protest, she picked up her legal pad and slid it into her briefcase. "Look, as far as your case is concerned, I think you have sufficient grounds to win in court. If you're telling the truth about your conversion and your new faith, then you can argue that the principles and missions that these donors supported are in place today. Their money is going exactly where they wished it would."

"I'm telling the truth," he assured her. "And I'm prepared to prove it. To a judge or anyone else who wants to know."

"Then I think you have a very strong case."

"Are you willing to try it for me?"

She dropped her pen into her briefcase. "I think the reason Mr. Benton recommended me to you is because I told him recently that I was thinking about going back to litigation. The climate at the White House is very uncertain. My work there is rewarding, but I miss the courtroom." She smiled. "I guess there is some of my daddy in me after all."

"Then you'll do it?"

"Yes. I have to warn you, though, that I've been out of the game for four years. I don't know how sharp my skills are. I'm a member of the D.C. Bar, but Theo Carter is one of the most respected lawyers in the city."

"He's got a lot less experience in the courtroom than you do," Marcus countered. "I hired him out of Harvard because he was bright and articulate and ambitious. He's never actually tried a case."

"But he's on so many of those commentary shows, I guess I just assumed—"

"Theo Carter is twenty-eight years old. I'm ashamed to say that he learned most of what he knows about deceiving people from me."

She seemed to consider that as she snapped her brief-case shut. "Why did he leave your organization? Why the lawsuit?"

"Because the night of the Rapture, I told him things were going to be different, that New Covenant was going to start standing for and doing what we'd advocated all these years. Theo couldn't accept that. He was angry at me. He felt betrayed, as did the few members of my staff who are still here."

With a nod, Sanura stood and extended her hand. "Then I'll take your case, Reverend. Just promise to give me a break on the preaching."

"I'm afraid I can't do that." Marcus rose and took her hand. "If I did, I wouldn't be half the man I promised God I was going to become."

She looked at him a moment, then shook her head and chuckled. "All right. We can argue about it later. For now, I need you to start making a list and pulling together all the information you have on these donors. I'm going to see if I can get any family members to talk to me."

"Thank you, Ms. Kyle."

"You can thank me when we win, Reverend. I'll be in touch."

★   ★   ★

Brad made his way along the crowded downtown street to the Los Angeles Central Library. Harmon Drake had called him again that morning and insisted, in spite of Brad's protests, that he put two West Coast–based agents on surveillance duty. The generic beige sedan Brad had spotted as he'd driven from his neighborhood confirmed that Drake's men were back on the case.

Brad didn't like the tail.

He especially didn't like the idea that people at the White House were aware of his activities in L.A. . . . even Harmon Drake. That's why he'd decided to return to Washington. This stop at the library was his last before he left the City of Angels.

Last night, after he'd returned from his meeting with Liza and George Ramiro's friend at the rail yard, he'd spent several hours on the Internet looking for background information about South Range. That research had filled in the blanks in Brad's somewhat sketchy memory of the case. Defense and weapons contractors had always been eager to tap the Department of Homeland Security's deep pockets with antiterrorism systems and devices.

A prominent Texas businessman, Victor Rudd, head of the Fortune 500 contracting firm Defense Technology, Inc. (DTI), had been among the top bidders on a massive computer-driven monitoring system that would allow the department to track the location and movement of air, land, and sea traffic in and surrounding the United States.

At the time, technological naysayers had protested the enormous cost of the system and pointed out the near impossibility of its effective deployment. But ally nations had expressed an interest in the technology. Some had even proposed a previously inconceivable system of international financial support from private and government investors.

After several months of intense debate, the Senate Armed Services Committee had tentatively agreed to consider the possibility of joint development. The decision was made to run the financing for the project through the Federal Reserve Bank, where foreign deposits could be made in gold rather than in more volatile foreign currencies.

For the first time since the Nixon administration, America's gold reserves had been opened for inspection and verification. The supply at Fort Knox had been carefully inventoried and verified before large transfers were made through the South Range facility for dissemination through the Federal Reserve Bank network.

Congress had awarded Rudd the multibillion-dollar contract, with the unprecedented promise of preliminary payment from international investors. In the media, the project became known as South Range because of the unusual nature of the financing. The once-small Texas town where DTI's central development offices were located had become the Silicon Valley of the Southwest. Soon after that, Rudd's company was turning out technological marvels that had made the smart bombs and stealth technology of the nineties look like medieval warfare.

After several years, however, progress had begun to fall well short of expectations. Rudd's organization had come under fire for alleged discrepancies in financial records. Under increasing pressure from foreign investors, the U.S. began demanding answers from Rudd. DTI's detractors charged that the corporation had used off-the-books partnerships and complicated accounting to hide losses from stockholders, clients, and investors. Some foreign banks claimed that the U.S. could no longer account for the gold transfers that had been made in the early days of the project.

A federal investigation had been launched to expose the structure and oversight of thousands of partnerships created at DTI that hid the company's debt and inflated the bottom line. As the story developed, Congress held hearings to determine whether federal government agencies such as the Securities and Exchange Commission and the Federal Energy Regulatory Commission conducted sufficient oversight of DTI's operations. The Federal Reserve conducted an internal audit to determine the security of the gold deposits.

For several months, DTI's outlook had been grim. Most observers had expected multiple federal indictments for securities fraud and conspiracy against Rudd, DTI, and several of Rudd's upper-level executives. If the Fed revealed that the gold transfers had somehow been violated, then a slew of top government officials faced indictment and probably jail time.

But in a stunning—and, some thought, suspicious—announcement, the Securities and Exchange Commission, the Federal Reserve, and the independent counsel had announced that while Rudd's business practices may have been risky, no illegalities were found. DTI filed for federal bankruptcy protection under Chapter 11. The Fed, with the backing of the White House, declared that the international gold deposits were complete and uncompromised. Subsequent investigations into Victor Rudd's personal financial practices also failed to reveal any wrongdoing. The South Range project was scrapped, and DTI continued to procure lucrative defense contracts from the U.S. government.

At the time, there was speculation about government corruption in the case, but soon enough another scandal captured the media's attention, and the public lost interest in South Range.

But if Liza's source was to be believed, the South Range issue was still alive and threatening to haunt Victor Rudd.

Brad entered the quiet interior of the library. The impressive eight-story atrium of the Bradley Wing with its oversized art and architecture swallowed him. A small crowd lingered in the atrium and hovered around the in-

formation center. A man in a dark suit sitting in the shadow
of a towering palm caught Brad's eye. Was it his imagination, or was the man's apparent interest in a copy of the *Los
Angeles Times* unconvincing?

When he spotted the library directory near the glass elevators, Brad ducked his head and hurried across the atrium.
He found the depository for government documents on the
directory and stepped into the elevator. The man in the suit
made no apparent move to follow him. Brad breathed a
sigh of relief as the elevator moved slowly up its shaft.

It took him a few minutes to locate the information he
wanted on the library's vast computerized system, but once
he'd found the series of reports on the South Range project,
he printed the pages he needed. He'd read them during his
flight.

Liza had promised to see what she could dig up about
the case through her own sources, while Brad had decided
to pull whatever original documentation appeared in the
logs of the Federal register where the independent counsel
had filed his report.

He paid the library clerk for his copies and slipped them
into an envelope. As he descended in the elevator, he noted
that the man in the dark suit was no longer in the atrium.
He strode through the atrium and exited quickly onto the
crowded sidewalk. He spotted the beige sedan still parked
across the street as he walked toward his car.

The afternoon was warm, and heavy crowds swarmed
up and down the sidewalks. Brad wended his way through
the throng, a strange sense of urgency making him hasten
his step. *Lord,* he thought, *am I going to feel this way forever?
Are they really hunting me?*

He kept a brisk pace through several blocks until he
reached the entrance to the parking garage. He was about to
give his ticket to the young female attendant when a reflec-

tion in the cashier's window caught his eye. Across the street, standing in the shadow of a lamppost, was the man in the dark suit.

"Sir? You need your car?" the cashier prodded him.

Brad stared at the reflection.

"Sir?"

Brad made a quick decision. "Um . . . no." In his peripheral vision, he spotted the beige car inching along the curb. "No, I forgot something at the library. I'll be back in a minute."

"If you want, we can bring your car around to the Sixth Street side. It's closer to the library. Then you can use the library's Sixth Street rear entrance."

"The garage has another side exit?"

"Yes, sir. It's gated. Monthly permit parking only, but . . . uh . . . the valets all have carded access. If you pay here, I'll ask them."

The underlying suggestion was unmistakable. Brad handed the pretty cashier his ticket and a fifty-dollar bill. "That should cover the parking and the trouble."

The cashier grinned. "Yes, sir. No problem."

"Have the car there in five minutes," Brad instructed. "Tell the valet to keep it running and wait for me. If it's ready for me, there's fifty bucks in it for him, too."

"I'll take care of it," she said.

Brad slipped away from the window and headed back toward the library. In the glass walls and doorways of the office buildings and stores, he monitored the progress of the man in the black suit. He was definitely following him. The beige sedan, now stuck in traffic, had been unable to make a U-turn yet. Brad took the stairs to the library's terrace level two at a time. He ducked inside the impressive glass doors and headed for the stairs. The library's rear exit was down two levels from the main entrance.

Brad clutched his envelope while he raced down the stairs. He had to navigate his way through a tour of library patrons who were admiring one of the enormous murals.

"Sorry," he muttered as he nearly careened into a woman who stood near the second set of stairs searching through her purse.

"What's the hurry?" she called as Brad darted down the stairs behind her. He shrugged in answer, then shouldered his way through the crowd in the lower lobby and into the revolving glass door. When he stepped onto Hope Street, he looked left, then right for any sign of the man in the dark suit or the beige sedan.

Nothing. Brad took a deep breath and dodged three cars as he cut across the center of the street toward the parking deck. The valet emerged with Brad's car just as Brad neared the garage's entrance. Brad thrust his hand into his pocket for his billfold.

"Here you go, mister," the valet said, holding open the door for him.

Brad muttered his thanks and slapped the promised fifty-dollar bill into the man's hands. Then he jumped in the car and threw it into gear before the valet even had the door closed.

As Brad sped down the street, he saw the beige sedan cross Hope Street and continue on. He sent up a prayer of thanks. God had protected him once again.

Brad tossed the envelope containing the fruits of his research onto the passenger seat so he could pull his cell phone from his jacket pocket. He punched speed dial, and Liza answered the phone on the first ring.

"It's me," he told her. "I'm on my way to the airport."

"Did you get it?"

"I think so." He paused as he negotiated his way onto the expressway. "I was followed."

"You said you were expecting a detail."

"There was someone else besides the detail."

"You're kidding. Did they come after you?"

"I only saw one guy. I noticed him when I went into the library and again while I was waiting for my car. I had the valet bring my car around back, and I lost him by using the Sixth Street exit." Brad could still feel his heart pounding.

"What about your detail?"

"Lost them, too. It doesn't matter. I'm taking a military flight back to Washington." With commercial air traffic still recovering, Brad had been forced to pull a few strings to arrange the flight on a C-20 out of LAX.

"Hmm," she mused. "You know what I can't figure out about all this?"

"What?"

"Who sent you the pictures."

"I've been thinking about that myself." Brad stopped at a light and searched the cars in his rearview mirror. Still no sign of the beige sedan.

"Any ideas?"

"No. What gets me is, whoever sent me those pictures wanted me to know George had been killed. But in order to take the pictures, that person had to know where the body was."

"True," Liza concurred. "You know, Joe *did* say the body had been moved."

When the light changed, Brad rushed through the intersection. "And you figure two, maybe three people at most know where it is."

"The killer and whoever helped him move it."

"So the killer must have trusted whoever took these pictures."

"Unless the photographer witnessed the murder and followed the killer to the drop spot."

"Possible," Brad said. "But then, why not just call the police? Why involve me?"

"Good point."

The traffic in front of Brad had begun to slow, and he carefully negotiated his way around a delivery truck that had stopped in the right lane. "I don't know. I'm going to review the South Range case tonight on the plane. Maybe I'll find something."

"Just be careful, Brad. If I didn't believe it before, I do after last night. Whoever killed George Ramiro is after you."

"Then I'm not the only one who has to be careful. You're up to your neck in this."

"I know."

"If you see anything—*anything*—you think is suspicious, go straight to the police. You understand?"

"Yes."

"Good. I'll call you when I land in Washington," he promised.

"Brad, do you really think you should be going back there right now?"

"It doesn't matter where I am. They're going to find me."

"I know, but in D.C.—"

"I'll be closer to the source of this story. Trust me, Liza. I know what I'm doing." He saw the signs for the interstate straight ahead.

She hesitated. "Okay."

"And about the other—what we talked about last night." He'd taken the opportunity to talk to Liza about his newfound faith. She'd been skeptical and flatly unreceptive.

"I told you how I feel about that," she said, her tone becoming guarded.

"I know. Just promise me you'll think about it."

"Yeah, okay. I'll think about it."

"That's all I can ask. I'll call you from Washington." Brad ended the call and slid the phone back in his pocket. He felt sick with guilt about leaving Liza in possible danger—especially when he knew she was not a believer. God had given him a chance to reach Emma. Was it too much to ask for His protection of Liza, too?

Lord, he prayed as he sped toward the airport, *please protect her as You do me. Soften her heart toward You so I can share with her again.* He prayed for his friends in Washington, for Emma, for the world he knew that was lost and dying. And, as his gaze fell on the envelope, he prayed for insight and wisdom.

He was now convinced that if he didn't soon determine who had killed George and why, then his life and the lives of friends he'd involved in this were all in peril.

He was approaching the on-ramp to the interstate when his cell phone rang. Brad hit the talk button. "Benton."

"Mr. Benton, this is Jane Lyons, George Ramiro's former assistant."

"Yes?" Brad's pulse quickened. He'd had a brief discussion with Jane the night of the shooting in the White House parking garage. Jane had been fired by the new press secretary, Forrest Tetherton, and had told Brad she was on her way home to somewhere in the Midwest.

"I hope you don't mind that I used this number. I just spoke to Liza Cannley, and she gave it to me."

"No problem. What can I do for you?" Brad merged with the oncoming traffic.

"Well, Mr. Benton, I wouldn't even have thought to mention this to you except that Ms. Cannley called last week asking about George and if I knew anything."

"Yes?"

"I didn't at the time. Maybe I still don't. But I was just

going through some files and things from my office, and I found something."

"What is it?"

"Some notes. They're in his handwriting. I must have picked them up from his desk by accident."

Brad's grip tightened on the steering wheel. "What kind of notes?"

"From a phone conversation. George always took meticulous notes on every phone conversation he had. That's one of the things that made it easy to work for him. If he gave you anything to follow up on, you had all his notes to go from."

Brad ignored the blaring horns behind him as he aggressively negotiated his way around a slow-moving dump truck. "Do you know who this conversation was with?"

"Well, no. I only have the second page, which means I don't have the date either, but here's the weird thing. It seems like the notes are about some court case. There are a couple of things about affidavits and depositions. Then at the bottom, he wrote, 'Pull Rudd file and check for September/October soft money contributions.'" Jane paused. "That's got to be Victor Rudd."

"No doubt." Brad's pulse raced, but he kept his tone deliberately calm.

"What's weird about this is that because of the gag order about that case . . . I forget the name of it."

"South Range," Brad supplied.

"That's it. The whole thing was settled before I came on board, but it had something to do with one of Rudd's contracts and the Federal Reserve Bank. International transfers or something like that.

"The SEC dropped the investigation, I think, but we were under absolute instructions not to discuss Mr. Rudd or anything related to the case or his party affiliation with

anyone outside of White House counsel. Every now and
then Rudd's name would come up. The press was always
trying to tie Rudd's legal problems to the administration.
That's why I can't understand why George would have had
this conversation with someone else."

"You said you didn't have the first page. How do you
know it wasn't an internal call?"

"Because these notes are on regular legal pad paper.
George always used internal communication report pages
for White House calls."

Brad thought that over. "Maybe he didn't have any at
the time."

"Maybe," Jane said, sounding doubtful, "but not likely.
George was very meticulous about things like this. He used
to tell us all the time that when we consider that a lot of
what we wrote was going to end up in a presidential library
or the national archives, it should put a new perspective on
things. If he had made these notes in a rush, I think I know
him well enough to say that he would have immediately
transferred them to the right form, and then destroyed the
original."

Brad made his way across traffic lanes toward the airport
exit. "Jane, can you send me a copy of those notes?"

"Yes." She paused. "I'll send you the originals if it comes
to it; I don't have any use for them. That reporter said you
think George might be dead, that he didn't just disappear
along with everyone else that night. Is that true?"

"I'm looking into things. I don't have any answers yet."

"If he was digging up information on Victor Rudd, then
I'm not surprised."

The remark took Brad off guard. "Why not?"

"I don't know a lot about this. But what I do know is
that with the exception of George and Mr. Swelder, everyone else who had intimate knowledge of the case is dead.

One of the White House counsels died of cancer the week before I got there. Another was mugged outside her apartment in South East. Two of Rudd's upper-level executives were killed in a plane crash when they were on their way to Washington for a meeting. And Phillip Hurst from the independent counsel's office died in a car accident. If you ask me, that's an awful lot of coincidence."

"Have you told anyone else about those notes?" he asked.

"No, no one except you and the reporter."

"Good. Don't."

"Mr. Benton, I'm a little scared."

"As long as no one knows you have any information, you're fine, Jane. I assure you."

"Where do you want me to send this and how?"

Brad thought that over. He'd have to stay in a hotel in Washington until he found a new apartment, and he couldn't very well ask her to send them to him at the White House. "Do you have access to an overnight carrier?"

"Sure. I live in a small town, but it's not Siberia," she said.

"Okay. Send them via an overnight service to D.C. and have them held at the carrier's office. If you e-mail me the tracking number, I'll pick the package up at the depot."

"No problem."

"And don't tell anyone about this conversation."

"Don't worry. I'll get the package off to you today."

"Thanks, Jane." Brad ended the call as he drove down the ramp to I-105. Jane's call had confirmed his growing suspicion and sense of urgency to get to the bottom of George's murder. Victor Rudd was a man with vast connections and unspeakable power. A man whose financial empire had been built on determination and ruthless ambition. A man who had the clout and connections to make someone like George Ramiro disappear.

A man, Brad thought, *who wouldn't think twice about killing anyone who threatened to expose his secrets.* But whoever had sent Brad those pictures had ensured that he was irrevocably drawn into the case. He was in way too deep to turn back. So as he headed back to Washington, he had the feeling that this terrified determination must be exactly the way David had felt when he'd faced Goliath with nothing more than a slingshot and a pouch full of rocks. He would take down the giant or die trying, because God had called him to do it. He'd promised Christine that he was through being a coward.

He and Marcus had talked about the story of David a couple of days ago on their morning run. He couldn't remember the verse exactly, but Marcus had told him that David's words to Goliath were something like, "You may come after me with a sword, but I come to you in the name of the Lord God Almighty."

In His infinite wisdom, Brad realized, God had given him a promise to hold on to to bolster his courage. Victor Rudd might be powerful enough to murder George Ramiro, but he was simply no match for the Lord God.

It was after 9 p.m. when Daniel Berger and Mariette finally finished their meeting. They'd spent over an hour talking about the possibilities of Marcus's plan. Daniel seemed genuinely excited. The rest of their time had been spent strategizing about New York's myriad of problems.

Mariette had to admit that the task was daunting—probably one of the most difficult she'd ever faced. The sheer size of the population and its density in the city made the crisis severe. Coupled with many of the as-yet-incomplete infrastructure changes that had followed the most recent terror attacks and the severely hampered airline traffic, Daniel was facing a monumental recovery effort.

They agreed to wrap up for the night and meet again the next morning. Mariette was packing her briefcase when her cell phone rang. "Yes?"

"Mom, don't freak." Randal's voice was controlled. "I'm at home. Somebody broke into the house."

★　★　★

"Mr. Benton?"

Brad nodded at the airman first class as he hoisted Brad's suitcase into the back of the jeep. He'd returned his rental car at the commercial lot, then called the military services office for transport to the air force hangar and runway. Even with the Los Angeles Air Force Base a few miles away, most nonstrategic flights took off from LAX. Brad's C-20 flight was headed for Andrews Air Force Base in Maryland that evening. Brad slipped into the passenger seat.

"I'm Airman First Class Seaborne, sir. Nice to meet you."

"Thank you, Airman. Thanks for coming for me."

"No problem, sir." The young man pulled onto the airport access road.

"Am I late?"

"No, sir. Actually, there's been a change in plans."

Brad tensed. "What kind of change?"

"The C-20 you were supposed to hop had to leave earlier than planned. But we've got a Galaxy leaving in twenty minutes. It's headed to Andrews, too." He shot Brad an apologetic look. "Won't be the most comfortable ride, but it'll get you there."

Brad released a pent-up breath. "It's fine." During his years in the navy, Brad had flown in one of the massive C-5 Galaxy transport planes only once. Then he'd been assigned to accompany the transport of an observation submarine to the Persian Gulf. "I've flown in a Galaxy before. What's in the belly?"

The airman turned sharply toward the military hangar. "Beats me. Orders are classified. All I know is we loaded the thing a couple of hours ago, and whatever we rolled into it was crated and sealed."

"How big's the crew?"

"Six," the airman supplied. "You've got two loadmasters and two flight engineers, besides the pilots."

As they neared the hangar, Brad could see the nose of the C-5 beyond the steel structure. He'd been hoping for some time alone on the flight to study the papers he'd collected at the library. He certainly ought to find that time and space in the cavernous interior of the Galaxy. The length of a football field, with a cargo capacity of nearly three hundred thousand pounds, the C-5 was the workhorse transport plane in the military's arsenal. It could carry 329 troops in wartime and was capable of transporting massive machinery and tactical vehicles.

The airman drove past the hangar toward the runway and stopped planeside. The sixty-five-foot-high tail towered over them.

A lieutenant hurried toward them and saluted Brad. "Evening, sir. I'm Lieutenant Ford. You're right on time." He looked at Seaborne. "Stow Mr. Benton's bag in the hold."

"Yes, sir." The airman rushed to comply, and Brad walked with the lieutenant toward the rear loading area of the aircraft.

"Sorry about the change in plans, sir," Lieutenant Ford said. "We couldn't reach you in time to catch the C-20."

"Like I told Airman Seaborne, it's no problem. I haven't flown on one of these in a while." He looked at the treaded cargo ramp. "But I think I can handle it."

The lieutenant nodded. "Then you know what to expect. We'll try to fly above the turbulence, but the Galaxy's built for transport, not for comfort."

"I understand." Brad headed up the ramp. "You want me on the forward deck?"

"Yes, sir. We're flying with ten, so there's room topside. As soon as you're settled, we're cleared to go."

"Thanks, Lieutenant." Brad clutched the manila envelope and hurried up the ramp. As he cleared the ramp, the massive winches activated to pull shut the cargo ramp and seal the lower compartment. Brad climbed the stairs and quickly found his place in the upper deck. The pilot was completing his preflight checks. He took a moment to welcome Brad aboard, then headed for the cockpit.

Brad leaned back in his seat with a sigh of relief. Cocooned in the aircraft, he felt safe for the first time in days.

★   ★   ★

Mariette dropped her keys and briefcase onto the bed of her hotel room with a weary sigh. Her day had started early. With air service in and out of most major airports still severely hampered, she'd taken a 5:00 a.m. shuttle from Reagan National to LaGuardia.

She was still reeling from her conversation with Daniel Berger—not to mention Randal's call about the house. Though he'd assured her everything was okay and that the police were on their way, she still didn't like the idea of his staying there alone. Especially not when she was fairly certain who was behind the break-in.

She crossed the small room to the dressing table and pulled off her earrings as she studied her reflection. She looked rumpled, and dark circles stained her eyes. This, she thought, should come as no surprise after the day she'd had. According to Randal, the house was a mess, but as far as he could tell, nothing was missing. He had guessed immediately, as had she, that this was no ordinary burglary. Someone had been looking for Brad's briefcase. She was more relieved than ever that she'd decided to place it in the vault of the Russell Building, where senators stored valuable gifts and documents before they were officially turned over to the Smithsonian and the General Accounting Office. After telling Max about her car getting broken into, he'd agreed that the seldom-seen vault was the safest spot for Brad's possessions.

Mariette finished removing her few items of jewelry, then released the clip that held her hair off her neck. It felt good to shake out the thick mass of waves. Whoever had broken into her car and home was still desperate to find the briefcase, which meant Randal was at risk if he stayed in the house. He'd insisted, though, rationalizing that since the intruders hadn't found what they were looking for, they wouldn't be back.

Against her better judgment and maternal instinct, Mariette had relented. She'd reminded herself half a dozen times since that she'd already placed Randal in God's care. For the most part, it didn't really help much—she still worried. If she hadn't had the distraction of Daniel Berger and his city full of nearly insurmountable problems, she would probably have gone mad.

She unbuttoned her suit jacket and gave herself a stern look in the mirror. "Worrying never got you anywhere."

As she headed for the closet to hang up her jacket, it occurred to her that maybe that was why God was putting her through this. Was He trying to teach her that worrying was nothing more than a lack of trust? Hadn't she had that very thought this morning on the plane as she'd prayed about Marcus's vision and her response? She shucked off the jacket and hung it on one of the hotel hangers.

That's why Daniel Berger's revelation that he'd accepted the Lord and his interest and apparent readiness to help had hit her with the force of a head-on collision. Would she ever learn to expect God to answer prayer in such an immediate and dramatic way? Her mother had often talked about praying while believing. But somewhere along the way, Mariette had discovered that when most people talked about God answering prayer, what they'd really meant was that God answered yes.

In her experience, no was the answer far more often than yes. And yet, as she'd lain sleepless in her bed last night, she'd asked God for a tangible sign that He was calling her into the potentially dangerous web of Marcus's vision. The risks, she knew, were enormous. From what she'd read in Revelation, it appeared that the persecution of the believers would be even worse than the Holocaust. Hard as it was to believe, the mass slaughter of the Jews during World War II would pale by comparison to the Antichrist's war against the tribulation saints.

She stepped out of her low-heeled pumps and entered the bathroom. Under the bright fluorescent light, she looked even worse than she had at the dressing table. "You look old," she told her reflection. "You should do something about the gray hair at least." The reflection seemed to taunt her, as if the idea of worrying about gray hair when the world had seven years left on its eternal clock was too ridiculous to contemplate.

Though Randal, with his fervor and rock-solid faith had willingly committed himself to the task, Mariette had been unsure. She believed beyond any doubt that God had saved her soul through Jesus' death and resurrection, but her confidence in His provision still remained shaky after years of feeling disappointed and bitter. She'd confessed that to no one. Faith seemed to come so easily to Randal and Brad and Marcus. And to Daniel Berger. They didn't seem to harbor the same fears she did.

So she'd needed proof, something real and unmistakable. And God had sent her Daniel Berger—the most unlikely person in the most unlikely position.

Mariette changed into a flannel robe she'd hung on the back of the bathroom door when she'd checked in. One thing she'd learned from her years of travel—whether she planned to be somewhere one night or twenty, she always unpacked and she always carried a bathrobe. It made the time on the road more tolerable.

She made a quick call to room service and asked for a pot of hot chocolate and a bowl of mixed fruit before she flipped on the TV. For security purposes, she liked to leave the television on while she showered in hotels. Anyone who happened to listen from the hallway would assume there was someone else in the room.

Mariette hurried through her shower, not wanting to miss her room-service delivery. She was out of the shower and toweling her hair dry in less than five minutes. The TV was tuned to a political talk show on which the host was commenting on the rumors surrounding Carpathia's alleged deal with the Israelis and Palestinians regarding Jerusalem. Randal had told her about that yesterday on the phone. Intrigued, she listened as she rubbed the thick towel on her wet hair. The commentators ridiculed the treaty plan as "beyond belief" and "impossible even for Carpathia."

A knock on her door sounded a few minutes later. "Room service."

Mariette hit the mute button, grabbed a two-dollar tip from her wallet, and headed for the door. The dead bolt was not engaged on her door, she noticed. Could she really have been so tired that she'd forgotten something as simple as throwing the lock? That wasn't like her. With a brief shake of her head, she opened the door for room service.

"Ms. Arnold?" he asked.

"That's me." She indicated the dressing table with a wave of her hand. "You can put it over there."

"Yes, ma'am."

Mariette absently studied the lock on her door.

The employee put the tray down and turned to leave, then said, "Ma'am, you know you have a note here?"

Mariette frowned as she walked toward him. "What?"

He picked up a sealed envelope and read, "'Mariette Arnold.' That's you, yes?"

"Yes." Mariette took the heavy vellum envelope. "Where did you find this?"

"Here on the dressing table. I uncovered it when I moved aside the hotel guide to lay out your tray."

Mariette's hand trembled. She was certain it hadn't been there when she'd removed her jewelry. She'd placed the hotel guide on the table when she'd taken it from the drawer to call room service.

"Is everything all right?" he asked.

The dead bolt had not been locked. She never stayed in a hotel room without locking it. "Um . . . yes. Yes, it's fine."

The young man looked at her curiously. "Well, then, have a nice evening."

She clutched the note as a chill went down her spine. "I will. Thank you." She handed him the tip.

After he exited, Mariette threw the dead bolt on her door. She stood for several seconds, forehead pressed to the door, as she pulled in great gasps of air. She'd been alone and unaware in the shower, and someone had been in her room. That was the only explanation for the note on the dressing table.

Taking herself firmly in hand, she checked the lock again, then went to the desk to study the envelope. It had her name and room number written in neat script on the front, but no return address. She flipped it over, but nothing on the back indicated who might have sent it. With a frown, she slit the seal with her index finger.

Inside was a folded card of expensive vellum paper with the seal of the United Nations embossed on the front. Mariette's heart pounded as she flipped open the note. In neat clean handwriting, the note read:

> Ms. Arnold,
>   Though I am new to New York myself, I feel I should welcome you here on behalf of my newly adopted city. I am aware of the extraordinary efforts you and your agency have made to make life more tolerable in this city following the tragic events of a few weeks ago. I wanted to personally extend my thanks to you and Mayor Berger for your continued efforts and offer you the full support and resources of my office and my staff. If there is any way that I can assist you in your efforts, please do not hesitate to ask.
>
> Sincerely yours,
> Nicolae Carpathia
> Secretary-General

Mariette clutched her throat with one hand as she sank to the bed. She reread the note. It was more difficult this time because her hands were trembling so much the paper wobbled. The harsh realization that Nicolae Carpathia not only knew she was in New York but apparently knew her hotel and room number would have been disturbing enough. But someone had come into her room to deliver his note. Suddenly cold, Mariette hurried to the thermostat to adjust the temperature.

Though she'd suspected along with Marcus that Brad—and maybe even Randal—might one day have to come into contact with this man, in her wildest imagination she had never dreamed that Carpathia would have any direct contact with her.

She pulled her robe tighter around her and sank to the bed, where she buried her face in her hands. *God,* she prayed, *I believe this man is evil. I believe he is the enemy Your Word describes. He knows where I am. He knows what I'm doing. I'm so scared. I've never felt like this before. I need to know You're going to protect me—to protect Randal and Marcus and Brad and Daniel. God, I thank You so much for sending Daniel to me today, but this . . . this is more than I can handle. I need to know what you want me to do.*

Though God didn't answer her audibly, she did feel a sense of security and peace return as she rocked back and forth on the bed. She struggled with the idea of calling the front desk and asking to be relocated to another room—or better yet, trying to catch the last shuttle home to Washington—but she soon dismissed the thought as cowardly. She had never been a coward. She wasn't about to become one now.

She was sure she wouldn't sleep tonight, but she would not give in to the enemy by fearing him. Cable TV, a pot of hot chocolate, and the knowledge that help was a phone call away would help her make it through the rest of the night.

Mariette picked up the note and started to toss it in the trash can, but she stopped as she realized that she should show it to Daniel. He'd been mentioned, too. He had a right to know. She slid it into the side pocket of her briefcase, then went to the bathroom to wash her hands. They felt suddenly dirty. With the water as hot as it would run, she scrubbed them hard with soap. When they finally looked pink, she shut off the water.

She was drying her hands when the phone on her nightstand rang. She stared at it for several seconds, her heart pounding. *He knows the room number,* her subconscious screamed. *He knows where you are.* Mariette forced herself to pick up the receiver. "Hello."

"Mariette? It's Brad."

"Brad." She dropped to the side of the bed. "Hi."

"Are you all right?" he asked. "You sound out of breath."

"Yeah, I'm fine."

"Are you sure?"

"Um . . . no. Not really. Where did you get this number?"

"Randal. I tried to reach your cell phone—"

"Some of the systems are still down here in New York. The coverage is spotty."

"Makes sense. Randal told me about your house. I'm sorry."

"It's okay."

"I understand why you're upset."

"It's not that." She leaned back against the headboard. "But don't worry about it. Your things are safe."

"I can't tell you how much I appreciate what you did for me."

"What are friends for?" The normalcy of the conversation was beginning to calm her nerves.

"Are you on your way home?"

"Yes. I was able to get on a MAC flight out of LAX."

"Did you find what you were looking for?"

"I think so. Listen, Mariette, I don't know how busy you are, but do you have time to do me a favor before you head back to Washington?"

She glanced at the television. Though the volume was muted, the commentators were obviously arguing hotly about something. She studied their angry faces. "Sure. What do you need?"

"I need a copy of the last five quarterly transcripts from

the Security and Exchange Commission's report on the international gold deposits at South Range. The deposits were made through the Fed in New York, so the city archives should have the reports. I could get them through the SEC office in D.C., but it'll raise less suspicion if you get them in New York."

"I've got a meeting with Daniel Berger in the morning. I'll ask him about it."

"That might not be a good idea," Brad said. "He might want to know why you want it."

"I can trust him," she responded.

"You sound sure."

"I am. I'll tell you about it when you get home."

"Okay. Just be discreet. When do you think you're coming back to Washington?"

Mariette's gaze dropped to her briefcase where Carpathia's note rested in the side pocket. "As soon as I possibly can."

★ ★ ★

Brad tapped his pen on the report he was reading. The SEC had certainly made its case that both Rudd and the Federal Oversight Committee had not mishandled the international gold deposits at South Range. Other than some unorthodox bookkeeping practices, the entire scandal appeared to be based on unsubstantiated allegations and political paranoia. Fitzhugh's political enemies would have loved to take down Rudd and the president in the wake of the scandal, but lack of evidence had caused the matter to die. When the *New York Times* reporter who'd broken the story had resigned after admitting to falsifying his sources and printing unsubstantiated evidence, interest in South Range had apparently died.

Though Rudd and DTI were major contributors to Fitz-hugh's campaigns, Brad still couldn't figure out what about the case had captured George Ramiro's attention.

Suddenly, the sound of a warning siren split the still air. Worried, Brad gathered up his papers and put them back in their envelope.

The three crewmen who shared the compartment with Brad scrambled from their seats. "Stay seated, sir," Lieutenant Ford called as he raced toward the cockpit.

Brad grabbed the manila envelope with his papers in it and stuffed it down his shirt. Then he gripped the sides of his seat like his life depended on it . . . and just in time. Seconds later, a loud popping sound reverberated through the aircraft as a rush of wind blasted through the compartment. The force of the gale threatened to tear Brad from his seat belt. The telltale popping in his ears told him they were losing cabin pressure fast. He glanced at the altimeter at the front of the compartment. They were at thirty thousand feet. Without oxygen or a massive drop in altitude real fast, this wasn't going to be pretty.

The cockpit door flew open, and Lieutenant Ford, fighting the draft, made his way toward Brad.

"What happened?" Brad yelled above the noise of the sirens and the roar of the wind.

"Our sensors indicate that the aft door in the lower compartment is open," the lieutenant told him. "We're going to drop down to fifteen thousand feet so we can check it."

Brad nodded. The plane began a sharp descent. The cockpit door opened again, and another crewman signaled the lieutenant. Brad couldn't hear their conversation above the deafening noise in the cabin. The lieutenant glanced at Brad, then at the pilot visible through the open door. He made a signal with his hand that seemed to satisfy the other airman.

Lieutenant Ford fought his way back toward Brad. "I'm sorry, sir! The engineers say we've lost an engine. The pilot is going to try and land." He released the buckle on Brad's belt. "We're going to have to evacuate you from this seat."

"Does the pilot know what's causing the problem?"

"About the engine? No, sir. But he's pretty sure the decompression's to blame. He thinks we might have blown a door. That would create a pressure overload on all the other locks." Ford guided Brad toward the stairs. The wind and the steep incline of the rapidly descending plane made the going hazardous and difficult. "After you, sir."

Warning sirens continued to blare while Brad made his way down the steel stairs, the young officer following close behind him. "According to the engineer," the lieutenant continued, "when we lost the aft door, he thinks it severed some of our hydraulics systems and flight controls. But Commander Reese thinks he can land. Meantime, we want you in the safest part of the plane."

But to Brad, at least, it didn't look any safer where they were heading.

In the lower compartment, the damage was obvious. Though the rear cargo compartment was partially sealed off from the forward part of the plane, the force of the pressure had torn at the contents of the hold, flinging ropes and loose cargo all over the plane's hull. There was a long row of parachutes still lined up neatly, carefully clipped to a rack. Brad took special note of them. He'd used parachutes before in navy Special Ops, of course, but it had never been a favorite form of transport for him. He wasn't one of those people who felt that jumping out of a perfectly good plane was a great idea. He'd much prefer to wait this mess out in a nice, safe seat. This plane, however, was feeling progressively less safe with every passing minute.

He was glad he knew the drill: *One cord's your chute; the other's your backup. Just remember that if you need to jump.* He hoped he wouldn't need that knowledge.

"Where do you want me to strap into a seat?" he asked the lieutenant. "This doesn't exactly look like a good place to be if the plane goes down."

"Sorry, sir. Orders. I'm getting the deck ready for you right now." Ford busied himself with something at the back of the plane. "Hang on to the safety strap for a second."

Brad looked at the digital altimeter on the compartment wall while he waited. They were at seventeen thousand feet and still descending. He clutched the strap and watched the altimeter as it fell to fifteen thousand feet.

"Here we go, sir," the lieutenant shouted. He'd clipped himself to the deck, Brad saw—not a bad idea in this situation. He himself could hardly wait to sit down and strap in. Ford pulled a lever. But instead of a seat revealing itself in the hull, the huge cargo door began to open with a groan, pushing against the pressure of the outside air. As the icy draft rushed into the compartment, Brad felt the pull of the wind against his body. It dragged at him, grasping like some angry beast. If he couldn't hang on, it would be the death of him. Fifteen thousand feet was a long, long way down.

An agonizing second passed as Brad clutched the safety strap, hoping against hope that he could hold on. He looked around for something he could use to clamp himself in. Still maintaining his grip on the safety strap, he reached for the parachute rack.

Then the lieutenant looked at Brad. "Sorry, sir. Orders." Then he pushed Brad free of the safety line.

"Help me!" Brad hollered.

Ford simply stepped back out of reach and secured himself against the cabin wall.

Brad lunged desperately for a handhold, scrambled to grab anything to stop his fall. For a millisecond, he thought he'd done it, that he'd gotten a secure hold on the plane. Then his grip shifted under him and he pulled free. He flew down the deck, dragged by wind and gravity. The force of the wind knocked him off his feet and he landed on the ramp. The draft did the rest of the work. It pulled him out of the hold into the frigid thin air.

He fell earthward.

He was going to die.

He panicked. Then he closed his eyes and began to pray. *Jesus, my Savior, I need You with me.*

A strange sense of peace enveloped him.

Lord Jesus, I give my soul into Your keeping. I'm Yours. Save me a place in heaven.

Not yet, said a voice in his brain.

Shocked, he opened his eyes. He was even more shocked when he realized what he was clutching—the very last thing he'd grabbed for as he'd fallen. He had a parachute in his hands. As the wind whipped around him, he fumbled it onto his back, trying to secure it properly as he hit terminal velocity. He was still high enough. He might just get out of this mess alive.

As he fought his way into the chute, he prayed again. *Jesus, I'm in Your hands. If it's Your will that I survive this, help me now!* The drills from Brad's navy days echoed through his head, though he'd never tried to put a chute on like this before. This strap here, this one here, attach this here and here. Careful, careful—don't let anything slip!

Trying not to think about anything but the chute—and certainly not about the ground rushing up to meet him far too fast—he fastened the closures, tightened everything up, found the rip cord, and pulled.

The olive drab chute flew out of the bag, silhouetted against the sky like an angel's wing.

It opened. For a terrible few seconds nothing happened; then he slammed hard against the harness. That bruising force was one of the finest sensations he'd ever known.

He was going to make it.

Brad seized the shoulder straps of his chute. In his mind, he could hear the faint echo of his jump instructor yelling orders at him. *"Chin on your chest. Elbows tight into your sides. Hands over the ends of your reserve parachute with your fingers spread. Bend slightly forward at the waist. Keep your feet and knees together with your knees locked to the rear."*

A rush of relief poured through him as he reached up to secure both toggles and pull them down to eye level. He rotated 360 degrees to check the canopy.

The plane had disappeared over the horizon, still fighting for altitude. Apparently the plane's malfunctions hadn't been a ruse. That plane was in trouble. Whoever wanted to get rid of him wasn't taking any chances that he'd survive this crash. His enemy was clearly planning to kill his messengers as well.

God, Brad prayed, *please protect them. Let them live. If I can find them, I can track them back to whoever is behind this nightmare.* He strained his eyes but could see nothing in the semidarkness to indicate the fate of the aircraft.

While he drifted downward, he scanned the ground for something that might indicate where he was. Large agricultural fields stretched over the earth in a quilt of corn and wheat. The amber waves of grain, Brad thought ironically, didn't appear so welcoming or so awe-inspiring tonight.

To his left, he spotted a cluster of farm buildings. He angled his body to head toward the grouping. The closer he landed to civilization, the less difficulty he'd have finding out where he was and making a plan to get home.

He wondered who would be the most surprised at his continued survival. He couldn't wait to see the faces at the White House when he walked back into the office.

The ground was rushing toward him now. He gripped the lines of his chute and tried to steer himself toward a small clearing. Though he bent his knees and prepared for the impact, his body still felt the shock of the jolt. He had been a lot younger the last time he'd done this. His chute fluttered down and covered him in a sea of nylon.

Thank You, Lord. Brad lay still for several seconds, taking mental inventory of his bones and muscles. Everything seemed to be intact. When he felt the strength return to his shaken arms, he began pulling at the parachute, clawing his way free of the canopy.

He forced himself to his knees as he fought with the tangle of nylon and cords. When he finally brushed the chute aside, he saw two teenage boys watching him intently.

One trained a bright flashlight on Brad. The other wore what looked like a cheap pair of night-vision goggles. The one with the flashlight looked like an athlete, while the other was smaller and thinner. Even with the night-vision goggles, something about him suggested he was the brains of the operation.

They were staring at him, dumbfounded.

Brad wiped a hand over his forehead. "Where is this place?"

The taller boy tucked his flashlight under his arm and announced, "Earth. Welcome."

10

Brad decided his assessment of the two teenagers had been correct when the one with the goggles whacked his friend on the arm. "He's not an alien, moron."

"How do you know?" the other one protested.

"Well, for starters—" the boy pulled off the goggles—"he's got a U.S. military parachute." He walked toward Brad, hand extended. "Hi, mister. My name's Willy."

Brad struggled to his feet. His legs still felt shaky, but he shook Willy's hand. "I'm Brad." In the darkness, he had trouble making out the boy's features, but the wire-rimmed glasses on his nose reinforced Brad's initial impression that the kid was a techno-wizard. "Who's your friend?"

Willy pushed his glasses up the bridge of his nose with a slender index finger. "Gus. He plays football," he said, as if that explained everything. He tapped the side of his head and lowered his voice to a conspiratorial whisper. "You know. Helmet damage."

Brad unfastened the safety harness and removed the rig for his parachute. "I see."

"Are you sure you're all right, mister? Gus and me, we

were out by the barn where I have a telescope. We heard all
that racket from the airplane. Did you crash or something?"

"I . . . jumped before the plane crashed," Brad explained.

"So the plane crashed? Is there wreckage?" Gus sounded
eager.

"I don't know." Brad glanced at the horizon. "The pilot
was going to try to land. I lost sight of the plane as I came
down."

"No smoke. And no flames." Willy folded the night-
vision goggles and slipped them into his back pocket. "He
might have made it."

"I hope so."

"We could have sold that wreckage," Gus said.

"Salvage?" Brad asked.

"No, eBay," Willy said.

Gus was eyeing Brad's parachute. "What about that
thing? You still want it?"

Willy smacked his arm again. "Cut it out, Gus."

"But we're only a couple hundred bucks short," Gus
protested. "We could probably get at least eighty bucks for
that."

"I'll make you a deal," Brad volunteered as he began
gathering up the chute. "You help me get out of here, and
I'll give you the chute."

"Deal," Gus said. "Where were you headed?"

"Washington, D.C." Brad checked the GPS beacon in
the front pocket of the rig. It was still working, giving anyone monitoring it, at least for the moment, his location.
"So where am I?" he asked Willy as he began stuffing the
voluminous chute into the rig. "Besides earth?"

"In Longford." Gus supplied. He dropped the flashlight
and started grabbing handfuls of the parachute for Brad.

"Kansas," Willy added.

That, Brad thought, explained the amber waves of grain. "How close is Longford to any place I might have heard of?" He saw the outline of a farmhouse silhouetted in the moonlight about a hundred yards from the spot.

"Not very," Willy admitted. "We used to be the Whiskey Capital of the United States, at least until Prohibition. Then the whole town just went downhill. We've got a population of about a hundred now—101 if you count old man Beasley who farms just outside the town limits." He thrust his hands into the pockets of his denim overalls. "'Cause of that Prohibition business, folks around here don't like Washington too much." His eyes narrowed. "Say, you're not one of those ATF agents are you?"

"No."

Willy looked disappointed. "Well, that'll make it easier for me to explain you to my dad anyway."

Gus helped Brad cram the rest of the chute into the pack. "I'll carry that for you, mister." He glanced at Willy. "Eighty bucks, don't you think?"

"Maybe," Willy told him. He looked at Brad and tipped his head toward the farmhouse. "The house is this way. And since you ain't going anywhere tonight at least, Mom can find you a bed. You need to call your base or something—let 'em know you're all right?"

"Not right now," Brad said. What he needed was time to think and plan. By now, the Galaxy had either managed to land or had crashed. If it had crashed, he might have twelve hours or so before recovery experts realized he wasn't aboard. If they'd landed, word was already out. Either way, somebody would be scouring Kansas for him by sunup.

"Come on inside, then," Willy said. "It's fixin' to get dark as pitch."

"And Miss Clara'll feed you some pie," Gus added.

★ ★ ★

Fifteen minutes later, a weary Brad was seated at a massive wooden table with a large piece of apple pie and a glass of milk. Bill Gleason, Willy's father, he'd learned, farmed close to four thousand acres—all of it planted in sorghum. He'd gotten out of the wheat business before the prices fell—or so Willy said.

Bill Gleason was a large man who looked like he'd worked hard for most of his life. His face was dark and creased from days under the hot sun, and his hands had a blunt, sturdy look. He wore a T-shirt and a pair of overalls that matched Willy's, along with a battered John Deere cap and dust-covered boots. His wife's only complaint about the boots in her pristine kitchen had been a cluck of her tongue and a quiet, "I told you to change your shoes."

Bill was straddling the back of a chair watching Brad with keen interest. "Willy tells me you're from Washington."

Brad swallowed a bite of his pie. "Actually, I'm from North Carolina. I live in California and I work in Washington."

"I already asked about the ATF, Dad," Willy assured him.

"He ain't no agent," Gus chimed in. He was on his third piece of pie.

"The boys say your plane went down," Bill said.

"I was on a military flight back to Washington. We had some mechanical trouble." Brad downed his milk.

"No wreckage," Willy told his dad. "I didn't see any smoke. Me and Gus just heard the racket from the barn."

Bill nodded, thoughtful. "Well, Mr. Benton, there's not much we can do for you tonight. Closest major airports are Topeka and Wichita."

"Two hours," Willy supplied.

Clara Gleason refilled Brad's milk glass. "You sure you don't want to make a phone call, Mr. Benton?"

"No, it's all right." Here in the middle of Kansas, he mused, no one knew or cared that he was the White House chief of staff. If his ego had needed deflating, this could do it. "Nobody's going to look for me until tomorrow morning."

"No family?" she prompted.

"No." Brad's throat clenched. "No family." The latter came out as a husky whisper.

Bill Gleason's face registered comprehension. "You lost your people in this mess, didn't you?"

"Yes," Brad affirmed. "My wife and three kids."

Clara walked around the table and wrapped her arms around Gus's shoulders. He was staring at his pie. "Gus lost his folks. That's why he's here with us now."

Bill folded his wide forearms on the back of the chair. "So the president says we've been attacked. That still the word out of Washington?"

"That's the official position at the White House," Brad said.

"Do you believe it?" Clara asked, her expression earnest.

"No," Brad said, "I don't."

"See, Willy?" Gus said. "Aliens. Just like I told you."

Brad gave the young man a sympathetic smile. "I don't think so. Though I have to admit, I think the alien explanation is more plausible than foreign attack."

"So what do you think happened?" Willy pressed.

With four faces watching him intently, Brad marveled for a moment at the wisdom and grace and providence of God. How divinely fortuitous that he'd literally dropped from the sky into the middle of a field owned by a farmer and his family who were ready to hear the Word of the

Lord. Brad tossed his napkin onto the table and leaned back in his chair, only too eager to tell the Gleasons what he believed.

★   ★   ★

"Thank you, Officer." Randal closed the heavy oak door and sagged against it. The house was a wreck. Drawers had been dumped in the kitchen and all the bedrooms. Furniture cushions littered the floor of the den. His mother's extensive book collection now lay in a heap at the base of the floor-to-ceiling bookcases in her study. And though he'd checked twice, he couldn't determine what, if anything, was missing.

The Maryland police had written up the report as random vandalism.

"Random," Randal muttered in disgust. He stepped over a pile of coats that had been ripped from the hall closet and made his way to the kitchen. Whoever wanted Brad's briefcase was behind the break-in. He was sure of that. He pulled open the refrigerator to stare at the mostly empty shelves. Both he and Mariette had been too busy to stock it lately. He was going to have to take care of that soon.

He finally grabbed a bottle of root beer. As he twisted off the metal cap with his hand, he noticed his mother's favorite dishes shattered on the floor. The cabinets had also been searched and ransacked. And he had to believe that whoever had done it had wanted Mariette and him to know this wasn't random. If they'd been trying to cover their tracks, they would have swiped the DVD player, the stereo, *something*. But everything of value was still firmly in its place.

This had been a campaign of terror, and he was pretty proud of his mother for the way she'd taken it. She'd sounded only mildly hysterical when he called her. She'd gotten pretty hot when he'd told her that he planned to stay at the house tonight, but after a few minutes of verbal sparring, she had finally admitted that she was all the way in New York and had no say in the matter. Given the tension between them the past couple of days, that was a minor miracle.

Randal wiped a hand through his hair and surveyed the mess. Of course, she hadn't seen the house when she'd agreed to that. He'd lived in a fraternity house one semester, and even that had never looked like this.

He downed half his root beer, then plunked the bottle on the counter. The only thing to do now was to clean up as much of the mess as possible before his mother got home. Otherwise, Mariette's case of mild hysteria was likely to become full-blown when she laid eyes on the place. And the slight argument they'd been having lately about his ability to handle the risks and potential danger of working for Brad would turn into World War III.

★   ★   ★

In his office the next morning, Daniel Berger examined the handwritten note with a scowl. "You got this last night?"

"Around ten," Mariette confirmed. She told him the story about the note.

"You're kidding." Daniel looked as horrified as she'd felt.

"I wish I were."

"And you stayed in the room? What were you thinking?"

"That I didn't want to let him scare me."

"Mariette—" he sounded exasperated—"someone broke into your room. At least tell me you contacted hotel security."

"What were they going to do besides tell me I had to be mistaken? There was no way someone could have come in that room if the dead bolt had been locked."

"And you're absolutely sure the note wasn't on the table before you went to the shower?"

"Positive."

"Oh, man." Daniel rubbed his eyes. "I don't know how you managed to stay there."

"I sat up all night." She managed a slight smile. "Like a kid watching for monsters in the closet."

"Except that these monsters happen to be the enemy of God. You should have called me. Why didn't you call me?"

"It was late."

He looked appalled. "Someone *broke into your room.*"

"I'm scared enough already, okay? I made it through the night without more visitors. Can we just leave it at that?"

"How do you think Carpathia knew where you were staying?"

"It's possible that someone from my office called someone in his office to find out information about his travel plans. Rumor has it that he's making a trip to Washington. I'm sure my boss is trying to get on his schedule."

Daniel raised an eyebrow. "For what?"

"Carpathia's organization has been putting out feelers about the possibility of revamping the UN's international relief efforts. Word has it he's very interested in some of FEMA's policies and procedures. Besides just a general case of arrogance and hero worship, I think my boss has delusions about getting a job."

"Ah." Daniel dropped the note on his desk. "So if your boss—what's his name again?"

"Bernie Musselman."

"Musselman. Right. I remember talking to him last year when we had floods up the Hudson."

"He's been at the agency for three years," Mariette said. "Fitzhugh brought him in after Willard resigned."

Daniel tapped his long fingers on his knee. "If Musselman is trying to squeeze himself onto Carpathia's Washington agenda, then it makes sense that he'd have someone calling the UN to check on the schedule."

"It's the only explanation I can think of," Mariette confirmed.

Daniel nodded. "Do you have any idea when Carpathia's supposed to go to D.C.?"

"It hasn't been announced yet—not by the White House or the UN—and talks about it have to be very top level or it would have leaked to the press by now."

A smile played at the corner of his mouth. "I suppose you know about it because your son happens to be the driver for the White House chief of staff."

"Yes," she affirmed.

"And you're heading back to Washington today?"

"On the two o'clock shuttle."

"Good," Daniel said. "You need to get home."

"I know. I'm worried about Randal. I still don't know what shape my house is in. And I'm not going to stay another night in that hotel."

"That's not what I mean," he said. "If it were as simple as security, I could have you moved to a hotel where I don't think the CIA could find you."

"I've got plenty to do at work, too," she assured him. "My assistant is having a rough time with all this. I wouldn't have made this trip if it weren't so important. I don't think David's really in a place to handle too much leadership responsibility right now."

"I'm sure that's true, but that's not what I was thinking either." He gave her a pointed look. "What I was thinking is that if Carpathia's going to appoint a head of an international relief effort, he should at least get someone competent."

Mariette stared at him for several seconds, confused. "What?"

Daniel's smile was warm if a little sad. "If Carpathia's going to meet with anyone from FEMA, I assume you'll be in the meeting."

"Not necessarily." She wasn't sure she liked where he was going with this.

Daniel stroked his chin. "But you could be?"

"I guess so. Bernie Musselman doesn't generally view me as a threat."

"Moron," Daniel muttered. "So if the secretary-general of the UN is going to establish an international organization modeled after FEMA, it would stand to reason that he'd want an administrator who has significant field and office experience."

Mariette held up her hands. "Don't say it. Don't even think it. There is no way I'm going to work for him. I can't believe you'd even bring that up after what happened last night."

Daniel's expression turned serious. He pulled a notepad from his top desk drawer. "Hear me out, Mariette."

"I can't believe that you would suggest—"

"Just wait a minute," he urged. He handed her the notepad. "I couldn't sleep last night either. All I could think about was what we discussed yesterday afternoon." He lowered his voice. "The shelter."

Mariette cautiously took the pad. "What about it?"

"One of the things that makes the idea feasible is the high-level positions of the contacts. With Benton at the White House and me here in New York—"

"You here in New York? Then you're going to join us?"

"I didn't say that. I want to meet Dumont first."

"I can arrange that."

"And if I feel good about him and if I pray about it and still feel good about him, then yes, I'm in. I can't sit by and watch this man perpetrate evil without doing anything." He leaned toward her, hands clasped, eyes full of passion and determination. "My grandfather lost most of his family in one of Hitler's concentration camps. He was able to survive because a courageous man risked his life to smuggle my grandfather out of the country. As far as we know, the Nazis executed that man for treason a year later."

Daniel searched her face for a moment. "It's my legacy. I owe it to my grandfather, to the man who gave his life to save him." He paused. "And I owe it to the Lord."

The quiet strength and dignity in his voice pulled at her heartstrings. "I understand. And you're right. Having you here and Brad in Washington will make us more effective."

"Then you can't deny that if you were to accept a position in Carpathia's organization, we'd have intelligence and unparalleled access."

"That's different," she protested. "No. Surely you can see it's not the same thing. You and Brad would be using your contacts to work against Carpathia. You're suggesting I work for him."

"I'm suggesting," Daniel said quietly, "that maybe God put you in this time and in this place with your particular background and skills because the job you have to do is best done in the shadow of the enemy. If you'll take the job, just think of what good you could do. You'd know where Carpathia was, what he was doing and planning. You'd know the truth about things like that murder at the UN. You'd be in the best position to keep us all informed and prepared."

Mariette glanced out the large windows. The weather was perfect today, one of those rare late spring days in New

York when the clouds didn't come, the rain didn't threaten, and the humidity minded its own business. The natural beauty seemed in stark contrast to the cloud of doubt that had hung over her head since last night. "I don't know, Daniel," she hedged. "I can't even imagine—"

"Look, the opportunity might not even present itself. I'm just saying I think you should consider it." He tapped the note with his index finger. "Carpathia is obviously already impressed with you. And between Brad Benton and me, we've got the political connections to make sure he hires you."

As repulsive as the idea was, Mariette reluctantly admitted that Daniel's words held a ring of truth. And hadn't she promised the Lord yesterday that if only He'd give her a sign, she'd follow Him wherever He led? She closed her eyes and released a long sigh. "I can't think about this right now."

When she looked at him again, he was leaning back in his chair and studying her with a warmly sympathetic gaze. "I'm still so rattled from what happened last night, I just can't go there."

"I understand."

"There's Randal. My house. My job. I-I'm not sure I can face the idea of leaving all that behind and relocating."

"Then just promise me you'll pray about it."

That's exactly what had gotten her into this mess in the first place. She was very glad that God had a sense of humor and that He loved her despite her own neurosis. "I will."

"Good." Daniel indicated the notepad he'd given her. "Then while we still have some time, I want to talk to you about that. It's some notes I made last night about Dumont's idea."

Mariette briefly scanned the list. "I can't believe I'm

about to say this, but I think you're more detailed than I am."

"I'll take that as a compliment," he said, rounding the desk.

She flipped the page, skimmed the list, then looked at Daniel. "You're going to like Marcus. A lot."

"I'm sure I will." He sat down next to her. "Let's get to work."

★　★　★

"All right, boys," Brad said as he handed Gus the homing beacon. Bill Gleason was going to drive Brad to Wichita, where there was one plane leaving at noon headed for Denver. Willy and Gus had searched the Internet last night to work out a way to get Brad back to Washington. With limited air traffic in and out of most U.S. airports, it hadn't been easy. He was booked on the noon flight, then on a 4 p.m. flight from Denver to Detroit. From Detroit, he'd have to connect through Memphis to LaGuardia, then finally to Reagan National on a shuttle flight.

If everything ran on time and he didn't get delayed anywhere, he might make it to D.C. by one in the morning. With a generosity and trust Brad found refreshing and inspiring, Bill Gleason had accepted Brad's promise of cash repayment and paid for the tickets so Brad wouldn't have to use his credit card. The charges would have made it easier for his adversaries to find him.

"Here's what I want you to do," Brad said.

Willy examined the beacon with keen interest. "Is this thing really a GPS homing device? It looks kind of small."

"Yes." Brad showed him the switch. "And once you activate it, someone's going to come looking for me."

Gus scratched the side of his leg, his expression dubious. "So why do you want us to turn it on after you leave?"

Willy whacked him. "Because somebody's looking for him and he don't want to be found." He grinned at Brad. "Like he said."

Brad had told Bill and Clara some of the details of his situation. He'd wanted to inform them enough to protect them, but not so much that he put them in peril. The three had agreed that Willy, especially, was better off in ignorance. His curiosity probably wouldn't let him leave the subject of Brad's sudden appearance and precipitous departure alone.

"You're in some kind of trouble, aren't you?" Willy asked.

Brad thought about how to explain his predicament. Last night when he'd shared with the Gleasons his new faith and his beliefs about the Rapture, he'd found them receptive and attentive. Though Bill had been slow to come around, the three and Gus had all prayed to receive Christ. Taking his cue from Marcus, Brad had led the small group in Communion. He'd made careful note of their address, not only to repay the money he owed for his airfare but to send them Bibles and other materials—along with a much-coveted signed picture of the president—once he got back to Washington.

Now he wasn't sure how much to reveal to the two boys. He didn't want to put them in danger, but he also didn't want to lie. "I learned something about what happened to a friend of mine. It's something that a handful of very powerful people don't want anyone else to know."

"Like a team's secret football plays?" Gus said. "You don't want that stuff to get out."

Brad smiled. "Yeah. Sort of like that."

"And these people," Willy probed. "They're evil, aren't they?"

"Yes," Brad affirmed. "They are."

"Are they trying to kill you?" he pressed.

Brad nodded. "I think so."

Willy's eyes widened. "You think they had anything to do with your plane going down?"

"I don't know yet. But it's possible." They'd watched the late news and the early shows this morning, but as of yet, there'd been no reports of the downed Galaxy.

"That's why you didn't want to call anybody," Willy remarked. "You want a head start before they start looking for you."

"That's exactly why."

Gus tapped the top of the beacon. "So what do you want us to do with this thing?"

"By now, if the Galaxy crashed, they've searched the wreckage and know I wasn't in it. If it landed, they know I jumped somewhere in this area. I was supposed to activate that beacon to alert the rescue team to my location. If they come looking for me here, that may buy me enough time to make it home to Washington before I'm back in their sights."

Gus exhaled a long breath. "You can count on us, Mr. Benton."

"I know, boys. That's why I trusted you with this."

"How do we turn it on?" Willy asked, studying the gadget with earnest intent.

Brad showed them the activation switch. "Wait until nightfall, then take it way out into one of the fields along with my parachute rig and activate it. It should take about three to four hours before someone comes looking for me."

"What do you want us to tell 'em when they come asking?" Willy asked.

"The truth," Brad said. "By that time, you'll have no idea where I am."

Willy laughed. "True enough. We got you booked through half the airports in the country."

Gus looked concerned. "You sure you're going to be all right?"

Brad clapped him on the shoulder. "I'll be fine, Gus. God is looking out for me."

"You want us to e-mail you if we find out anything about the plane?" Willy asked.

Brad didn't point out that he was headed for the information and intelligence capital of the world. If that plane had gone down, he'd know about it long before they did. The boys were eager to help, and he didn't have the heart to dim their enthusiasm. "That would be great."

Willy pushed his glasses up the bridge of his nose and tucked the beacon under his arm. "No problem. We'll handle everything on this end."

Had he not been utterly aware of the seriousness of the circumstances, Brad might have been amused by Willy's conspiratorial tone. "I know you will."

Bill Gleason had walked out of the house and was loading some empty feed bags in the back of his red pickup. "You 'bout ready?" he called to Brad. "I've got to drop these on the way out of town."

Brad thanked the boys again, then headed for the truck. "I'm ready."

Clara threw open the front door and hurried toward Brad, a brown paper sack clutched in her hands. "Hold on. Bill, I told you I'd just be another minute."

"We're not leaving without your supplies, Clara," Bill said. "I wouldn't dare."

She gave him a slightly chastising look as she handed Brad the bag. "It's just some food for the trip. I know you're going to be on and off a lot of planes, and you might not get another good meal until tomorrow."

Brad started to thank her, but Clara threw her arms around him and hugged him fiercely. "We might not see you again here on earth, Mr. Benton. But thanks to you, we've got hope about the future now. I don't know how I can ever thank you." She stepped away and mopped at her tear-filled eyes.

"Pray for me," Brad told her. "Just like I'll pray for you. And study and learn everything you can about Jesus and His promises. That's all the thanks I need."

She managed a watery smile. "You're a great man."

"No, I'm a pretty average guy who just happened to give my life to the greatest man that ever lived." Brad brushed a stray tear from her cheek. "And I *will* see you again, Clara. In glory."

"In glory," she whispered.

Brad thanked God again for dropping him in the middle of Longford, Kansas.

11

Marcus flashed his clergy badge at the nurses' station as he headed toward Emma Pettit's room at George Washington Hospital. He'd promised Brad he'd look after Emma in his absence. He'd visited her twice since Brad had left. Both times, she'd been asleep. Her sister had arrived and had been by her bedside, so Marcus had explained his friendship with Brad and left his number for the two women to call if they had any needs.

Emma's sister had called this morning with the news that the doctor had finally released Emma and she was going home that afternoon.

Marcus knocked on the open door before he entered the room. "Good morning." The curtains were pulled back, and Emma was sitting up in bed sipping a cup of tea. There was no sign of her sister.

She smiled at him over the rim of the cup. "You must be Marcus Dumont. My sister said you were coming."

Marcus went to the bed and put a hand on her shoulder. "It's nice to meet you, Emma. Where is your sister?"

"Getting coffee. She can't get through a morning without it." Emma motioned to the chair at the bedside. "Sit. I'm so glad to finally meet you."

"Brad asked me to look in on you while he's out of town."

"Did he finally make it back to California? I felt horrible that he got called back to Washington so quickly." She shook her head. "That Max Arnold doesn't care about much besides his political aspirations."

"He's home for a few days," Marcus affirmed. "It's good to see you up. Your sister tells me you're going home today."

"Yes, thank goodness. I'm sick to death of this place and I'm bored besides. To tell you the truth—" she lowered her voice—"I'm hoping to be back at work by the time Brad returns to Washington."

Marcus laughed. "I don't mind telling you that he's missed you, but I think if you show up at the office, he'll have your hide."

"Posh. That man worries too much. He's determined to make an old woman out of me."

Marcus linked his hands together around his knee. "I think he's just worried. You scared him to death."

"I imagine." She set her cup down on the bedside table. "I probably would have been rattled too if I'd been conscious."

Marcus was beginning to see exactly why Brad liked Emma so much. She had a sharp sense of humor, a dry wit, and, if Brad were to be believed, was second to none when it came to running his business life.

Emma tidied the folds of her blanket before meeting his gaze again. "So how's he faring without me?" She held up a hand. "Consider that before you answer."

"He's lost," Marcus admitted. "Can't keep anything straight."

"I'll bet." She shook her head. "That boy never has been good with dates and times. Do you know that when we first came to Washington, I had to get him a pager so I could inform him that the president wanted to see him?"

"No kidding?"

"No kidding." She clucked her tongue. "I have definitely got to get back to the office."

"Brad will nag," Marcus warned her.

"I'm sure he will. He'll get over it." She shifted slightly in the bed. "What I really want to know is what you told Brad that Sunday morning after the hearings that had such an effect on him."

Marcus leaned forward and placed both hands on the side of her bed. "I introduced him to my best friend."

She looked at him speculatively. "God?"

"You bet," Marcus said.

Emma nodded, her expression thoughtful. "He told me about that before he left."

"He said he thought you were listening that day."

"I was." She glanced out the window. "Looking death in the eye makes you think of things a different way."

"Emma." Marcus waited for her to look at him. "I know Brad told you that you can have eternal life. That if you are willing to let Jesus be Lord of your life, He promises you eternity in heaven."

"He did," she admitted.

"But you're not sure?"

"To be honest, Reverend, I've never really worried much about death. Even when I faced it, the idea didn't bother me much." Her forehead creased. "It's here and now that bothers me. I'm kind of glad in a way that I've been out of it these past few days. My sister says things are awful out there."

"There are a lot of hurting people," Marcus acknowledged.

"And Brad says that God is responsible. That this was some kind of supernatural event where God took His believers—like Christine and the kids."

"Yes. That's what I believe too."

"Then you tell me, Reverend—why would I want a God like that? Doesn't that seem cruel to you?"

"Emma, the Bible says that God is loving and merciful, but it also says that He's holy and just. All of us had the chance to acknowledge Him as Lord at one time or another, but through our own sin, we rejected Him. He made the consequences clear."

"I've never seen Brad the way he was that morning he came to see me," she said. "For as long as I've known him, he was restless and unsettled."

"He has direction now."

"Yes." She drummed her fingers on the top sheet. "And you think that because he—what did you say it was again?"

"He realized that he needed Jesus in his life—that the only way to have any hope was to acknowledge Jesus as his Lord and Savior and allow God's grace to save him from his sin."

"As long as I've known him, Brad never seemed to need anybody."

"He's a changed man," Marcus assured her.

Emma nodded. "I know. I saw it in him that day at the office. I didn't want to listen then, but I saw it. He's more peaceful. More content."

"That's because he trusts the Lord to lead him."

She sighed. "Then I want you to explain this to me. Because the way things look right now, I have to tell you I don't really want to face this world without knowing that someone greater than me is in charge."

Marcus smiled and leaned back in his chair. "As it happens, that's my favorite subject." With a silent prayer for wisdom and clarity, he pulled a pocket New Testament from his suit jacket and opened it to the book of Romans.

★   ★   ★

"You still haven't heard from him?" Charley Swelder asked Randal. They were seated in Brad's office, where Randal had found Charley looking through some files when he'd arrived.

"No," Randal said. "Mr. Benton's not in the habit of checking in with me. You know, I just wait until he needs me, or I work out of the pool."

Swelder, he noted, looked agitated. And furious. He'd demanded to know if Randal had any news from Brad the moment Randal entered the office. Randal wanted to ask what Swelder thought he was doing plowing through Brad's files, but he already had a pretty good idea. And he'd bet his last dollar it had something to do with why somebody was so eager to get his hands on Brad's briefcase.

Charley leaned back in Brad's chair. His shirt stretched tight over a stomach that had enjoyed one too many beers at one too many victory parties. "Young man, I don't think I have to tell you that we brought you on at the White House because of Mr. Benton's personal recommendation."

"No, sir. I know that."

"So I can understand why you might feel a certain loyalty to him."

"Is there any reason I shouldn't feel loyal to him?" Randal asked innocently.

"No," Swelder said. "But I'm afraid that loyalty might be clouding your judgment."

"Sir?"

"Mr. Arnold, I believe Mr. Benton could be in serious danger. I also believe you know where he is and you don't want to tell me because you think you're protecting him."

"I can honestly tell you," Randal insisted, "I have absolutely no idea where he is." His mother had phoned this morning to check on him and informed him that Brad had called her last night from an airport. All Randal knew was that Brad was expected back in Washington sometime today.

Charley Swelder's gaze bored into him. "You realize his life might be in danger?"

"Do you think so? Really?" Randal figured that the dumber and more innocent Charley Swelder thought he was, the more likely the man would be to reveal something.

"I'm afraid so," Swelder said, his tone sickeningly sincere.

"Oh, I guess I just figured that you folks would know where he is. Or how to find him at least." He gave Charley an ingenuous look. "Can't you call the FBI or something?"

Swelder's face reddened. "I assure you," he said, his tone pure acid, "we're using a number of avenues to trace him."

"I hope so. I'd hate it if anything happened to Mr. Benton."

"Which is exactly why you're going to tell me if you hear from him."

"Oh yes, sir. You can count on that."

Swelder studied him a moment longer, then slapped his hands down on Brad's desk as he stood, apparently satisfied. "I'm sure you will." He walked away from the desk and put a beefy hand on Randal's shoulder. "Why don't you get back to work for now?"

"You're sure there's nothing else I can do to help?"

Randal stood, unable to bear the feel of the man's sweaty hand through his shirt.

"We've got the situation under control. I just wanted you to be aware."

"You could try asking his secretary," Randal added helpfully as he walked with Swelder to the door.

The look he received was chilling. "I'll do that." Swelder opened the door for Randal and practically shoved him through it.

When the door closed with a decisive click, Randal hurried through the outer office toward the side stairs that would take him out of the West Wing. He pulled his cell phone from his pocket and clutched it as he raced along the corridor toward the exit.

When he was finally clear of the building, he hit a speed dial number on his phone. He shook his free hand impatiently as he listened to the ringing. "Come on. Pick up. Pick up."

"Hello?"

"It's me," Randal said. "I think Brad is missing."

★   ★   ★

Mariette thumbed through her stack of phone messages with a frown. "You're sure this is all?" she asked David. Brad had not called. When he'd called her from the airport last night, she'd assumed he'd be home today. She knew he was eager to retrieve the items she held for him as well as the report he'd asked her to get. But according to Randal, no one, including the White House, seemed to know where he was.

"As far as I know." David dropped into the chair across from her desk. "So tell me how much extra work New York is going to dump on us."

Mariette studied the messages again, then set them aside. *God,* she prayed, *please let Brad be all right. Please take care of him.*

She told herself not to worry, that there could be any one of a dozen reasons why he was late returning to Washington. There were even more reasons why he had not alerted the White House to his whereabouts. As sporadic and unpredictable as air traffic was these days, he'd probably been delayed—despite the fact that he'd told her he was flying military aircraft. Most MAC flights still used civilian airports, and the entire aviation system was a mess. *Please bring him home,* she prayed. *We need him.*

"Mariette?" David prompted.

She shook her head, forcing herself to set aside the grim thoughts. "Sorry. I'm a little tired, I guess."

"I'm sure you are."

"Berger's got enormous problems," she said as she pulled the report from her briefcase. "But I think we came up with some things."

"Great." He tapped his pen in a rapid, agitated rhythm on his notepad.

Mariette noticed the stress in the action and in his eyes. Carefully, she broached what she already knew was a tough subject. "David, before we start, I'm assuming that you went to see—"

"The shrink. Yeah. She said I was nuts." His laugh sounded hollow.

"David—"

He held up a hand. "I thought you said you weren't going to ask for the report."

"I didn't." She paused. "I'm asking you. As your friend and as your boss. How did it go?"

"Fine." He looked irritated. "I'm fine. I told you everything was okay. I'm just stressed and tired and sick of Musselman calling up here and making our lives wretched."

"Did something happen while I was gone?"

"You could say that," he said bitterly. "Bernie decided he had to know exactly what was going on at the UN. Like we've ever cared about the UN. When he found out you were in New York, he went ballistic."

"He knew I was in New York," Mariette protested. "I e-mailed him the TDY papers."

"Well, news to you, he doesn't know how to access attachments on his e-mail."

"Great."

"So he showed up here in some kind of freako mood and started demanding that we track you down. I kept telling him you were meeting with Berger all day, but he was determined to find out if you had any appointments at the UN, and he wouldn't take our word for it. I tried to get him to call you, but he wanted to hear it directly from the secretary-general's office. It took three staff members most of the day just to verify that you didn't have a meeting I already knew you didn't have. What's going on, Mariette? What's he up to?"

She shook her head. "It's just gossip. I don't know anything for sure."

"But you know something?"

"Maybe." At David's relentlessly expectant look, she finally gave in. "Daniel Berger told me there's a *rumor* that Nicolae Carpathia might be planning to reorganize the UN international relief division into an organization more closely patterned after FEMA. Musselman might be angling for the job."

David's expression went from stunned to incredulous to annoyed to amused in less than two seconds. He burst out laughing. "You have got to be kidding."

"Like I said. It's just a rumor."

"Has anyone bothered to mention to Bernie that he doesn't have a clue about how this agency works?"

"That's all I know about it," Mariette answered. "Nothing more."

"If I'd known that, I would have called the secretary-general myself and said, 'Hey, did you know this guy you're thinking of hiring is a total moron?'"

"I don't know that Carpathia is thinking of hiring him," she insisted. "I don't even know for sure that there's a job."

"Yeah, well, if there is, Nicolae Carpathia would be a fool to hire Musselman. If he's half as smart as everyone says he is, he should hire you."

Mariette swallowed. Hard. "It's all speculation and a waste of time." She handed David a copy of her notes. "So let's worry about what we can fix. Okay?"

★ ★ ★

Brad flashed his membership card at the reception desk in Denver International Airport's business lounge.

The young woman behind the desk inspected it and greeted him with a warm smile. "Welcome to Denver, Mr. Benton."

"Thanks." Brad scanned the lounge for signs of an open computer terminal. It was more crowded than he'd expected. "Busy today?"

"Busy every day lately. Flights are so restricted that people are waiting hours for connections. How 'bout you?"

"Four p.m.," Brad said.

Her gaze dropped to his nearly empty hands. All he had was the paper bag Clara had given him when he'd left Longford and the manila envelope with the photocopies of articles he'd retrieved from the library. "You're traveling light."

"Short trip. Do you think you have an open computer? I'm going to need a printer and a fax machine."

"Let me check." She punched a few keys on her computer. "Yes, sir. Number twelve is open. There's a printer at that station, and I can send a fax for you whenever you're ready." She handed him a card imprinted with his temporary access code.

"Thanks."

"No problem. Just let me know if you need anything else."

Brad stopped by the refrigerated case and helped himself to two bottles of water. When he found the terminal, he breathed a sigh of relief that the wall bordered it on one side, and there was no one seated at the adjacent terminal. It would make his task a little easier.

By now, he knew, his friends in Washington had been alerted that he was missing. Harmon Drake was probably out of his mind trying to find him, and in a few hours when Willy and Gus activated the security beacon, things were going to get worse.

He made quick work of logging on to the terminal. He typed a deliberately vague note to Marcus and hit the print key. The fax machine, he figured, was his best bet for contacting Marcus without being overheard or traced. When the page printed, he scrawled Marcus's fax number on the top, then crossed the room in a few quick strides to deliver it to the receptionist.

With that necessity behind him, Brad dug into Clara's bag for a sandwich, then opened the manila envelope. He'd already perused nearly half the materials, and the picture that was emerging was as sinister as it was sobering. If his hunch was right, it was no wonder George Ramiro had ended up with a bullet in his head.

Nor did he doubt that whoever was after him wouldn't rest until Brad was permanently and irrevocably silenced.

12

The jarring ring of the telephone sliced through the stillness in Marcus's home.

Phone calls at two in the morning always brought news.

He'd been around long enough to know that. At the first ring, Marcus frowned as he lifted his head to check the clock in his study. In the few days following the Rapture, he'd slept better than he had in years, but it hadn't taken long for his habitual insomnia to return. These days, though, he spent the long nights praying and studying until the small hours of the morning instead of poring over his business plan to see how he could boost his TV ratings and fund-raising profits.

Please let it be Brad, he prayed as he reached for the phone. Brad's fax that afternoon had been too vague to shed any light on why he'd gone missing. He'd simply said that he'd contact Marcus as soon as he reached town. "Hello?"

"Hi, Mr., um . . . Dumont?"

The caller was a woman whose voice he didn't recognize. "Yes?"

"This is Mindy McGavin. I work at the Wholly Donut."

He recognized the name of the coffee shop a block and a half from his house. "Yes?"

"I swear this is not a crank call. There's a guy here who says he knows you. He tipped me to call you and—"

"Is he there now?" Marcus asked.

"Well, yeah. You want to talk to him?"

"No. Tell him I'll be there in ten minutes." Marcus hung up the phone and reached for his shoes. Brad was behind the phone call. He was sure of it.

He made quick work of tying his shoes, then sped down the polished wood stairs and out the door. He checked over his shoulder as he secured the dead bolt. Georgetown was never quiet at night. The area was one of the most popular in the city for nightlife, but Marcus's home was on a side street with a gated entrance. Though he could hear the music coming from the clubs in the next block, he saw no one on his street.

He hurried toward the safety of the bustling M street traffic, checking twice to see if he was being followed. In recent days, the shadows of darkness and the unknown dangers they could hide had become menacing. Every snapped twig, every rattling leaf sent his pulse racing. He picked up his pace to a brisk walk and finally emerged onto M Street where partygoers milled about and the overflow crowds from clubs and bars spilled onto the street. Bouncers guarded the doors of the hot-ticket clubs where lines of young adults and teenagers waited for admission to the inner sanctum of the cool and beautiful.

The Wholly Donut was down the street and over a block, so Marcus determinedly made his way through the heavy crowd.

"What's the hurry, pop?" a woman asked him as he squeezed between a light pole and cluster of people.

Marcus glanced at her and revised his opinion. She was little more than a girl—a girl with too much makeup whose revealing blouse and tight-fitting leather pants could not disguise the fact that she was nowhere near twenty-one. "How old are you?"

That earned him a frown. "None of your business."

The exchange drew the attention of her friends in the small crowd. "What's goin' on?" one of the boys demanded. "This guy bothering you?"

"No," she said, still glaring at Marcus.

The boy turned to Marcus. "Get lost, old man. You don't want any trouble."

The rest of the crowd had picked up on the conversation and was now watching the drama unfold.

The bouncer near the club door shouldered his way toward them. "Something going on?"

Marcus grabbed the girl's arm. "This young lady is underage."

"Hey!" She angrily jerked her arm free.

The bouncer frowned, glanced at the girl, then at Marcus. "You know her?"

"Well enough to know she's not twenty-one."

"Shut up!" She looked at the bouncer. "I've never even met him."

The bouncer gave her a hard look, then jerked a thumb toward the street. "Beat it, kid. I'm not letting you in." He turned to the rest of her friends. "The rest of you either. Out of here. All of you."

Amid the grumbling and protests, the girl gave Marcus an angry look. "Thanks a lot."

Her boyfriend slung an arm over her shoulders. "Somebody should teach you to mind your own business," he said, the menace in his tone dimmed by his glasses and youthful face.

"I live in this neighborhood," Marcus told them. "Underage drinking is my business."

Their friends urged them to head down the street to another club where they might gain admittance. The girl looked like she wanted to argue. She continued to glare at Marcus.

"I know a good donut shop down the street," Marcus told her.

She made a disgusted noise as she turned her back to him, flinging her hair over one shoulder. He watched her teeter as she walked on her high heels down the brick sidewalk after her friends.

Marcus shook his head. *God, please look after these children. They know not what they do.*

The bouncer was now dealing with another small crowd but acknowledged him with an appreciative nod.

Marcus waved, then made his way toward the Wholly Donut.

The small shop was nearly deserted. A woman sat near the door, and there was another man at the counter. Marcus spotted Brad seated in the back, looking tired, disheveled, but except for a scrape across his cheek, mostly in one piece. Marcus stopped at the counter to get a cup of coffee.

"You the guy that man asked me to call?" the girl at the counter asked.

"That's me," Marcus said as he handed her his money.

"He wouldn't tell me why he wouldn't call you himself. Is he like a spy or something?" She dumped his change into his hand.

"Or something." Marcus grabbed a cream and two artificial sweeteners.

"Are you serious?"

He shot Brad a look over his shoulder, then leaned toward her. "Does he look like any spy you've ever seen?"

"Well, no."

"Do you have any reason to believe that a spy would pick the Wholly Donut for a rendezvous?"

"No way, mister. This is the most boring place on earth."

"Then you're going to have to trust me when I tell you he's not a spy. He just doesn't like to use the telephone."

She gave him a blank look, then nodded, her expression knowing. "Oh. One of those."

Marcus didn't bother to ask what that meant. He took his coffee and went to join Brad. "Sorry I'm late. I was detained by my citizen's duty."

Brad took a sip of his coffee. "No problem. I can't tell you how good it is to see you."

Marcus slid into the seat opposite Brad. He studied the younger man as he tapped the two sweetener packets against his palm. "You look terrible."

"Falling out of an airplane will do that to you." Brad scanned the occupants of the shop while Marcus finished preparing his coffee.

"I guess it would." Marcus set his plastic stirrer aside and leaned back in his seat. "What's going on, Brad? The White House reported you were en route to Washington when your plane went down. You're supposed to be dead. If I hadn't gotten your fax—"

"That's why I sent it to you."

"And I assume we're here instead of at my house," Marcus said, looking around, "because there are some people you aren't ready to let in on the fact that you're still in one piece."

"Uh-huh. I thought about coming to your place first, but the more I thought about it, the more I realized there's a *chance* you might be under surveillance. They're looking for me, and unless I miss my guess, they're pretty desperate right about now."

"I figured that. And I suspected the surveillance too. Lately, it feels like . . ." Marcus shook his head. "I can't explain it."

"You don't have to. What I've heard from security experts is that hunches like that are usually right. If you feel like you're being watched, you probably are."

"Maybe. So what happened in California?" Marcus took a sip of his coffee.

Brad checked the coffee shop once more, then leaned across the table toward Marcus. "I think I'm on to something. I got some information in L.A. that's beginning to make me understand why somebody wants me dead."

"You think the plane crash was intentional?"

"It would have to be a pretty big coincidence if it wasn't." He dropped his voice to a whisper and said, "I was on a MAC flight, Marcus. Did they announce that on the news?"

"No, I don't think it did. I don't remember how the report was worded, but something about it made me assume it was a private aircraft."

"It's not going to surprise me to find out that no one at the Pentagon has any official information about it either." Brad quickly told him the story of the change in aircraft he'd discovered at LAX. "So if someone did this deliberately, then he had the clearance and connections to sabotage a military jet."

"Oh, Brad—"

"That's why I needed to meet you here first. Somewhere safe. In case your place is bugged."

"You've got to sleep somewhere tonight."

Brad reached in his shirt pocket and produced a small

electronic gadget about the size of a pager. "I picked this up at LaGuardia."

"What is it?"

"It finds bugs—listening devices."

"You can get that kind of thing at the airport?"

Brad gave him a look. "These days you can get them at Wal-Mart."

"I never thought of it that way."

"If someone's listening or watching your house, it's not going to take them long to come down on you once they know I'm there." He handed Marcus the device. "You can sweep the place with this."

"I've seen these advertised in magazines." Marcus turned the device over in his hand. "This thing works?"

"Better than you'd think. Another little amenity I received along with the bombproof briefcase when I went to work at the White House was one of these things. That one got blown to bits in the apartment."

Marcus flipped the switch on the top of the device. Three LEDs flashed a random sequence until finally just one remained lit. "How does it work?"

Brad tapped the LEDs. "It's green now, which means neutral. Take it inside the house and walk slowly through the main floor. If anything's hot, the other lights will flash. Red's for audio. Yellow's for video. When you're within ten feet of the listening device, whichever indicator light is activated will burn steady."

"I only have to do the main floor?"

"It's sensitive enough to pick up any signal in the building. If the downstairs is clean, so's the upstairs."

"What about the phones?"

Brad tilted his head toward the girl at the counter. "That's why I didn't call you myself. If your phones are tapped, we can check them later. For tonight, I just want to know your house is clean. For your sake and mine."

Marcus nodded slowly. "Makes sense."

"You leave first, and I'll come after you in a few minutes."

Marcus took one of the napkins and used the pen in his shirt pocket to scrawl a code on it. "After hours, you have to have a code for the gate. There's a small alley that runs between the first two houses inside the gate. If you go down that alley, you can cut through the backyards to my house. One of the neighbors has a fence, but it's gated on both sides. No dogs."

"Good."

"If anyone's watching my house from the front, they won't see you approach."

"There's a back door?"

"Only on the deck on the second level, but the house has a half basement. I'll go downstairs and open the basement window for you."

Brad gave Marcus an apologetic look. "I'm sorry to drag you into this."

"Don't be." He took another long sip of his coffee, then slid out of the booth. He put one hand on Brad's shoulder. "God sent you into my life to be my brother and my friend. I wouldn't dream of doing anything else." He put the detection device into his pocket. "Give me a five-minute head start."

A few minutes later, Marcus let himself into his house. He flipped the power switch on the device and waited for the lights to sequence. Both the red and yellow lights continued to flash. Slowly, he walked toward the living room. The lights blinked faster.

As he moved around the room, their speed varied slightly—it reminded him of a high-tech, high-stakes version of hotter/colder. When he stood directly beneath an overhead vent, both lights stopped flashing and burned steady. Marcus grabbed a screwdriver from the drawer of the sideboard. He pulled a chair beneath the vent, slipped the detector in his pocket, then stepped up onto the chair to detach the vent cover. Inside, perched at a delicate angle on the edge of the duct, was an electronic device the size and shape of a cell phone. Three wires exited the device and headed up the duct. They probably tapped into his household wiring for power.

A surge of anger gripped him. A very private man, Marcus had few close friends by choice. He rarely shared intimate moments, and the idea that strangers had violated his life and his space enraged him. He seized the device and yanked it until the wires snapped.

When he pulled Brad's detector from his pocket, only the green light was illuminated. To be sure, he switched it off, waited five seconds, then turned it back on. The lights sequenced, but after a moment the red and yellow lights went out, leaving only the green light glowing.

Satisfied, Marcus quickly replaced the vent cover and the chair. He double-checked his curtains and blinds and switched off all but one light in the living room. He tossed the screwdriver into the sideboard and grabbed a flashlight. Quickly, he headed for the basement stairs.

He moved through the semidarkness in the basement to open the casement windows. He had barely cranked it open when he heard movement in the backyard.

Brad crouched down by the window. "Clean?"

Marcus handed him the device he'd removed from the vent. "It is now."

Brad examined it. "Where was it?"

"Den. In the air vent. I switched off the detector, then

turned it back on just to be sure. Green light only. You're sure I don't need to check the upstairs?"

"Yes. If there'd been more than one device, it would have indicated it."

Marcus signaled him to come in through the window. "Then it's clear. Come on in."

Brad handed Marcus a manila envelope and the deactivated surveillance device. He swung his feet through the opening, braced his hands against the foundation wall, and slowly lowered himself through the window.

When he was clear, Marcus cranked the casement shut again. "Your fax was a little vague. What were you doing in Denver?"

"It's not easy to get to Washington from Longford, Kansas, when the airlines only operate about half the scheduled flights."

Marcus laughed. "I can imagine. It was probably hard enough when the air schedules were normal."

"I still wish I knew what was in the belly of that MAC flight."

"You don't know?"

"They loaded it before I arrived at the hangar. It was in the front section under the nose. They put me out the back hatch. The weird thing is, I know the pilot made an emergency landing, but I don't think the plane crashed. The C-5 is a huge plane. It was only at fifteen thousand feet when I jumped. If it had crashed, I'd have seen the smoke plume."

Marcus briefly closed his eyes and thanked God again for His providence. "Thank God you're all right. I've been praying since I got your fax."

"I felt it," Brad said. "I've felt shielded and protected all day, actually." He clasped a hand on his friend's shoulder. "In the shadow of His wings. It feels safer than I dreamed."

"I'm glad." Marcus indicated the stairs with the flashlight. "Let's go upstairs. The drapes are drawn, the blinds are closed, and you look like you could use a rest."

"I'm whipped."

They climbed the steps and headed for the den where Marcus listened as Brad told him the story of his near miss at the L.A. Central Library, the Galaxy, his jump, the Gleasons, and the beacon he'd given Willy and Gus.

"It's a miracle you're alive, Brad."

"Literally," Brad told him. "I'm not sure I believed you before, but this has shown me that God has His hand on me."

"It would seem so. What I don't understand is why you asked the boys to activate the beacon. Wouldn't it buy you a little more time if the authorities continued to believe you were dead?"

Brad shook his head. "It's not going to take them long to figure out that I wasn't on board. Like I told you, I don't think the plane crashed, but the thing landed in the middle of nowhere. Once the crew was rescued, the authorities would know I wasn't on board. To tell you the truth, I'm surprised the news wasn't out before this evening."

"Maybe it was," Marcus agreed.

"But you said—"

"I said the news media reported that you were dead. Which means the White House and the Defense Department had to tell them you were dead. An official statement came from somewhere." Marcus gave Brad a close look. "It's a lot easier to explain someone's death if there's a plausible explanation. If the public believes you died in a plane crash, who's going to question when you don't show up at the office?"

"Like George Ramiro," Brad concurred. "I think so too."

Marcus thoughtfully stroked his chin. "You think the plane was sabotaged?"

"The pilot was forced to make a crash landing—apparently, at least. But the crew had time to put me off the plane—a plane that was in such danger, the pilot wasn't sure he'd be able to land it."

"But there was no apparent crash."

"Exactly. Which makes me think that the plane wasn't in serious difficulty. Once I was off, the pilot continued on to his original destination."

"Which may or may not have been Andrews Air Force Base."

"Right. But it raises the question of how deep this conspiracy goes." Brad frowned. "Did Randal tell you what he overheard when he drove those two men to the airport?"

"Something about Ramiro having an appointment in New York with some tell-all writer."

"I'm not sure his appointment had anything to do with a tell-all book." Briefly, Brad filled Marcus in on the details of the South Range case and his conversation with Jane Lyons. "The word at the White House was that the issue was officially and irrevocably dead. Never on the agenda. Never discussed."

"But you're not so sure?"

"I'll know more when I see the notes Jane is sending. I have a feeling that George was in a very small circle of people who knew exactly what had happened at South Range and that the administration had managed to squash the investigation, but there were still some unanswered questions. If someone was looking for answers to those questions, it makes sense they would have gone to George first."

"This is big enough to warrant murder, Brad?" Marcus pressed.

"If it means Victor Rudd—and maybe even Fitzhugh himself—might be looking at jail time it is."

"Oh, my."

"If George was asking questions, or worse, threatening to tell what he knew about South Range, then he could have made some fairly powerful enemies. Rudd's got broad enough contacts in the Defense Department to mean upper-level Pentagon officials might be involved. I have no way of knowing how far the circle of corruption could extend."

"And if you were put off that plane in order to make you disappear and not because of sabotage," Marcus mused, "then at least the pilot and the flight commander would have to know you weren't supposed to make it to Washington. Someone had to give that order and justify it."

Brad nodded. "I don't have to tell you that Fitzhugh isn't terribly popular with the Joint Chiefs of the military brass. If Fitzhugh's allies killed George to put the brakes on a South Range investigation, the Pentagon couldn't care less. But if South Range implicates someone in the Pentagon, then even the president might be at risk."

Marcus shook his head. "I have to tell you, Brad, it's more palatable to believe that there's one person after you than a government-wide conspiracy."

"I know," Brad said, "but the evidence says this is too broad to be a potential political scandal. The former chief of staff left the White House in a cloud of embarrassment. From the day I walked in the door, there were rumors the scandal that precipitated his departure was manufactured. Someone framed him to get him out of D.C. and out of the public eye. I'm beginning to wonder if he didn't set the whole thing up himself."

"Why?"

"Because his reputation is ruined, and his political career is over, but as far as I know, he's still alive."

"Unlike George Ramiro."

"Exactly." Brad gestured to the envelope on the table. "I think it's possible that George was asking too many questions and the wrong people started to get nervous. Someone wants the entire South Range issue buried and forgotten. If they were willing to kill George for looking into it, then they are willing to kill me, too."

Marcus linked his fingers together, propping his hands on his belly. "Have you talked to Randal today?"

"About his encounter with Rudd this morning? Yes."

"Doesn't it sound like the White House is planning on you taking the fall for this South Range business?"

"Maybe," Brad conceded, "which also makes me think that's why someone wants me dead. It'll be a lot easier to pin me with evidence if I can't defend myself."

"But if those two boys followed your instructions tonight, then by now, that beacon's been found."

"And they know I'm not in Kansas anymore," Brad said. "By morning, they'll know I'm here."

"Then you've got to get yourself seen by enough witnesses to make it known to the world that you're alive and well before you conveniently disappear like George Ramiro."

Brad nodded. "The last call I had from Randal, he told me Carpathia's scheduled to make a trip to D.C."

"Tomorrow." Marcus checked the clock. "Today, actually. That was on the news tonight, too."

"Did my precipitous disappearance at least make it earlier in the broadcast?" Brad asked.

"Sorry. Carpathia's visit was the lead story. You came after the weather."

"I'm not surprised."

"You were before sports, though."

"What a relief. Did they announce what time Carpathia's due at the White House?"

"No. I guess that's undecided."

"Or deliberately withheld. I'll call Randal in the morning. He may know something."

"Probably. He's turning out to be a natural at this intrigue business. I have a feeling he's going to love this little spy gizmo you have."

Brad shot him an amused look. "The biggest danger I might face is Mariette. I have the feeling she's not too pleased with Randal's involvement in this."

"There's some tension between those two, no doubt. Neither has told me anything about it, but I think Mariette is struggling with her maternal instincts and Randal is a little too eager to assert his independence."

"When you were twenty, did you think you were indestructible?"

"Absolutely."

"My mother didn't like it either." Brad folded his hands behind his head and leaned back on the sofa. "I'm sure the press'll be crawling all over the White House tomorrow. I'm sure that Fitzhugh is trying to time Carpathia's arrival so he can have one of those diplomatic welcome receptions on the front lawn. All I have to do is show up to get myself on camera. If I'm splashed all over CNN, someone's going to have a hard time claiming I disappeared in Kansas."

"True enough," Marcus agreed. "You might even get a decent night's sleep out of the deal." Brad, he noted, had sunk deeper into the cushions of the sofa.

"I probably shouldn't stay here." He indicated the surveillance device he'd dropped on the coffee table. "I could be putting you at risk."

"Forget it. If somebody torches my house, I'm covered—financially and spiritually. It's too late for you to check into a hotel anyway." He glanced at the manila envelope next to

the surveillance device. "Besides, it looks like you're traveling light."

Brad tried to stifle a yawn but failed. "I think the answer
to who killed George Ramiro is in that envelope. I've just
got to finish putting all the pieces together."

"Do you have proof?"

"Not yet, but if I'm right, I know where to get it."

"Good. The sooner the better."

"By the way, how's Emma?"

Marcus smiled when he thought of his last conversation
with Brad's assistant. "Well. Very well, actually. You'll be
glad to know your words didn't fall on deaf ears."

A peaceful look settled on Brad's face. "You talked to
her?"

"Yesterday, just before she went home from the hospi-
tal. Her sister called to tell me she was being discharged.
When I got there, her sister was out, so Emma and I talked.
She accepted the Lord, Brad."

Brad's eyes drifted shut. "Thank God. Thank God. How
can I ever thank you, Marcus?"

"You planted the seeds," he said as he stood. "I was just
there for the harvest."

"I'm eager to talk to her about it."

"You'll probably get your chance. She's threatening to
be back at work when you return to the White House."

"You're kidding."

"Afraid not. She's sure you need her."

"She's right about that, but I'm equally sure her doctor
told her it's too soon."

"She doesn't seem like the kind of woman who particularly cares what her doctor says."

"You have a point there."

Marcus laughed. "Maybe you can talk some sense into
her. Randal and I aren't having much luck."

Brad held up his hands. "I learned a long time ago that Emma might call me her boss, but she calls the shots. I can beg, I can even try to threaten, but I doubt it'll do much good."

"You're probably right." Brad's eyelids, Marcus noted, were starting to droop. "Let me get you a blanket." When Brad didn't protest, Marcus knew he was exhausted. By the time he returned with a pillow and a blanket, Brad was dead asleep on the couch. Marcus tossed the blanket over him and switched out the light.

He said a brief prayer thanking God for watching over them all once again, then headed for the stairs. He stopped in the foyer to double-check the locks. Whoever had placed that device in his ductwork had broken into his home already. Given Mariette's hair-raising tale of her experience in New York the night before and Brad's third calamitous brush with death, was it any wonder Marcus was having trouble sleeping?

★   ★   ★

"Explain to me," Randal said the next morning, "how you managed to make it back from California again without any clothes."

Brad took the dry-cleaning bundle from him. "Cute. Come in." He left Randal to handle the door as he retreated toward the den to dress. "Give me a minute, will you?"

"Sure."

Brad slid the hidden door that separated the den from the foyer shut and began to dress quickly.

"I'm glad you remembered you had that stuff at the cleaners," Randal called to him through the door.

"Me too." Brad swiftly checked his watch. He'd awakened early, despite his fatigue. He'd decided to risk being seen but not overheard, so he walked down the street to a pay phone to call Randal early and ask him to pick up his dry cleaning from the twenty-four-hour laundry near the White House. To his surprise, the college kid had actually sounded semialert despite the predawn hour.

"Mom said you could pick up the stuff she got from your apartment whenever you're ready," Randal told him now. "It's stashed in the vault of the Russell Building."

"But she has Christine's Bible?" Brad asked.

"Yeah. She hasn't let it out of her sight. Especially not after someone busted out her car window."

"How's everything at your house?"

"Okay. They didn't take anything. Nothing important got broken either."

"I was talking about your relationship with your mother."

"Marcus told you?"

"He said things were tense."

"Yeah. A little."

"She doesn't like you working for me."

"When I was ten, she wouldn't let me ride my bike past the end of our street. She forgets I'm not ten anymore."

"Cut her a break, Randal. She's your mother. And these people I'm dealing with have already murdered someone. They're capable of anything."

"I know that. It's just that I can't sit around on my hands and do nothing while this Carpathia guy takes over the world. It's driving me nuts."

"God has a plan," Brad assured him. "He'll use you in due time."

"Sooner would be better than later."

"Your mother is still entitled to worry."

"She could try a little harder to keep it to herself, you know."

"You could try a little harder to understand why this is putting her through an emotional wringer. She's worried."

Randal's sigh was audible through the closed door. "Yeah, I know. I know. I'm trying."

"Good. I was afraid I was going to have to remind you it's your Christian duty."

"Got it covered. Read the verse yesterday. Twice."

"Glad to hear it. In the meantime, we need to sweep your place for bugs."

"Are you serious?" Randal asked. "You think we're bugged?"

"Marcus was," Brad told him.

"Get out." Randal sounded more enthused than appalled.

"We found it last night." Brad had his pants and one of Marcus's clean T-shirts on. He reached for his dress shirt. When Brad had spoken to Randal that morning, he'd told him that Carpathia was due at the White House sometime early afternoon. Fitzhugh had stunned the White House staff and the press with the announcement that he'd agreed to send *Air Force One* to pick up the new secretary-general.

Brad pulled his shirt on, then slid the door open with his foot as he worked on the buttons.

Randal was studying one of the paintings in Marcus's foyer. "Marcus here?"

"He left me a note. Said he had an early meeting with Sanura."

"The lawyer," Randal said, his eyes gleaming. "Smooth move on that, Brad, I gotta tell you."

"Excuse me?" Brad buttoned one cuff, then the other.

"Don't tell me you sent Sanura Kyle to Marcus's office just because she's a good attorney."

Brad reached for his tie. "What other reason would I have?"

"Come on. You're not going to convince me that you didn't think about the fact that Sanura Kyle is drop-dead gorgeous, smart as a whip, and that Marcus could use the company. How long since his wife died?"

Brad looped his tie around his neck and hastily tied a Pratt Knot—which he preferred for its symmetry. "I'm not exactly sure. But Marcus asked me to recommend a lawyer, and I picked the best one I know."

"Yeah. Sure." Randal watched as Brad scooped up the manila envelope and his suit coat. "I hope Marcus buys that."

Brad handed the envelope to Randal so he could slip on his coat. "Let's go."

Randal hesitated. "You're sure you want to go in today? You could take one more day to get things settled."

"Definitely sure," Brad told him. "I'm not going to hide."

"Now you sound like Mom. She told you about the note from Carpathia?"

"Yes."

"Did you guys think you were the only ones old enough to worry about the people you love?"

"Did you think you were the only one young enough to have guts?" Brad teased him.

"No, but then, I didn't almost get blown up in an airplane the night before last either." Randal gave Brad the envelope as they walked toward the door. "The most excitement I've had is listening to that Rudd character try and set you up for the South Range deal. Are you going to explain that to me anytime soon?"

"Soon," Brad promised. "As soon as I understand it myself."

"Before or after someone else tries to splatter your guts on the pavement?"

Brad clamped a hand on his shoulder. "Don't worry about it, Randal. God is taking care of me."

"For how long?" he mumbled, his hand on the doorknob.

"As long as He's got work for me to do." Brad gave him an earnest look. "Are you sure you're doing all right with all this?"

"Sure. I guess. I just don't like feeling helpless. Mom was really scared when someone broke into our house, but I gotta tell you, I was just hacked off."

"I understand." Brad remembered his own sense of outrage when his apartment had been bombed. Once the shock had passed, a deep, abiding anger had set in.

"What's in your briefcase that they want so much?"

"Nothing," Brad told him. "It's what they think is in there."

Randal's eyes narrowed for a moment, then comprehension dawned. "Those photographs. The ones you got on my first day of work. You had them in California with you."

"Yes, but they didn't know that. By now, someone who doesn't want me asking questions about George knows I have them."

"But who sent them to you in the first place?"

"I haven't figured that out yet."

Randal shook his head and pulled the door open. "I hope you figure it out soon. I'm not sure how many escape-imminent-death passes you have."

"Enough to get me through this," Brad assured him.

They made their way down the front steps to the black sedan Randal had picked up that morning at the White House.

When they were seated inside, Brad remembered what

Marcus had asked him that morning. "As far as you know, do you and your mother have any plans tonight?"

"Not that I know of," Randal said. "Why? You want your Bible?"

"That, and Marcus thinks the four of us should meet. With everything that's happened over the last few days, he thinks we need to sit down together for some serious prayer and study time."

"I agree."

"And he wants to discuss the idea of a relocation shelter in more detail."

"We'll be there," Randal said as he merged into the heavy Connecticut Avenue rush-hour traffic. "God willing."

★　★　★

"Do you have any idea what this is about, Brad?" Harmon Drake leaned back in his ancient leather desk chair, sturdy hands linked behind his head. His broad chest and deep voice gave him a sense of authority and command that Brad knew many found intimidating.

"Not really," Brad hedged, not yet ready to reveal his suspicions—not even to Harmon Drake.

Drake's eyes narrowed. "Well, I can't believe you were picked at random. At first, we thought maybe some crackpot was just taking shots at the White House and you were in the line of fire. But now, with the sniper, the house, the plane—that's a major coordinated effort."

"Yes."

"If we were dealing with some freak out to pop a member of the administration, I don't think he would have gotten past the garage. That bomb at your apartment took some planning, but sabotaging a military aircraft—"

"That might not have been related," Brad pointed out.

"I don't think we can afford to rule it out."

"Me either."

"But here's the thing, Brad," Drake said. "I've spoken with several top-level Pentagon officials this morning. No one has any information about that C-5 leaving LAX the other night—let alone crash-landing."

"I didn't imagine being shoved out of an airplane," Brad insisted.

"I know. I know. I'm not saying you did. Ever since these disappearances, everything's in chaos over there. I think the Joint Chiefs can't decide if we've been attacked and the president is pushing them to name the enemy and the weapon."

"Something as inconsequential as a crashed Galaxy may not be on the radar; is that it?"

"You said yourself you're not sure whether or not the plane was able to put down. If it didn't actually crash, the report may not have made it to Washington yet. I'm still checking."

"I appreciate it, Harmon."

"I can double security on you," Drake promised. "Put a detail on your house."

"That's not necessary."

"Swelder's likely to insist. Losing an administration official is not something Fitzhugh wants to explain to the media right now." Drake shot Brad an apologetic look. "Don't mean to sound crass, but it's no secret you're not considered indispensable around here."

Brad shook his head. "No, don't apologize. I've known where I stood around here since the day I arrived in Washington. Fitzhugh brought me on to calm some nerves after that last scandal broke."

With a sigh that sounded more like a growl, Drake

planted his hands on his desktop and leaned forward. "I've got to tell you, I don't like the fact that this is going on in my house. You haven't talked to the police, have you?"

"No," Brad assured him. "I thought the matter was best left to you."

"Good." He uttered a colorful description of the D.C. police force that left no doubt about his contempt. "And by the way, what happened in L.A.? I had a detail on you. They said they lost you at the library."

"I used the rear exit," Brad said. "I was running late for the airport, and it was faster. I didn't think they'd have trouble finding me."

Drake shook his head. "It's that L.A. field office. Bunch of idiots. They know counterfeiting, but when it comes to protection detail, they're sloppy and useless. I shudder every time the president goes out there."

★   ★   ★

"Have you talked to Marcus yet?" Daniel Berger asked on the phone.

"I have a meeting with him tonight," Mariette said. David was standing at the door of her office so she waved him in. "I'm sure he'll be pleased."

"I'm serious about wanting to meet with him first," Daniel said.

"I know. I'm sure we can work something out—just not over a weekend. He preaches on Sundays."

David was watching her.

"Actually, I was thinking of coming to him instead. I heard him preach once—before all this, I mean. I think I'd like to hear him now."

"Oh." She wasn't sure why the idea of having Daniel in town disconcerted her. Maybe it had something to do with the trouble she had picturing him in one of Marcus's worship services.

Daniel must have sensed the wariness in her tone. "Mariette? Did I say something wrong?"

David idly thumbed through the report in his hand.

Mariette turned her chair toward the window and lowered her voice. "No, I'm sorry. There's someone in my office. Can I call you back?"

"Yeah, sure. No problem."

"Thanks." She hung up and faced David. "Hey. What's up?"

He took the seat across from her desk. "I could ask you the same thing." He tipped his head toward the office receptionist. "Cindy told me Berger was on the phone."

"He was."

"Hmm." David dropped the report on her desk. "I thought you might want some of the preliminary information we've been building on getting relief supplies into the city so I brought it in here. But it didn't sound like the conversation went that way."

Mariette reached for the report. She shrugged with deliberate nonchalance. "I'm looking into a personal matter for the mayor. He was calling to see if I'd made any progress." In her peripheral vision, she could see David's expectant look, so she gave undue attention to the chart on the third page. "This is very comprehensive."

David was undeterred. "Did that personal matter have something to do with the fact that Carpathia's expected in town today and rumor has it he's going to discuss his international relief plan with the president?"

"No." She gave him a direct look. "It didn't."

He searched her face for several seconds. "Musselman has already more or less announced he's taking the job."

"Good for Bernie." She held up the report again. "Can we get back to New York?"

David's eyebrows rose, but he nodded. "Sure. The biggest issue I see right now is the Teamster strike."

★   ★   ★

"Brad." Gerald Fitzhugh strode into Brad's office. "So you *are* back. Charley told me you were in the office today. I didn't believe him."

Brad stood and rounded his desk. "Mr. President. It's good to see you."

Fitzhugh shook his hand, then indicated the cluster of stuffed chairs near the small conference table. "You gave us all quite a scare with that airplane business." He sat down and crossed his long legs. "Don't know where that story came from, but Tetherton was running around here like a maniac trying to verify the report." He flicked a speck of lint from his trousers. "I still haven't heard how that all got started."

Brad took the seat across from him. "I'm not sure either. I was on a MAC flight that had some trouble over the Midwest."

Fitzhugh nodded, his expression thoughtful. "We heard it was a MAC flight but didn't want to release the details until we had more information."

"A C-5," Brad told him. "I was scheduled on that afternoon's C-20 out of LAX, but when I got to the airport, there was an aircraft change."

"That's the strange part," Fitzhugh told him. "According to the Pentagon and the LAX flight log, the C-20 took off on schedule and landed at Andrews. Charley talked to the pilot. He had your name on his manifest but said you never showed."

Brad felt a chill slip down his spine. "I reported to the MAC terminal when I arrived. An escort took me to the C-5 and told me there had been an aircraft change. I didn't think to question him."

"Some misunderstanding, I suppose. I talked to Dave Marsden about it yesterday afternoon and didn't get anywhere. He's his usual pompous self."

Disagreements between Fitzhugh and the irascible Marsden of the Joint Chiefs of Staff were legendary. Yet it came as no surprise that Fitzhugh had tapped Marsden for information. The general was arrogant, controlling, unpredictable, and widely recognized as the most informed and powerful member of the Joint Chiefs. The idea that a Galaxy with a loaded belly could leave LAX, drop a passenger in the middle of Kansas, and apparently set down somewhere else without Marsden's knowledge was laughable. What gave Brad pause was the idea that Marsden was brazen enough to stonewall the president of the United States.

Brad suddenly realized the president was looking at him expectantly. "I'm sure the Pentagon is having many of the same problems we are with communications these days. Everything is still fairly chaotic."

"It's possible . . . but you'd think the top brass would know if a White House official was nearly killed." He swore quietly. "They might enjoy killing a White House official, but you'd think they'd at least know about it."

Brad managed a slight laugh. "I think even Dave Marsden would tell you they have no intention of getting rid of any of us."

"Maybe." Fitzhugh's expression remained troubled, but he shook his head. "Charley is looking into all this. He'll get to the bottom of it."

"I'm sure he will."

"Drake tells me he's increased your security."

"Yes, sir."

"Good, good. Do us all a favor and cooperate, will you? The last thing we need right now is a major disruption."

The president didn't sound overly concerned about his welfare, Brad thought. "I understand."

"I'm sure you do. We've got a lot going on here, Benton, and I don't mind telling you, you're going to have to play a key role in this business with Carpathia."

"Sir?" Brad said.

The president nodded. "Hmm. You know we've sent *Air Force One* to pick him up?"

"I heard that."

Fitzhugh's expression soured. "Chafed me, I'll tell you, but the smarmy little cuss practically forced me into it. We weren't going to get him here until we sent the plane."

"When I initiated contact with his people, Carpathia indicated that was his preference."

"He may know a lot about the UN, but he hasn't figured out yet that the United States doesn't bow to it. *Air Force One* isn't an international taxi service for self-impressed diplomats."

"It's unprecedented," Brad agreed.

"Truth is, Benton, I never would have agreed to it if I hadn't gotten word that the new plane is ready to roll out of the hangar." Everyone at the White House was aware of Fitzhugh's fascination with the new *Air Force One*, which had been under construction for the past year. The huge new aircraft was a technological wonder, and the president had taken a personal interest in its design and details. "Boeing tells me they're ready to send the plane as soon as the paint dries and we authorize a pilot."

"That's good news."

"Especially with this treaty business coming up. Looks like we'll all be making a visit to Israel for the signing." The president shook his head. "Still can't believe Carpathia managed to get the Arabs to agree to surrender Jerusalem to the Israelis."

Brad had no trouble believing it. It was merely another of the many signs that Carpathia was, indeed, the prophesied Antichrist. "He's polished—and smart."

"I'll grant you that. You know he's calling for a religion summit? Some nonsense about a global partnership between the world religions?"

"I've heard that."

Fitzhugh snorted. "I guess getting the Arabs to the table on this Jerusalem deal has gone to his head."

"Perhaps."

"At any rate, there's no getting around the fact that we're going to have to make a trip to Israel for the signing, and I plan to make that trip the maiden voyage of the new *Air Force One*."

The plane, Brad knew, wouldn't officially be christened *Air Force One* until the president's first flight on board. The new jet was a larger class than the existing plane, and the pilot had indicated that he'd prefer to retire than go through the rigorous training to recertify. "Then we'd better scramble to find a pilot."

"Charley made some calls. We've got a short list of candidates. I'd like you to handle it as quickly as possible."

"Yes, sir."

"Charley will bring you up to speed on everything else. Carpathia is due here around two this afternoon. I'll greet him on the lawn before we sit down to talk."

"Who set the agenda?"

"We did. I'm not willing to head off to Israel without settling this antinuclear business. You know Arnold is putting us in an untenable position about signing the thing."

Max Arnold was one of Washington's most outspoken

critics of Carpathia's unilateral disarmament plans. With the majority of the American public swept up in Carpathia's rhetoric and the euphoria of his promises of global peace and harmony and the terror of the Rapture still ever present in their minds, Americans were desperate for hope, and Carpathia was obliging them.

"I'm sure," Brad said, "that Senator Arnold is just as eager as we are to make the best political use of Nicolae Carpathia's popularity."

"I don't have to tell you how much he's enjoying the opportunity to educate the American public on the constitutional requirements of treaty ratification. Nothing makes Max Arnold happier than to point out that he's got more power than I do."

Brad laughed. "I don't think I'd go that far."

"When it comes to ratification he does. It's a mess, Brad. If the Senate doesn't ratify it, I can't sign it. But will voters hold Arnold responsible for that? Of course not. They'll blame me."

"Depends on how outspoken Arnold's opposition is."

"The only way out of this, according to Charley, is for us to get Carpathia to agree to some terms we can tolerate."

Brad was doubtful that was possible. "I can't see Max Arnold agreeing to support any treaty that requires us to completely disarm and turn over 10 percent of our weapons to the UN."

"We've met with the Senate leadership. I think if Carpathia will agree to appoint me as the chairman of the disarmament committee, we might be able to make a go of it."

Brad thought that over. "It would be controversial. Carpathia would draw major opposition from the Russians, certainly, not to mention the Arab states."

"Maybe, but he can't make this work without us. We

may have to make a few concessions, but I think we'll get it."

Brad wondered what those concessions might be but didn't press for answers.

Fitzhugh continued. "And it isn't as if the blasted idea has a chance of working. I don't expect the thing to last six months. But the voters are buying it, and if we don't come off looking like we're cooperating, we're going to lose more than a few seats in the congressional elections this year."

"I agree."

Fitzhugh braced his hands on the arms of his chair. "Which reminds me, what have you heard about the possibility that Morrow's office is going to reopen the South Range investigation?"

Brad went still. "South Range?"

"Just heard about it. Swelder tells me that the congressional oversight committee is asking questions again. Seems Carpathia has opened a can of worms with all this disarmament business." He shook his head. "The rumors that the South Range reserves were compromised to give covert assistance to al Qaeda resistance groups are persisting. UN inspectors turned up some North Korean nukes in Afghanistan."

"They could have been there for years."

The president shook his head. "The technology is less than ten years old. No one's sure how they got there."

"And someone has suggested they might have been purchased with gold reserve from South Range?"

"That rumor won't die, it seems. I met with Rudd while you were out of town. He's understandably upset."

"I'm sure he is."

"I assured him it'll blow over. We've got the documentation from Morrow's office that shows they didn't find any discrepancies the first go-round. Tetherton has all the infor-

mation. Get him to fill you in, in case you get asked some
questions after the Carpathia visit."

"Tetherton's handling the post-reception press?"

"Yes. But I'm sure your phone will be ringing." Fitzhugh
glanced at the door. "Which reminds me, what's the news
on your secretary?"

"She's home from the hospital and eager to get back to
work."

"Good, good. I think you're going to need some competent office support soon."

Brad didn't bother to point out that he was far more
concerned about Emma's complete recovery than about
having his appointments scheduled and his correspondence neatly typed. "I'll let her know you're looking forward to having her back."

Fitzhugh stood. "Good. Excellent. Make sure your
schedule's clear this afternoon. I'm not sure how long
Carpathia's going to stay, but we're going to need to put our
heads together on getting this treaty ratified. I'd like to get it
done before we leave for Israel if we can. We need to have a
unified response."

Brad stood, too. "I understand."

"Fine." Fitzhugh clapped him on the shoulder. "I'm sure
I don't have to tell you that I know we've had our differences, but this is the time to be a team player. You didn't get
where you are without good political instincts, Benton.
You know that."

"Yes, sir."

Fitzhugh gave Brad's shoulder a slight squeeze before
dropping his hand. "I'm sure we can count on you."

Brad watched the president move toward the door.

With his hand on the knob, Fitzhugh turned to face
him. "By the way, Brad, I think Carpathia may be behind
this renewed interest in South Range. There's been some

talk that he wants to move any international gold reserves into a World Bank holding facility." His laugh was harsh. "He might get us to agree to this disarmament thing, but the failure of the euro should have been writing on the wall on where we stand on an international currency."

"I have the impression Costello is behind it," Brad said, referring to the secretary of the treasury.

"He's playing ball," Fitzhugh assured him, "but we've discussed this. Unless the dollar is the foundation marker for the currency, we're not going to endorse the plan."

"But you think Carpathia wants to relocate the international gold deposits from the New York Fed?"

"He's insinuated it. Costello says he has some backing for the plan. Naturally, that has everyone questioning what happened at South Range."

But George Ramiro, Brad thought, had been questioning it long before Nicolae Carpathia made his dramatic entrance on the global scene. "Could be."

"I know you weren't here when the story broke, so make sure you consult the counsel's office before you make any statements."

"I will," Brad said.

"I think Sanura Kyle is the point person on that. Charley will know."

"I'll ask him when we meet."

Fitzhugh's expression registered relief. "All right, then, let's see if we can get through this Carpathia business today without any incidents. Good to have you back, Benton." He pulled open the door and exited the office.

"Thank you, sir." Brad frowned as his office door swung silently shut. Though he'd told Marcus he wouldn't be surprised to learn that the Pentagon had no official statement on the flight that had left him stranded in the Midwest, Fitzhugh's revelation that David Marsden had denied knowledge of the incident gave him an uneasy feeling. Marsden might not like Fitzhugh or his politics, but he was a professional soldier who respected his commander in chief out of duty and honor. Marsden might not have been forthcoming, but he would not have lied to the president.

Brad thought it over a moment, then reached for the phone on his desk and punched an extension.

"Wells," came the voice on the other end of the phone.

"Colonel," Brad said, "this is Brad Benton. Have you got a minute in your schedule for me today?"

★   ★   ★

Randal adjusted the earbud of his listening device as he sped across the Wilson Bridge. With Carpathia's arrival scheduled at the White House today, most of the drivers were busy shuttling VIPs who were streaming to the White House for the president's welcome reception that afternoon. Everyone was eager, it seemed, to be seen on the platform with the new secretary-general of the UN. Brad had been asked to release Randal to the pool for the day to help supplement the beleaguered staff.

"Did he tell you anything else?" the woman in the backseat asked her companion.

Randal had picked up the pair at Andrews. He'd recognized Katrina Royal. She was a ranking member of the Subcommittee on Military Construction Appropriations. The young man with her reminded Randal of the slick political operatives he'd known while working on his father's senatorial campaigns.

"Nothing," the man said. "All I know is that Morrow's office is set to make an announcement by the end of the week."

Senator Royal made a sound of disgust. "I'm sure Swelder wishes I didn't have that information."

"I've got a call in to Morrow's aide," the young man assured her. "The last I heard, they plan to start taking depositions again as early as next month."

"Hmm. I wonder what kind of pressure Rudd is putting on the White House to kill the story."

"Severe, I understand. This all came up because of Carpathia's negotiations to make the World Bank the depository for an international currency standard. With the hemorrhage on Wall Street since the disappearances, it's no surprise the oversight committee and the Fed are nervous."

"No," Senator Royal said thoughtfully. "The only surprise is that Fitzhugh's lawyers aren't screaming that Morrow should be disqualified from the case. After the entire thing fell through last time, his objectivity is going to be questionable."

"True," the man agreed, "unless he can actually prove there was something to all this South Range business the first time."

"He'd have presented charges to the grand jury if it had been true."

"Maybe . . . or maybe he made a choice about his future and his well-being by dropping the charges."

"Morrow can't be bought," the senator insisted.

"But can he be terrorized?"

"Interesting question."

Very interesting, Randal thought as he negotiated through the city traffic toward the White House.

The rest of the conversation in the backseat turned to Carpathia's disarmament treaty, his meeting with the president, and the pending treaty signing in Jerusalem. Randal considered what he'd heard from Victor Rudd in light of this new information. Rudd had seemed certain that if the South Range scandal did resurface, then the White House would make Brad take the fall for it.

But if Thomas Morrow had been threatened or coerced
into dropping the charges the first time, had Rudd been behind it? And if so, why couldn't Rudd also be behind the
murder of George Ramiro?

He stopped at a security checkpoint and showed his ID,
then continued on through the restricted area toward the
White House. He pulled the earbud from his ear and
switched off the radio as he reached for his cell phone.
While in college, he'd used his contacts in the Congressional Research Service to request research packets for theses
and term papers. And though he now acknowledged with a
twinge of guilt that the practice had been less than honorable if not technically cheating, the contacts would serve
him well. He punched a number into his cell phone and hit
the call button. His phone digitally dialed the number and
he listened impatiently to the ringing on the other end.

The information Brad had asked him to retrieve from
the Federal Election Commission had revealed, as expected, that Rudd had several common ties to organizations linked to Constantine Kostankis, but Randal had
found no evidence that the two men had any direct contact.
The conversation he'd just overheard made him wonder if
Thomas Morrow's final report on the South Range issue
might contain some evidence that irrevocably linked Rudd
to Kostankis.

He heard the distinct click as his call connected. "CRS,"
came the voice on the other end.

"Ted? This is Randal Arnold."

"Hey, man. How are you?"

"Busy."

"Yeah. I heard you landed a White House job."

"I'm driving."

"Your old man pull that for you?"

Randal squelched his irritation. In Washington, political contacts and clout held the power of money in most of the world. While wealth and breeding equated aristocracy in normal cities, Washington determined its elite by tracing the strings of power. "My mother, actually," he said. "She knows Brad Benton."

"Oh. Makes sense. You like it okay?"

"Pays the bills," he said dismissively. "Listen, Ted, I know you guys are busy right now—"

"You can't imagine. Since the disappearances, we've got members asking for every conceivable translation of the Bible, every past issue of *Jane's*, and anything else they think might shed some light on this."

"Then I won't keep you," Randal assured him. "I just need a copy of the Morrow report on the South Range investigation."

"Seriously? What are you working on? Some kind of paper for school while you're on break?"

"Yeah, something like that."

"How studious of you," Ted said. "I think we still have a couple of bound copies lying around here somewhere. Let me get a pen and you can tell me where to send it."

★   ★   ★

Brad struggled to stifle a yawn as he listened to Charley Swelder finish briefing the staff on the afternoon's meeting with Carpathia. Carpathia had been late, incensing the president, and even now Fitzhugh had a disgruntled expression as Swelder hit the high points.

"We made some progress on the disarmament issue," Swelder assured the top staff.

Forrest Tetherton dropped his notebook on the conference table. "Can I tell the press the U.S. has agreed to chair that committee?"

"Carpathia hasn't offered me the chairmanship yet," Fitzhugh said. "We're meeting again after dinner."

Swelder tapped his pen on his copy of the briefing papers. "For those of you on the invitation list, we've got a State Dinner tonight. To the rest of you, I'm insanely jealous that you get to go home."

The quip was met with muffled laughter. Brad had never been more glad in his life to be an outcast than when he'd realized he'd be able to skip the tedious banquet tonight.

One of the speechwriters signaled for Charley's attention. "Are the president and Carpathia meeting on some of these same issues after dinner, or can we get started on the rhetoric?"

"You can start," Fitzhugh said. "No matter what we agree on or don't agree on, our position is the same. We're going to do what's in the best interest of the United States, and unless we have some control over this disarmament treaty, the U.S. isn't interested."

Tetherton shook his head. "I don't think we're going to be able to sell that to an American voting public who is still terrified that we'll come under attack again."

The speechwriter agreed. "Carpathia has a lot of support for the proposal."

"Sure," the president shot back, "until some terrorist organization gets their hands on a load of nukes and blows the snot out of somebody." His laugh was unpleasant. "We should have all known something like this was coming when Romania turned its government over to that poet— what was his name?"

"Hegel," Brad supplied.

"Yeah. That's the one. Hegel. I mean, who in their right mind thought some limerick writer was qualified to run a country? No wonder they dug themselves into an economic quagmire. They started throwing their money into all those fruity programs like children's art education. You know what I always say: the best way to defend your borders from the threat of hostile takeover is to have a nation full of kids who can draw." Fitzhugh continued his rant with a list of profane names for the former and current Romanian presidents.

Brad flipped a page to study the rest of the talking points. He reached the third item on the list, and his fingers trembled slightly. "Uh, sir—"

Fitzhugh stopped and glanced at him. He noticed that Brad was studying the second page. "Yeah, page two. The whole plan gets weirder, doesn't it?"

"Brad," Charley said, "we think you're our best point person on item three."

"Global religion," Fitzhugh said, his tone disgusted. "I tried to explain the concept of separation of church and state to Carpathia for over an hour, but I'm beginning to wonder how bright he is. He doesn't seem to understand that if all the religious nuts in the world want to get together and write their own Bible, then the United States couldn't care less. He wants us to recommend some representatives for the summit meeting."

"Is the meeting already scheduled?" Brad asked.

"Next week," Charley answered. "He wants it to happen before the treaty signing in Jerusalem. The delegates are supposed to gather in New York at the UN to open discussions."

"I don't know why he thinks it's going to work," Fitzhugh insisted. "It's like this Israeli treaty. The Arabs and the Israelis have been fighting over that hunk of mud for more than six thousand years. I don't know what makes him think it's going to stop now. Treaty or no treaty."

"The offer seems genuine this time," Forrest responded,

"although I'm not sure why it's only a seven-year peace agreement."

"Give 'em time to rebuild the temple," one of the speech-writers pointed out.

And fulfill yet another of the biblical prophecies, Brad thought.

Fitzhugh was clearly unimpressed. "How many peace treaties have the Arabs and the Israelis signed in the last fifty years? How many of those worked out? Before the ink's dry on the paper, the Palestinians will send some sui-cide bomber into a Jerusalem day-care building and the whole mess will start all over again."

Brad glanced at Charley Swelder. He'd never seen the man so irritated with Fitzhugh. Generally, the two worked in tandem, but something about the conversation was seri-ously chafing Swelder. It made Brad wonder what Swelder had to gain from the president's unconditional compliance with Carpathia's agenda.

"Besides," Fitzhugh continued, "he can't even get those two loonies at the Wailing Wall to cease and desist. What's he think he's going to do with the extremists in the parlia-ment?"

"I believe there's a plan to deal with the faction at the Wailing Wall," Charley said. "And if you remember, the secretary-general mentioned something this afternoon about discussions at the Knesset."

"A plan?" Fitzhugh laughed. "What kind of plan? If you can believe the media, every time somebody gets near those two nuts they melt 'em to ash. That report the day be-fore yesterday said that they melted a semiautomatic rifle into a puddle."

Charley's face had begun to turn red. "The secretary-general indicated that intelligence reports suggest that those reports are less than accurate."

"Intelligence," Fitzhugh scoffed. "If those two freaks are so easy to stop, then why are they still raving like loons all day? You want my opinion? I think Carpathia's just mad that they're stealing his thunder. For the first time in weeks, the media's got something else to talk about besides the Romanian golden boy."

"I don't think he enjoys all the attention," Charley said.

"Oh, come on, Charley. You don't believe that, do you? Since when doesn't an ambitious politician relish the spotlight?"

"He insists he wasn't looking for all this power," Charley pointed out. "And I'm inclined to believe him."

"Then he's got you hoodwinked like the rest of them." The president swore under his breath as he looked around the room. "Let's not forget what we're about here, people."

"To get reelected," one of the speechwriters joked.

He earned a scathing look from Swelder and a few muffled laughs.

Fitzhugh scowled for a moment, then looked directly at Brad. "I think we'll get the concession on the disarmament issue. Benton, I'm going to put most of the administrative responsibilities for that on you."

The announcement had the impact of a neutron bomb on the room of staff insiders who were all too aware of Brad's status at the White House. Forrest Tetherton, Brad noticed, actually started to sputter. Brad couldn't have been more surprised if Fitzhugh had just asked him to manage his reelection campaign. "Sir?"

"I'm going to tell Carpathia tonight that if he doesn't promise me the chairmanship, I'm keeping my finger on the button." Fitzhugh scrubbed his face with his hands. "But to get it, there are a few concessions he wants that I don't care about. So I'm just going to pacify him."

"What kind of concessions?" Tetherton asked.

"He's holding out on this global religion rot," Fitzhugh replied. "He's determined that the U.S. has to send a representative."

"Since Brad's the only one around here with any ties to religious fanatics," Swelder said, "we figured he could help us out with this."

One of the speechwriters snickered.

Brad ignored the gibe. "What are you looking for, Mr. President?"

"Find me a candidate. I already told him that as far as we can tell, most of the evangelicals are gone. I suggested a bishop or a cardinal, but he's already decided on Cardinal Mathews from Cincinnati."

"The secretary-general," Charley added, "feels the summit will be more effective if the Christian community is represented. He wants that representative to come from the U.S. evangelical movement." He paused as the occupants of the room reacted with a mixture of cynical laughter and disbelief. "He even offered to let us appoint more than one representative if we chose."

Brad's blood ran cold. He could well imagine why Nicolae Carpathia was so amenable. In the wake of the Rapture, the pool of candidates was understandably small. Most of the well-known evangelicals were gone, and those that remained had been left because their faith had not been genuine. God had sorted the wheat and the tares and left the tares behind to face judgment.

Brad was certain there were a few like Marcus who must have seen the light and realized the gravity of their situation, but increasingly, as the media continued to explore the different theories for the cause of the disappearances, many were coming forth with the heresy that the church had been purged. Among the detractors of this theory were men like Marcus who had surrendered their lives to Christ and were taking a bold stand despite the personal and professional risks. Nicolae Carpathia, Brad knew, would dearly love to have the names of these courageous and influential leaders on a short list from the White House. Brad's mouth went dry as he considered the implications.

"Get me a list of names," Fitzhugh was saying as he stood. He glanced at his watch. "Make some phone calls and have a list of candidates on my desk in the morning. After dinner, I can let Carpathia know that we're working on making a go of this."

"Sir—"

"It can't be that hard," Fitzhugh assured him. "Everybody seems to be in love with this guy. I'm sure there's some preacher somewhere who'd like the publicity and the fund-raising opportunity to be in on his parade."

Charley stood and moved toward the door. "We've got to go, Mr. President. The first lady is waiting for you in the residence."

"Yeah. Yeah. I know. Time to squeeze into the penguin suit." Fitzhugh looked at Brad again. "Good to have you back, Benton. Try to keep your head down this time, will you?"

★   ★   ★

"Amen," the four friends said in unison that night as they sat in Marcus's den.

When Mariette considered what the last week had been like, she thought it was a miracle they were all still alive. She glanced at Brad. "Randal said you hardly saw Carpathia today."

Brad nodded. He was holding the Bible—Christine's Bible—that Mariette had handed him the moment she'd walked in the door. He clutched it to his chest with one hand. "He insisted on meeting with Fitzhugh alone. I spent most of the day covering the press conferences with Forrest Tetherton."

"What a weasel," Randal said.

"He's not well liked, but I'm almost glad Swelder didn't take my advice and give the job to Jane Lyons. Whether she knows it or not, she's better off out of town."

"Lyons," Marcus mused. "Wasn't she sending you some notes Ramiro made before his death?"

"They're waiting for me at the FedEx office on U Street." He looked at Randal. "I'll need you to run me over there in the morning to pick them up. The distribution center opens at 6 a.m."

Randal groaned. "Why is it that everything in this town starts at the crack of dawn and shuts down in the middle of the afternoon?"

"Because," Mariette told him, "the federal government thinks that it can serve the public without keeping the same hours they do."

Brad laughed slightly. "That's probably true. If it's any consolation to you," he told Randal, "I had a tough time adjusting to the schedule when I moved here. California is a nine-to-five kind of place."

Randal shook his head. "Yeah, well, Penn State is a noon-to-3 a.m. kind of place, and this early-morning stuff is killing me."

Brad gave him an affectionate cuff on the side of the head. Mariette watched the interchange with mixed feelings of gratitude and fear. More and more, she saw Randal casting Brad into the paternal role he'd denied Max since her divorce. And though she couldn't have asked for a better role model for her son, she also knew that Randal was being drawn further and further into the web of danger surrounding Brad.

But her attempts to discuss her worries with Randal had only created tension between them. She had no choice but to rely even more heavily on God to calm her fears and protect her son.

Brad was telling the group about the outcome of the president's meeting with Carpathia, and Mariette deliberately dragged her thoughts back to the present.

"I think Carpathia has agreed to appoint Fitzhugh as chairman of the Disarmament Committee." Brad looked at each member of the small group. "They're finalizing the details tonight. The president has asked me to oversee the administrative responsibilities."

Shock registered on Randal's face. "You've got to be kidding."

"I'm afraid not."

Randal laughed lightly. "I would like to have been there to hear you tell him to blow it out his ear."

Brad's expression was curiously sad. "I told him I would consider it."

Randal's mouth dropped open. "Really?"

"No. I wanted to pray about it first."

"But wouldn't that be the same thing as working for Carpathia?" Randal challenged. "You might as well be on the payroll of the Antichrist."

"I'm not so sure," Brad countered. "I wanted to see what you all thought."

Mariette drew a steadying breath. "You're not the only one facing this dilemma." They looked at her in surprise. Randal, especially, looked shocked. She wasn't surprised. As difficult as it was for her to accept that he was an adult who could make his own decisions and take his own risks, she knew he found it tough to remember that her responsibilities and her life extended beyond motherhood.

She gave him an apologetic look as she quickly filled

them in on the possibility of the UN's new relief effort. "I didn't have time to discuss it with you first," she told Randal, then looked at the other two men. "Musselman wants the job, but there are some rumors among my staff that Carpathia may offer it to me."

"You're certainly more qualified," Brad told her. "I'm sure the White House would endorse you."

"But, Mom—"

"Don't get me wrong. I think Bernie would tell you this will only happen if I step over his corpse to get the appointment," she assured them. "And frankly, until I went to New York and received that note, I would have said the rumors were totally unfounded. I had no reason to think Carpathia even knew I was alive." She paused. "I liked it better that way."

Brad nodded. "I know exactly how you feel."

"It may not materialize," Mariette said, "but if it does, I'd have to pray hard about what to do. Like you, Brad. Even though my instinct says to flee and I can't picture myself working for him. How do I know this isn't what God has for me?"

"Working for the servant of Satan?" Randal protested. "That's insane."

Brad glanced at Marcus. A silent communication seemed to pass between the two men. "Now wait a minute, Randal. What if being a force for God in the enemy's camp is what the Lord has been preparing us for? What if that's the job He has for us in the time we have left?"

Randal frowned. "I don't think—"

"I think we have to consider it," Mariette stated firmly. "Had we known the Lord before the Rapture, we would have been spared the Tribulation." She looked to Marcus for affirmation. "Isn't that right?"

"Yes," he said gravely. "We'd be in heaven with the Lord now."

"But we're here," she told Randal. "I can't speak for anyone else, but in my case, I'm here because I made a conscious choice to reject God. God is merciful and good, but He's also holy and just. Choices have consequences."

"Be careful, Mariette," Marcus warned. "In our human understanding, it would be easy for us to think that God plans to exact judgment on us for the mistakes we made before the Rapture. Granted, the believers who accepted Christ before the evidence of the Rapture had a greater faith than you and I, but God's grace extends to everyone. We're all unworthy."

"I know," she assured him. "I guess what I'm saying is that I'm no longer content to walk outside of God's will for my life—no matter what it might cost me."

Marcus nodded. "I understand.

"So do I," Brad said.

Randal flopped back against the sofa. "Yeah. Me too."

The conversation turned to the events of the past few days, and the four of them related their individual experiences. Brad talked about California and his flight home. Randal reported what had happened the night their house had been burglarized and the conversations he'd overhead about the South Range project.

"Do you think they're really going to come after you for that?" Randal asked Brad.

"I don't know. If George died because someone didn't want him looking into South Range, then there's more here than meets the eye."

"Do you think Rudd violated the gold deposits?" Randal asked.

"If he did, he used Kostankis to facilitate it and hide it,

which means there's an international connection somewhere. Someone with the right contacts is in the middle."

Mariette considered that. "Someone at the White House,
you mean?"

"Maybe," Brad said. "But the way the president talked
about his conversation with Marsden . . ." He shook his
head. "Fitzhugh knew nothing about that plane. That much
was obvious."

Randal frowned. "Then who?"

"I don't know."

"And you're in serious danger until you find out," Marcus pointed out. He exhaled a long breath and reached for
the Bible in the center of the coffee table.

"I can't tell you why," Brad told them, "but I'm not
afraid. I really haven't been since I saw Carpathia murder
those two men at the UN. Something about that experience
made me feel the hand of God protecting me."

Marcus flipped open the Bible and turned to a certain
passage. "I believe that." He glanced up. "I believe that
about each of us, actually. In my Bible study this morning, I
spent some time meditating on this passage." He turned his
attention back to the Bible. "It says in Proverbs, 'Seek His
will in all you do, and He will direct your paths.' "

He let the power of the words sink in. After several seconds of silence, he shut the leather-bound Bible. "I've read
that verse a thousand times. I've even preached several sermons on it. But tonight, it means more to me than it ever
has."

Brad looked at him a moment, then nodded solemnly
as he turned to Mariette and Randal. "I called Marcus before I left the White House this evening and told him that
one of the things to come out of the president's discussions
with Carpathia is a summit Carpathia is organizing for the
world's religious leaders."

"Carpathia has asked the president to appoint an American evangelical leader as a representative to the summit," Marcus added.

Randal looked quickly between the two of them. "But isn't this what the Bible says about the single world religion? Isn't Carpathia's plan just fulfilling another one of the Tribulation prophecies?"

"Yes," Brad said. "And frankly, the president's choices are limited."

Marcus concurred. "Most American Christian leaders were raptured. The ones who weren't are like me. We're still here because we were living a lie."

"Then how can you even consider this?" Randal demanded. "Sure, Brad running the disarmament treaty is one thing." He glanced at his mother. "And I can even see you in charge of the UN's relief effort. You'd have the chance to help a lot of people get through what's coming. But this—" he spread his hands in genuine confusion— "what good could possibly come of something like this?"

Brad laid a hand on Marcus's shoulder. "I thought the same thing at first. And it also occurred to me exactly what Nicolae Carpathia could do if he had the names of evangelical leaders who might oppose him."

The thought made Mariette shudder. "The Nazis began keeping records of the names and addresses of Jewish leaders several years before the Holocaust began."

"Exactly," Brad said. "But I also know that when this summit takes place, I'd rather have God's voice represented by a man I know has given his life to Christ."

"My initial reaction was the same as yours," Marcus told Mariette. "I have plans and a life here. I feel God has definitely called me to build the shelter we've discussed and begin laying the groundwork to help the believers He sends my way escape persecution. The church is growing. There are people who rely on me. I have an entire flock that needs guidance and leadership. When I consider all that, I can't even imagine accepting something like this." He sighed. "Not to mention the stress of listening to the heresy at that meeting."

"But Brad is right," Mariette countered. "You *could* have tremendous influence." She thought of the arguments she'd already given herself against taking the relief job.

Randal shook his head. "No, Mom. He couldn't. The Bible says the one world religion thing is going to happen. It doesn't matter what Marcus might say at that meeting. Carpathia's going to make it happen anyway."

"That's true," Marcus replied. "But then, that could be said about all the prophecies of the end times. They're all going to come to pass. That doesn't mean that God's people should sit silent and ignore the evil. All through history God has raised up righteous men and women to oppose the forces of darkness."

"God has trusted us with His work during these times," Brad said. "I've never been more convinced of that than over the last few days."

"Like that family you met in Kansas," Mariette said. "That's an example. Arguably, God allowed your enemies to drop you in their field so you could share the gospel with them."

Marcus nodded. "We have no way of knowing what God has for us—only that He will direct our path if we allow Him to."

Randal leaned forward and braced his hands on his thighs. "So what are you saying, Marcus? Are you going to do it?"

"I need to check with Sanura first. I have to make sure my absence won't affect the case against New Covenant. More than ever, I have a vision and a passion for what the ministry can accomplish if we win this lawsuit. But if the president offers it to me, then yes, I plan to accept."

Brad released a deep breath. "I'm glad to hear you say that. It makes me feel a little better about my decision." His expression showed resignation. "I'm going to tell the president tomorrow that I'm accepting responsibility for the disarmament treaty if we ratify it."

For the first time that day, Mariette felt the peace of God settle on her as she considered the future. This feeling of incredible contentment and security in the midst of uncertain and daunting circumstances must be what the Bible meant, she realized, by the peace that passes all understanding.

"Mom?" Randal was watching her expectantly.

"I feel the same way, honey," Mariette told him. "As scary as it is, I know that if God opens this door for me, then I wouldn't be faithful to Him if I refused to walk through it."

Marcus's eyes closed for a moment. "When God brought us all together, I couldn't have imagined that this is where He was leading us."

"Neither could we," Brad said, "but it's like I told you when I called. Despite the challenges, the fact that someone wants me dead, and the way this South Range thing could ruin my reputation and maybe even cost me my life, I feel better about the future now than I have since the night of the Rapture."

"I do, too," Mariette confessed. "I feel like I have a purpose—not just seven years left to live."

"Me too," Randal said quietly.

"I have to agree." Marcus's voice, though sad, held a ring of hope. "And that's one of the reasons I'd like us to discuss the future. I think we can all agree that we have no idea of exactly what lies ahead."

"I've thought about that," Randal said firmly. "I've been

praying about it since we talked the other night. I think things are only going to get worse—not just for us but for believers around the world. And I definitely feel led to help you establish this mission shelter." He looked at his mother. "I know you want to protect me—"

Mariette held up a hand. "I want you to live God's will for your life, Randal. I don't have to like it, and I can't promise not to worry, but I do want you to do whatever God is calling you to do."

He gave her hand a slight squeeze that lightened her heart; then he looked at Marcus. "So I'm definitely in. I don't know what I can do or how much help I can be, but I'll do whatever I can."

"That's all God asks," Marcus assured him.

"And if I wasn't sure before today," Randal added with a grimace, "I was absolutely sure when I laid eyes on Carpathia. I was a hundred yards away at a diplomatic welcoming ceremony and he still made my flesh crawl."

Mariette's heart twisted as she accepted the bittersweet reality that her baby was a grown man of conviction and character. Twenty years ago when she'd nursed him and rocked him and held him, she could not have dreamed that he would grow into such a fine and honorable man.

"I've decided, too," she said to Marcus. "I told you I wasn't sure the night we met, but then I met Daniel Berger the next morning. When I learned he was a new Christian, it felt like the tangible sign I'd asked God to give me that this was the way He was leading. If Daniel will help us— and I think he will—then his contacts will be invaluable to us."

"I'm in, too," Brad said. "I've had plenty of time alone on airplanes and falling out of airplanes in the last thirty-six hours to think through this. And, Randal, I know exactly how you felt today when Carpathia was at the White House."

"You were even closer," Randal said.

"And after what I witnessed on the satellite feed the other day, I had no idea what was going to happen." He shook his head as if clearing the memory. "I felt that same presence of evil."

"Me too," Randal confirmed.

"I told Daniel Berger about that," Mariette told them. "He said he felt that way when he shared a platform with Carpathia shortly after the Rapture."

"That doesn't surprise me," Marcus said. "The Bible clearly says that Satan's forces will be unleashed on the earth during the Tribulation."

"All the more reason we need this shelter," Randal asserted. "Tell us what you're thinking."

For the next several hours, they talked through the challenges and demands of the undertaking. Marcus believed a major catastrophe—possibly even a nuclear attack—lay in the future. They would need a temporary place to ride it out.

The location would have to be far enough from Washington to remain safe if the city was attacked but close enough that they could reach it in time.

They all agreed that the shelter would have to be spacious and well stocked to accommodate a core group of believers for as long as two to three months if necessary. That meant laying in food, water, and other necessities. When Randal broached the issue of cost, Marcus pointed out that Sanura Kyle was optimistic about making significant progress in his legal battle. If the issue was resolved in his favor, they'd have all the money they needed for a project of this scope.

Brad, who had not spoken much during the conversa-

tion, listened attentively while Mariette talked about her
experience with shelters and the unexpected needs that often arose. She sensed his close scrutiny. "You were thinking
something?"

"It's what you said about federal and state emergency
shelters. It got me thinking."

Marcus gave him a curious look. "I don't think we'll
have access to—"

"We wouldn't." Brad straightened in his chair as he visibly warmed to his idea. "Not to an active one. But the most
significant cost in this is the construction of the facility.
Yes?"

"Of course," Marcus concurred. "The shelter structure itself, the wiring, the plumbing . . ."

"We'd have to be wired for a computer network,"
Randal pointed out. "All digital. I think we need high-
speed Internet access and wireless communication capabil-
ities."

"GPS tracking would be even better," Brad added.

"Naturally." Marcus's expression turned speculative.
"Then there's transportation and supplies. All that's going
to cost money. But as I said, Sanura is making excellent
progress. I don't think that'll be a concern."

"But what if—" Brad's voice was laced with excitement—"we could find all that already built—already up-
to-date with the latest technology and access to U.S. government computer systems. What if all we had to do was
move in?"

Mariette suddenly realized where he was headed. "A
place that has cutting-edge communications systems, is already designed to house a large group of people comfort-
ably for as long as a year, and is linked into the country's
defense and information systems."

Brad shot her a knowing look. "That has transportation infrastructure and is known only to a handful of people."

Randal glanced from one to the other. "What are you talking about?"

"The Cold War," Brad told him. "Before your time."

Randal frowned. "You mean one of those crazy bomb shelters people used to stick in their backyards? You're kidding."

"No," Brad said. "While the government was telling Americans to prepare for the bomb, the defense department and civil engineers were making sure the government was prepared."

"There are relocation facilities all around this area," Mariette said. "I don't know of many—I've never had clearance that high. But I know there was one for the president, one for the Joint Chiefs, one for Congress."

"Yeah," Randal protested, "but that stuff is like, ancient. I mean, the computers they put in those things weren't as powerful as a cheap laptop today."

"That would still be true," Brad said, "if we hadn't been attacked on September 11, 2001. The president was in the air at the time. For a while, he had to run the country from one of those shelters. The realities of the dated technology scared the Defense Department into undertaking a massive renovation and modernization project."

"Everything was updated?" Randal said.

"Over 90 percent of the cold-war facilities were brought up-to-date," Brad confirmed, "in a classified program called the Phoenix Project."

"But if everything's new," Randal insisted, "don't you think the government is going to want to use the facilities when these disasters start to hit?"

Marcus looked expectantly at Brad. "You know something."

"The modernization project took a few years—long enough for us to sink a barrel of money into the upgrades. Then the war on terrorism ended, new presidents were elected, the country went through some tough economic times, and generally the government got caught up in other national interests. Six months ago, four facilities were re-sealed."

"And you know where they are?" Marcus asked.

"Yes," Brad said. "I toured them along with two members of Congress and a representative from the Joint Chiefs before we made the decision. All four are considered permanently closed. There is no staff and no security at any location."

Randal was fidgeting with excitement. "So we could just like . . . take one over? I mean, who would know?"

"It's not as easy as just picking the lock," Brad admitted. "The doors are security sealed. We'd need the codes. The technology inside is top-notch, but of the four, only one is big enough to handle what we're talking about."

"Where?" Marcus asked.

"About an hour's drive west of Washington in the Blue Ridge Mountains."

"An hour?" Randal repeated. "If someone launches a nuclear bomb, they're going to do it from a submarine. We have—what?—eight minutes?"

"That problem arose in the early eighties while the facilities were still under federal funding and Ronald Reagan was referring to the Soviets as an evil empire. A few of the better-known facilities were deemed impractical and closed," Brad explained. "But the one I'm talking about was modified to accommodate the reality that a submarine strike would take a matter of minutes. The Army Corps of Engineers built a radiation-proof subway system that runs under the city all the way out to the location. The entrance is tapped into the city's Metro system."

Mariette nodded. "I've heard rumors about that. They circulate every now and then."

"I'm not surprised," Brad said. "Several years ago, the Metro Transit Authority announced it was expanding service to several outlying areas. The taxpayers and the press thought the plan was to reduce the traffic congestion—which it did. But what they didn't know is that the Metro expansion was a cover for a seven-billion-dollar construction project being conducted simultaneously to provide rapid transit escape for government officials in case of another terrorist attack. There were some rumors in the media, but nothing was ever substantiated."

Randal let out a low whistle. "Unreal."

"But the rails are in serious disrepair, and, as far as I know, the trains that were supposed to run on them have been decommissioned."

Marcus tapped his fingers on the arm of his chair. "Are the trains still there?"

Brad nodded. "I saw two of the engines and a few cars when we toured the facility."

Marcus briefly closed his eyes and appeared to mouth a word of thanks to the Lord. "Then fortunately, we have Solomon Grady."

"Who?" Mariette asked.

Brad grinned. "The maintenance man at the church."

"That nice old guy with the gold tooth?" Randal asked.

"Yes." Brad glanced at Marcus. "Didn't you tell me he was one of the original engineers for the Metro?"

"Uh-huh," Marcus said. "The Transit Authority made him take early retirement when the budget was slashed. I'm sure he'd rather spend his days working on subway trains than pushing a broom."

"So," Brad continued, "provided Solomon Grady can help us get the train system up and running, the other challenges are the security codes and the internal operations systems. The entire facility is run by Defense Department computers. We're going to have to be able to hack into the DOD system without being noticed just to turn the lights on."

"We'll need a pro hacker for that," Randal mused. "I'm sure the system is drum tight."

"No doubt," Brad said. "But every system has a back door. I'm sure this one does, too."

"I know a couple of computer guys, but nobody with that kind of skill," Randal said, then looked at his mother.

Mariette shook her head. "Me either."

"Then we'll start praying for one," Marcus said.

Randal looked doubtful. "I don't think hackers are the kind of people you bump into at the grocery store, you know. They call them the underground for a reason."

"I'm not trying to sound trite," Marcus assured them. "But one thing I've learned in this life—even before I surrendered to the Lord—is that God gets His work done. If this is what He has for us, He'll provide."

"I agree," Brad said. "I saw that in my family's life a dozen times." He leaned back in his chair. "In the meantime, Randal and I will work on getting the codes."

"Me?"

"Didn't you tell me you'd gotten to know that intern in the security office?"

"Bryce. Yeah. He's a good guy."

"I need you to get friendly enough with Bryce to get a look at the thermal security unit they have in that office."

"That thing they used to scan my palm print when I got my security badge?"

"Yes. To get the codes, we're going to have to take them

from the classified-files vault at the Pentagon. To do that, we'll need to get through the security doors without setting off the alarms."

"Bryce answers the phones and does some filing," Randal said. "I'm pretty sure he's not your mission-impossible type."

"All Bryce has to do is let you study the machine. I'm going to give you a minidisc to take in there with you. Once you insert it into the machine's bay, we can access it from the terminal in my office. We can upload our existing palm scans to the DOD system."

Randal's eyes widened. "You're kidding."

"Nope. And in the meantime—" Brad plucked his cell phone from his pocket—"I may not have a lead on a computer expert, but I think I can set us up with someone who can handle our commodity needs."

"Food, you mean?" Mariette asked. "A year's worth of supplies is a massive undertaking."

Brad started punching numbers into the phone. "Do you have some kind of formula for that? You know—x number of people times x number of weeks?"

"Sure," she told him. "We have several models we use for disaster relief."

He hit the call button. "If you get me the numbers, I'm sure I can take care of the storage, purchasing, and transportation."

"That's a massive job," Mariette repeated as Brad pressed the phone to his ear. "If we start stockpiling that much food, someone's going to get suspicious."

"But what if a Kansas farmer with four thousand acres of sorghum enters the picture?" Brad held up a hand when his call connected. "Bill? Hi. Brad Benton."

13

Brad handed a yellow slip of paper to the clerk behind the counter at FedEx's U Street office. "You're holding a package for me. I have a tracking number."

The clerk glanced at the number, then punched it into the computer. He frowned, punched some numbers into the keyboard again, then studied the monitor with a perplexed look. "Did you come in earlier to pick this up? Like yesterday afternoon, maybe?"

Brad's pulse tripped into overtime. "No. According to your Web site, it didn't get here until midnight last night."

The clerk typed some more numbers. "You didn't call?"

"No. Why?"

"It says here that you called yesterday and inquired about this package. There's a note in here to divert it to our southwest facility."

Brad struggled to remain calm. "Did you?"

"Divert it?" The clerk looked at him. "Well, if it was scanned in yesterday, it might still be in the back. The trucks aren't loaded yet."

Brad's gaze dropped to the young man's name tag.

"Look, Lowell, could you check, please? It's very important."

Lowell punched a few more numbers into the computer. "I think this came in with the hot shipment last night. I should be able to find it." He glanced at Brad. "Do you have ID?"

Brad nodded and produced his license.

Lowell studied it for a moment. "Bradley Benton." He looked up. "Like the White House Bradley Benton? Chief of staff?"

"Yes," Brad said warily.

"Cool. My mom used to work the switchboard there. Fifteen years." Lowell handed him his license. Something about his expression told Brad that Lowell's mother was among the missing. "Betty. Her name was Betty Johnson."

"She's gone?" Brad asked quietly.

"Yeah. With everyone else. It's just me and my sister now. My sister was an elementary schoolteacher out in Montgomery County. But you know—" his face twisted slightly—"no kids."

The impact of the statement hit Brad full force. Until that moment, he hadn't even considered the impact the Rapture had had on educators and professionals who'd given their lives to working with children. "I'm sorry," he said, though the words felt grossly inadequate.

"She's taking it hard. They still got her on the payroll, but I keep telling her she needs to find some volunteer work or something. You know, just to keep her mind off stuff." Lowell shrugged and rolled the yellow slip of paper between his fingers. "Wait here, Mr. Benton. I'll see if I can find that package for you."

"Thanks." Brad watched Lowell disappear through the back door of the facility. He snatched his cell phone from his pocket and punched in a number.

"Hello?" came the sleepy voice on the other end.

"Jane?" Brad said. "I'm sorry I woke you. This is Brad Benton."

"Oh, hello, Mr. Benton. I'm glad you called. Did you get the package?"

"I'm picking it up now," Brad told her. He cast a glance over his shoulder. Through the tinted glass, he saw Randal waiting for him in the idling government-issue sedan. "Listen, Jane, did anyone else know you were sending me this package?"

"No," she said slowly. "After what you told me the day I called, I didn't mention it to anyone. Why? Is something wrong?"

"It could just be a mistake," he answered. "You're sure you didn't mention it to anyone?"

"I'm sure. I mailed the package and e-mailed you the tracking number. No one knows what's in that envelope except you and me."

Brad's fingers tightened on the phone. "Okay. Thanks, Jane."

"Mr. Benton, I found something else. It might not be anything, but I stuck it in the envelope anyway. Just in case."

"Something else?"

"Yes. It's a diskette. When I found it, I remembered that George had given it to me one afternoon and told me to file it somewhere safe. He said it had some access codes to archived briefing statements and things—stuff I might need if I ever had to step in for him."

Brad inhaled sharply. "When did he give it to you?"

"It wasn't long before the disappearances," she told him. "I didn't really think much of it at the time—but it makes me wonder now if he didn't know something was wrong."

"Maybe he did," Brad said, noncommittal.

"I hope it helps."

"Thanks. I'll let you know if I hear anything else." Through the plate-glass walls that separated the warehouse from the office, he saw Lowell making his way toward him. He held an envelope in his hand. Brad flipped the cell phone shut and jammed it in his shirt pocket.

"Here it is," Lowell announced as he reemerged behind the counter. "You were lucky, though. The driver was about to load it to send over to southwest. You'd have had to wait until this afternoon before we could have rerouted it."

That confirmed his worst fears. Brad accepted the envelope. "Thanks, Lowell." He was about to leave when he had a sudden thought. He reached into his back pocket and produced his wallet. Removing a business card, he handed it to Lowell. "I think you probably went above and beyond the call of duty for me. I appreciate it. Here's my card."

Lowell looked at it. "Thanks."

"I like to think of the White House staff as an extended family," Brad told him. "And that includes the staff I haven't had time to meet yet—or in your mother's case, didn't have time to meet. If you and your sister need anything from the White House—I hope you'll call me."

Lowell's shoulders squared. He gave Brad a look of profound gratitude. "Thank you, Mr. Benton. Have a great day, okay?"

Brad sprinted toward the waiting sedan. He tore open the envelope as he dropped into the passenger seat. "Go," he told Randal.

Randal looked at him with raised eyebrows but threw the car into gear and hit the accelerator. "Something wrong?"

"Someone was looking for this package," Brad said, dumping out the contents. There were two pages of handwritten notes, the diskette Jane had mentioned, and her explanation for it on a yellow sticky note. Brad slipped the disk into his shirt pocket.

"What do you mean—looking?"

"According to the kid behind the counter, someone called yesterday afternoon and requested to have the package rerouted to another facility on the other side of town."

Randal let out a low whistle as he accelerated through a yellow light. "No idea who?"

Brad shook his head as he scanned the notes. "I called Jane Lyons. She says she didn't tell anyone she was sending this to me."

"Then how—?"

He glanced up. "I think someone's monitoring my e-mail."

Randal frowned. "At the office?"

"She sent the tracking number to my personal address, but someone could hack it through the Web." Brad looked at the notes again. "Whoever it was, I know why they wanted these notes."

"Revealing?"

He finished scanning the second page. "Revealing enough to get George Ramiro murdered—and to send Victor Rudd to prison."

★   ★   ★

Marcus gave Brad a dry look as his friend loped down the hill to join him for their morning run. During Brad's trip to California, these early-morning fellowship times in Rock Creek Park were what he'd missed the most. "You look rotten."

"I picked up Jane Lyons's package this morning." Brad looked over his shoulder as Randal eased back into the morning rush-hour traffic. He'd sent him on to the White House. "Someone was after it." He quickly told Marcus about his conversation with Lowell.

Marcus shook his head and started to jog down the path. When Brad fell into step, he said, "What about the diskette?"

"If it is what I think it is, I'm guessing George wasn't entirely forthcoming with Jane. We have an electronic archive system at the White House. If you have the access codes, you can pull old files and records."

"You think they were records about South Range?"

"I know the counsel's office kept files—which are classified, but accessible—but it's possible there are other records, too. It seems hard to believe that anyone would store something with incriminating evidence, but then Nixon didn't erase the Watergate tapes, either. White House personnel are notorious for hanging on to explosive information."

Marcus had lived in D.C. long enough to know the truth of that statement. "What are you going to do with it?"

"Try it out. See what it lets me get to. In the meantime, I'm sure someone's monitoring my e-mail. Maybe I can use that to my advantage."

"They're closing in on you, Brad," Marcus said gravely. "Getting closer."

"I know. Morrow's supposed to make an announcement soon. I expect to get subpoenaed."

"You and I can share a lawyer," Marcus said, grinning a little.

Brad expelled a long breath. "Just as long as we don't share a grave. The notes Jane sent confirmed that George was definitely looking into South Range."

"Anything helpful?"

"A few names. Kostankis's name is on there. I'm still try-ing to make sense of it."

They ran in silence for a few paces, the only sound the distant hum of morning traffic and the cadence of their feet on the path. "Any ideas yet on who might have sent you those pictures?"

"A few, but I'm still missing the most crucial piece of ev-idence in the whole picture. I'm almost positive Rudd vio-lated the South Range gold reserves. I also suspect he had an accomplice at the Pentagon, and the entire thing had something to do with a covert international operation. Rudd used Kostankis to funnel the money."

"But Morrow concluded—"

"Kostankis is well connected and rich enough to have helped Rudd rebuild the reserves before Morrow's investi-gation was concluded. Or—and I'm beginning to think this is more likely—Morrow was either blackmailed or coerced into dropping the charges before he finished his investiga-tion. Randal's studying his report to see if he can turn any-thing up."

"If that's true, though, why is Morrow coming forward now?"

"I don't know," Brad admitted. "That's another part of the puzzle."

"Any chance that Tommy Morrow sent you the pictures of George Ramiro?"

Brad shot him a quick look. "I've thought of that. If someone used those pictures to try and scare Morrow into silence, it would make sense that he would have them."

"But why send them to you?"

Brad shook his head. "No clue."

Marcus frowned as he thought through the events of the last few days. "Whoever is behind this has ample enough resources to pull off your near miss on that Galaxy. Still no news on that?"

"No. I've got someone looking into it."

"The sniper. The bomb at your apartment. The plane. Not to mention a bug in my house," Marcus said. "Randal found one last night at their place. Did he tell you?"

"Yeah. I think he was psyched about it."

"I doubt Mariette felt that way."

"Me too."

"And now you think your e-mail is being intercepted. They're thorough," Marcus said. "I'll give them that."

Marcus wiped the sweat from his forehead with the back of his hand as their pace began to drain him. Spring had turned to early summer in Washington in the last few days, and the morning air had an unpleasantly humid bite. "What's your next step?" Marcus asked.

"I'm going to see if I can make some sense of Ramiro's notes. I hope they're going to be the key to whatever records are locked away behind those access codes. I'll have to wait until tonight to try the codes. The central server monitors keystrokes and terminal access for security. If I log on to the system from my terminal, all someone would have to do is request the activity log to know I'd been trying to access the archives."

"How are you going to get past that?"

Brad's mouth twitched at the corner. "Believe it or not— Emma's going to help me."

"Emma?"

"Umm. There's a reason I brought Emma from California. She's not just incredibly competent; she's smart and she watches my back. Not long after we got to the White House, she spent some time figuring out how to protect me against whomever might want to see me taken down. One day, she let me know that she'd procured an unassigned terminal code in case I needed to log on anonymously and see what was being written about me." Brad's breath had begun to come harder as they headed up an incline. "I laughed at her then. I couldn't imagine—"

"You think she still has it?"

"Emma still has copies of my first campaign literature. She's got files on everything and everyone who's ever crossed my path. I'll go by and see her this afternoon. I need to anyway. I want to make sure she's doing all right."

They crested the hill, both of them lengthening their strides when they headed down a long stretch of the sloped path. Marcus prayed for his friend's safety as he thought about the web of intrigue that seemed to be closing around him.

"So," Brad finally said, breaking the silence, "when are you going to tell me about your meeting with Sanura Kyle?" His breathing sounded ragged.

"I told you last night; she's doing a great job with the case. She's very competent," Marcus answered.

"Hmm. That's not what I mean."

"I didn't think so."

"You liked her," Brad said. "Admit it."

"She was an interesting recommendation."

"She's sharp," Brad said. "I understand she was an incredible litigator before she went to work at the White House. In fact, she's the lead counsel on the South Range issue. I talked to her about it for a few minutes yesterday."

The path turned upward again, and Marcus picked up the pace as they ran uphill. He didn't want to have this conversation, had, in fact, studiously avoided even thinking about his opinions of and reactions to Sanura Kyle. But he had a sinking feeling Brad wasn't going to let him off the hook—so he put off the inevitable by pushing his endurance with long-legged strides. Beyond the slope, Marcus could see the towering monolith of the Washington Monument.

Brad matched Marcus stride for stride until the path evened out. "Did she tell you anything about herself? About her background?"

"Her father was a preacher," Marcus said. "She lost nearly everyone in the Rapture."

"That's what she said." Brad shook his head. "My heart went out to her. I know how she feels."

Marcus gave him a knowing look. "Is that why you forgot to mention when you gave me her number that Sanura Kyle is—?"

"A knockout?" Brad said with a grin. "So you did notice."

"I'm reserved and conservative. I'm not dead."

"Glad to hear that."

"You were worried?"

"Curious. And I didn't tell you because I wasn't sure you'd see her if I did."

That made Marcus frown. "What's that supposed to mean?" The humidity and sweat had his T-shirt clinging to his shoulders and back. When they neared the fork in their familiar path, he wrestled with his discomfort. Brad couldn't imagine how close he was treading to a chasm of deep, unfathomable pain Marcus had consciously avoided for years.

"Your wife died a long time ago, Marcus," Brad said quietly.

"It doesn't feel like a long time ago." Marcus couldn't keep the edge off his voice. "How long's the time limit before you quit missing the people you love? When are you going to be ready to move on now that you've lost Christine?"

Brad pulled in a harsh breath but didn't respond.

Several seconds of silence passed. Marcus's limbs had begun to protest the exertion of their unusually fast pace, but he pushed on, deliberately punishing his body in the hope that it would numb the rising swell of pain in his soul.

"You don't have to stop loving your wife in order to give a little of yourself to someone else," Brad said.

Marcus came to an abrupt stop. He bent over, hands braced on his thighs, and drew in several ragged breaths. Brad had run six more strides down the path before he realized he was alone. He stopped to face him. Marcus wiped his forehead with the sleeve of his T-shirt. "I'm sorry," he said to Brad. "That comment about Christine. It was out of line."

Brad tipped his head in silent acceptance. "I hit a nerve. I didn't mean to, but I did, obviously. You hit back. It's natural."

"But not godly." Marcus shook his head. "I'm supposed to be above that."

"Above what? Being human? None of us could stand you if you were."

Marcus managed a slight laugh. "Point well taken."

Brad held up his hands in mock surrender. "Look, it's not what you think. I swear. I wasn't trying to shove you out of your comfort zone. I just thought you and Sanura would have some things in common."

"She's a very interesting woman."

"I thought so. And heaven only knows she desperately needs the Lord. I thought you might be able to relate to her background. And you needed a good lawyer. She's the best I know. As for the other, well . . ." He shrugged. "Maybe nothing will come of it. All I'm saying is, I think you've isolated yourself for long enough."

Marcus had to struggle for a moment to clamp down on

another wave of irritation. While part of him wanted to lash out that this was none of Brad's business, another part knew that his mounting anger had more to do with his fear of facing this subject than his feeling of having his privacy violated. Restless, he started to jog again, this time at a more leisurely pace. Brad fell into step beside him. Marcus carefully chose his next words. "Don't you think that in the situation the world now faces that it's a little shortsighted to think about something like that?"

"Like a relationship, you mean?"

"Yes."

"No," Brad said emphatically. "If that were true, then it would be useless to make any connections at all. You and Mariette and Randal—you're my family. I care about you as much as anyone I've ever known. I feel the same way about Emma. To a certain extent, I even feel that way about Liza Cannley. I know it's risky. You've taught me to read the Scriptures—to study the prophecies. I know there's a chance I could lose them all before this is over."

"There's no way of knowing how many of us might make it to the end," Marcus pointed out. They rounded a corner where the path neared the Parkway. Marcus noticed a blue sedan parked at one of the pull-offs. A man sat in the car, apparently reading the newspaper. He tipped his head toward the car. "That's not your security detail, is it?" he asked Brad.

Brad studied the car for a second. "It's a Lexus. Secret Service details use American-made sedans."

Marcus shook his head as he looked at the car. Soon they could no longer see it through the trees that lined the path. "This is making me paranoid."

"You and me both." Brad glanced at him as they continued down the path. "And to tell you the truth, what keeps me sane—even with all this intrigue and danger—is having the support and fellowship of my brothers and sisters in Christ. It's how I deal with my grief about Christine and the kids. It's how I face every day knowing someone wants it to be my last. It's what keeps me going."

Marcus didn't respond.

They ran in silence for several moments before Brad spoke again. "What keeps you going? Besides your faith, I mean."

"There are a lot of people who rely on me." He gave Brad a serious look. "I have to be many things to many people."

"I know that," Brad assured him. "And no one appreciates your spiritual guidance more than I do. But you're more than my friend, Marcus; you're my brother in Christ. And what kind of brother would I be if I saw something in your life I thought was keeping you from experiencing all the blessings God has for you?"

Marcus thought about telling him that the reason he'd preached to people for most of his life was because he didn't like listening to anyone else's sermons. The only person who'd ever had minimal success in getting through his thick head was his late wife. He deliberately pushed aside the twinge of guilt that told him Brad's words had hit a nerve. "I'll consider it. Maybe you're right."

"Sorry. I can't let you off that easy," Brad said, shaking his head. "There's something to this or you wouldn't be trying to clamp down on it."

"What do you want from me, Brad? You want me to slit an artery?" Marcus heard the edge of desperation in his voice.

Evidently, Brad heard it, too. "You're angry—or at least irritated. I noticed it last night, but I didn't want to get into it in front of Randal and Mariette."

"Thanks for that."

"If I offended you by not telling you about Sanura before you met her, then I'm sorry, but I think we should talk about what's really eating you."

Frustrated, Marcus ran a hand through his damp hair. "I'm tired. You're tired. We're both under a lot of pressure. I don't think this is the time or the place for this conversation."

Brad tilted his head to one side and watched Marcus speculatively. "That's where I have to disagree with you." He looked around at the lush setting as they made their way through the park. "We've had a lot of crucial conversations in this park. You *baptized* me in this park, for crying out loud. I don't know about you, but I consider this place kind of sacred."

Marcus hesitated. His breathing was harsh, and the sound of it punctuated the otherwise still air. "So do I," he finally admitted.

"I've had a lot of time over the last couple of days to think about some things. Being home in California, especially after that explosion in my apartment, it just reminded me of how easy it always was to let things get in the way of keeping my priorities straight." He paused. "I got to be so good at avoiding difficult conversations that I never even had them with myself. It cost me everything. I don't want that to happen to you."

Marcus remained silent.

"My family was always a lot better to me than I was to them," Brad said quietly.

Marcus knew the feeling all too well, but he didn't say so. His only hope for extricating himself from this conversation with a shred of dignity was to keep his mouth shut. He didn't have a list of smooth answers and Scripture-based responses that would steer the attention in a new direction. Brad had caught him unprepared. Vulnerable.

Everything in him screamed that Brad was leading him

down an emotional path he should do everything in his power to avoid, but at the back of his mind, he saw an image of Isack Moore and the condemning look on his face. Isack, Theo, and who knew how many others had labeled him a fraud.

Hadn't he vowed not to live that way anymore? Yet if he begged off of this conversation with Brad, wouldn't he be just as hypocritical as he'd been all those years when he'd preached a message he didn't believe? Brad was right. Marcus would not have let him off the hook so easily. He'd have forced him to look deeper and explore the things in his life that were keeping him from fully surrendering to God's will.

"Okay," Brad said, "since you're obviously not in the mood, I'll talk. You listen."

Marcus said nothing and kept his gaze trained on the asphalt path and the cut grass that littered the black ribbon of pavement.

Brad was obviously undeterred by his silence. "I'll admit that you have a point about how unsettled everything is. None of us has any guarantees about the future. Nobody knows that better than I do. I've cheated death three times in two weeks, and I still don't know who's after me."

Marcus concentrated on synchronizing his breathing to the steady cadence of their footfalls.

"Well, for that matter," Brad continued, "if you argue that forming deep bonds with people isn't advisable simply because we know the clock is ticking, then you'd have to say that Jesus shouldn't have invested Himself in the disciples or Mary and Martha or anyone else. He knew exactly how long He'd have with them—and exactly how difficult His death would be for them. But Jesus gave them as much of Himself as He could during His life."

Marcus winced as the words sunk in. For years he'd used

biblical examples and analogies to drive home a point. He wasn't prepared to be on the receiving end. "I'll give you that," he admitted.

"So all I'm saying is, I don't think God intends for us to live out the rest of our time without emotional fellowship."

"No, but that's not the same as romantic involvement." He gave Brad a probing look. "That *is* what you're talking about, isn't it?"

"I don't know. Maybe. To be perfectly honest, I didn't think about it that hard. Sanura just seemed like the kind of woman you might find interesting."

"I did." The admission made him uncomfortable.

"You're really good at getting people to open up to you, but you never really reveal much about yourself. You've got a bunch of sheep you take care of—that's true enough." Brad wiped the sweat from his forehead. "But who takes care of you, Marcus? Who is responsible for making sure you're doing okay spiritually and emotionally? Who holds your arms up when you get weary? Who encourages you from the corner?"

Marcus pulled in a ragged breath. The question sent a shaft of pain and loneliness through him that was overwhelming. Brad lapsed into silence as they continued to run along the path while Marcus wrestled with the demons of the past. In his mind, he saw his wife as clearly as the day he'd met her. How many times had she deliberately slipped into his shadow, willingly blended into the background, lovingly and gently supported him while remaining his most avid and courageous advocate? How would she feel, he wondered, if she knew he was now a victim of his own cowardice—so afraid of the pain that he'd learned to stop feeling in the years since her death?

His limbs aching and weak, his lungs screaming for air, and his throat raw with unshed tears, Marcus found his voice. "I met Lily when I was putting myself through college," he told Brad.

Brad looked at him sharply. "Your wife?"

"Yes." He waited for the tight fist of grief that rose in his throat to pass. Brad didn't push him, and Marcus was grateful. He'd done nothing, he knew, to deserve the friendship Brad readily offered him. When the knot finally eased, Marcus continued, "We were students at Morris College. Sumter, South Carolina."

"I know the place," Brad said. "Been around awhile."

"Founded in 1908. It's a Baptist college." He was drawing three breaths to every stride now.

"Lily's parents were Baptists—I remember you told me that."

"Yes. And Lily was a perfect Southern lady in a time when black women had to work hard for dignity. She always reminded me of this one china dish my mother owned. We kept it on the top shelf of the kitchen cupboard, and Mama only let us use it on special occasions. It was valuable and delicate and just touching it was a privilege." Marcus pressed his lips together to fight a wave of emotional pain that far outweighed his mounting physical fatigue. "Lily was like that. Being around her made me feel like a two-bit farm kid who'd grown up in foster care and scammed my way through life."

From the corner of his eye, he saw Brad's smile. "How'd you meet her?"

"At Morris, the women's college was separate from the men's college, but the professors taught both. Lily was taking a math class from one of my professors." Marcus managed a slight laugh. "The woman was brilliant, but calculus nearly killed her."

"And you bailed her out?"

"My professor asked me to tutor her. To tell you the

truth, I don't know why she gave me the time of day. I think I babbled like a fool the first day I met her at the library."

"But she got past it."

"Yes. I was poorer than dirt. I couldn't have afforded to take her on a date if my life depended on it. For a long time, we just met at the library."

"Who finally broke the ice?"

"Lily," Marcus admitted. He shot Brad a wry look. "I've always been a coward about women."

Brad shook his head. "Want to explain to me how a man who can sit at state dinners with presidents and heads of state has trouble asking a college girl for a date?" The path took a sharp turn, and Marcus and Brad headed up another incline.

"Easy," Marcus told him. "I don't especially *like* presidents and heads of state."

That made Brad laugh. "But you liked Lily."

"I was crazy about her." Marcus negotiated around a tree branch that had fallen across the path. "But she was just like that china dish. Nice to look at and terrifying to touch."

"She asked you out?"

"Sort of. I think she knew how broke I was. She didn't want me to be embarrassed, so she invited me to meet her for a weekend picnic. We had this gazebo on campus—"

"Many a college romance has been started and ended in a gazebo."

"Isn't that what they're for?" Marcus shot back. "We met that weekend and the next and the one after that. And then when things started to get serious, we had a place on the edge of campus we'd go at night and sit up in a tree where we could watch all the couples walking underneath. We sat up there for hours. Lily had a way of getting me to tell her things I usually shared with no one. Dreams. Plans. Goals. She's the one who encouraged me to pursue the ministry."

He wrestled for a moment with a surge of guilt. Lily had always credited him with more than he was worth. "With her father's help," he went on, "I got accepted at the theology school at Union Seminary. Lily and I got married two weeks after we graduated from Morris, and in August I was in classes in Richmond. She worked as a cafeteria cleaning lady and took in laundry to put me through school." Marcus still remembered seeing Lily come home, her body weary but her smile always ready. He shook his head. "She had a college degree, and the only work she could get was cleaning floors."

Marcus took several deep breaths before he continued. "It made me angry that she had to do menial labor, but I was so wrapped up in myself and my ambitions that I never even thought to ask her how she felt about it, what her dreams were, or what she'd hoped to do with her life. The only thing I knew for sure is that Lily wanted children."

"You never had kids, though," Brad said, thoughtful. "Life got in the way?"

"Lily couldn't have children," Marcus admitted. "But I'd be lying if I told you I wasn't relieved. By the time I graduated from seminary, I was tired of being poor and tired of seeing Lily work herself to death. I'd made some political connections in Richmond, and opportunities were beginning to open up for black men with ambition and education. There were plenty of corporations and organizations that felt guilty enough about past discrimination that it almost became vogue to put a black man on their board or on their speaker's platform. The timing was right for an ambitious black preacher to walk onto center stage and steal the spotlight."

"I can see that."

"I grabbed it with both hands. I made a name for myself, and before I knew it, Lily and I were in Washington with our names on every invitation list in town." As his feet continued to pound the asphalt, Marcus remembered the irony. "The first party we went to, I had to borrow a tuxedo from a friend of ours who waited tables at an upscale restaurant. I met some people that night who were willing and eager to give money to any cause that made them look good. That's when I learned that fund-raising is more about image than substance."

"How did Lily feel about all of that?"

"She stayed out of the limelight," Marcus said. "She kept to herself except when I asked her to accompany me somewhere. She was supportive and encouraging—more than I ever deserved."

Several moments passed as they ran in silence.

"When did she get sick?" Brad prompted.

Marcus felt the pain drive a shaft deep in his gut. He stopped running so abruptly that Brad ran ahead of him again. He turned back to look at Marcus. "You all right?"

Marcus shook his head and indicated the shade of a large tree with his hand. "Mind if we sit? I don't know if I can get through the rest of this while we're running."

Brad nodded. When they were settled on the grassy slope with their backs against the tree, they sat in silence for a few minutes while their breathing slowed and their heart rates returned to something near normal.

Marcus finally found the strength to continue. "New Covenant really started to peak. We were taking in major donations and getting ready to expand into television. When Lily was diagnosed with breast cancer, I took it hard. She kept telling me not to worry. The doctors caught it early. Treatments were better than ever. She was going to make it." He balanced his forearms on his bent knees, his hands dangling loose, and stared at the thick shrubbery that lined the babbling Rock Creek. "For the first three years, I believed her. She lost her hair, and I still believed her. She was sick and weak from the radiation and the chemo, and I still believed her."

He struggled for a moment, fighting a surge of tears. They came readily when he allowed himself to remember that time in his life. "I believed her until we were sitting at the table one morning. I was complaining about some article in the newspaper that hadn't painted me favorably, and she was buttering a piece of toast. I looked at her and I knew she wasn't going to make it through the year."

Brad sighed. "Oh, Marcus. I can't imagine the pain."

"People were praying for her—people I didn't even know. For the first time in years, I actually threw myself on God's mercy. Then I told Him that He had to heal her. When she got worse, I started arguing with Him. And when she died, I stopped talking to Him altogether."

They sat in silence for a long time. "Lily would have been disappointed in me if she'd known that," Marcus admitted.

Brad seemed to think that over. "Do you think she would have wanted you to cut off the rest of the world?"

"I doubt it."

"Look," Brad said, pushing himself to his feet and extending a hand to Marcus, "I couldn't care less whether or not you decide to take an interest in Sanura Kyle." Marcus took his hand and Brad pulled him up. "All I'm saying," he continued, "is that you could stand to let yourself feel some things again."

"It hurts," Marcus said quietly. "I don't like it."

"Tell me about it." Brad inhaled a deep breath of the grass-scented air. "Not a day goes by when I think that I can't wait for this to be over. I'll see Christine and the kids again. . . . It starts to feel like there's not much to live for sometimes."

"I'm sure it does."

"But you told me yourself, God's not finished with me yet. Well, He's not done with you either, Marcus. And if getting to know Sanura Kyle will help her realize that you're a godly and honorable man who has committed your life to Christ, then what's the harm in that?"

"You make that sound so easy."

"Like falling off a bike. And one way or another, you're going to have to call her. If the president approves your appointment this morning—"

"I don't suppose there's any chance he won't?"

"Hardly," Brad scoffed. "He was just thrilled that I gave him a name."

"You neglected to mention when you talked to me about this that the summit was the day after tomorrow."

Brad's expression turned serious. "You won't be gone long. According to Carpathia, the meeting is just a preliminary discussion. The representatives are supposed to hammer out a unity statement."

"What makes him think that after six thousand years of bickering about the person of God almighty that a bunch of religious leaders can agree on anything?"

Brad shook his head. "He got the Muslims to agree to move the mosque on the Temple Mount. Now he's flying in Cardinal Mathews from Cincinnati to chair this summit. I think Carpathia's expectation is that it's all a formality."

Marcus wiped a hand through his damp hair. "It is, I guess. Hard as it is to believe, the Bible is clear on the fact that the world will turn to a common religion—some kind of Unitarian code."

"That's why I especially wanted you to go."

"I won't be able to stop it from happening, Brad," Marcus said carefully. "You know that."

"Sure. But after I witnessed Carpathia murdering those two men in cold blood and getting away with it, I feel like it's crucial we have an eyewitness at this summit." He shrugged slightly. "I don't know, Marcus. It just felt right—like God was telling me you needed to be there."

"I felt the same thing."

"I probably won't have a chance to talk to you before I have to leave for Israel for the treaty signing. The president is flying over on Saturday."

"I'll call and let you know what happens."

Brad cuffed him on the shoulder. "This might be the last time I see you . . . for a while."

Marcus didn't think he imagined the hesitation before Brad added the end of the sentence. He, too, was acutely aware of the increased danger his friend faced. "I'd like to pray with you before you go."

"I'd like that, too." Brad gave him a solemn look. "Marcus, there's no way I can ever thank you for—"

Marcus held up a hand. "We've got an eternity to settle up on who owes whom." He placed his hand on Brad's shoulder. "In the meantime, I'd like to anoint you with a prayer of protection and guidance if you'd let me."

"I'd be honored."

★   ★   ★

"Musselman wants to see you," David informed Mariette with a tilt of his head in the direction of the FEMA director's office.

Mariette frowned. "He's in this early?"

"Been here since 7:30. Can't be a good sign," David said, handing her a stack of papers. "I think he finally decided he'd better quit telling the press all the wonderful stuff we're doing until he knew what he was talking about."

She accepted the inch-thick sheaf of that day's briefings with a groan. "Great. Can't he stay uninformed on his own time?"

"He wants to be briefed." David moved past her toward his desk. "And he wants it from you."

Mariette sighed as she pushed open the door of her cramped office. A meeting with Bernie Musselman was not on her agenda for today. She was up to her neck trying to put together the contacts and resources she needed to address Daniel Berger's problems—not to mention the relatively minor earthquake that rumbled through San Francisco yesterday. Normally, the quake would have caused minimal damage, but with an infrastructure and ecosystem still recovering from the shock of the Rapture, hysteria had ensued. She'd taken calls from the mayor, the governor of California, both senators, and a gaggle of legislators wanting to know if and when they could expect federal disaster aid from Washington.

With most of the country's major cities in near chaos, the agency's funds couldn't begin to cover all the needs. She had already scheduled several appointments with members of the House Appropriations Committee to request an increase in budget, but her prospects of getting it were not good.

And now Bernie Musselman had finally decided to do his job. Maybe he could make the begging trip up Capitol Hill, she thought. She dropped the stack of papers in her in-box, scanned her desk for any additional messages, and pocketed the one from Daniel Berger. He'd called several minutes after she'd left the office yesterday. It couldn't have been overly pressing, or he would have called her on her cell phone.

Squaring her shoulders and reminding herself that Bernie Musselman's inefficiency and incompetence were the president's problems and not hers, she headed for his office.

He was dictating a letter to his secretary when she walked in. One of her first impressions of the man was when he'd informed her that he didn't use—and never planned to use—a computer. Mariette had wondered then, as she did now, how someone that out of touch with the modern world could hope to address the daily changing needs and challenges of the agency.

"You wanted to see me?" she asked him from the door.

He motioned her into the room as he finished dictating the letter. "See if you can get those to me by noon, will you, Corrine?" he told his secretary.

He might as well have called her "babe," Mariette thought.

Corrine assured him she'd try as she hurried from the office.

Bernie picked up a designer fountain pen and leaned back in his too-large executive leather chair. In his tailored suit and silk tie, he looked more like an advertisement for Brooks Brothers than a relief specialist.

"So . . . ," he said as he rolled the pen between his fingers. His expression was speculative, and, in her opinion, slightly hostile. "How was New York?"

"Busy. The mayor has some significant problems I think we can help him with."

Bernie nodded slowly. "Good. Good. See anyone else while you were up there?"

"Anyone else?"

"You were there what, two days?"

"Not quite. A day and a half."

"You spent the whole time in Berger's office?"

"I didn't take in dinner and a show if that's what you mean."

"No," he said, "that's not exactly what I mean."

"I think you lost me."

He sifted through the few papers on his desk until he found the one he sought. Even from the back side, Mariette recognized the impressive embossed seal at the top. It was an executive memo from the White House. "'From Charley Swelder,'" he read. "'Senior Policy Advisor.'" He glanced at Mariette over the top of the sheet. "I've known Swelder for fifteen years. You wouldn't think he'd feel the need to remind me of his title."

She didn't bother to point out that the federal correspondence manual mandated that appropriate titles be used in all official correspondence for the purpose of archiving. "I don't know," she said.

Bernie looked at the paper again and continued to read. "'As you know, the president met this afternoon with Secretary-General of the United Nations Nicolae Carpathia. The secretary-general was very complimentary of FEMA's efforts during this difficult time, and the president has asked me to offer you his thanks and appreciation.'"

He looked at her again. "I gave Fitzhugh $5,000 in the primary and $5,000 in the general election. My wife and both my daughters gave him the same amount."

Federal election laws, Mariette knew, prohibited higher contributions. The way businessmen like Bernie got around the rule was to give donations in the names of relatives.

"If he wanted to thank me," Bernie said, "he could have done it in person."

She didn't know how to respond, so she waited for him to continue.

Again, he read from the paper. "'The secretary-general

also indicated that he is interested in exploring with us the possibility of a joint project with FEMA and the UN that would streamline the UN's global relief efforts into the more efficient and effective type of organization FEMA is here in the U.S. The president assured him that your agency would fully cooperate in any way possible, and Secretary-General Carpathia was very insistent that your deputy director, Mariette Arnold, should be included in any and all meetings.' "

Bernie paused dramatically. "Carpathia wants to be briefed on Thursday."

Mariette frowned. "As in the day after tomorrow?"

"Yes. He's leaving for Israel for the treaty signing on Saturday. He wants to have some of the framework for this already in place by the time he leaves."

"What's the rush?"

Bernie shrugged. "Who knows? Maybe he knows something you and I don't know. Maybe he's had a divine revelation about some pending disaster."

Not exactly a divine revelation, Mariette thought with a shudder.

Bernie continued, " 'The president assured him this would pose no difficulty for the agency and that he could expect your full support.' " He finally set the paper down on his desk with careful precision. "You seem to be drawing some impressive attention these days, Mariette." He leaned forward and braced his elbows on the polished surface of his desk. "How is that, exactly, when we have an agency policy that I make all public statements on behalf of FEMA?"

"I have no idea," she told him honestly, thinking, *his policy*. One she'd eagerly complied with, relieved to be able to do her job and ignore the demands of the press. In that way, she and Bernie Musselman were very well suited to one another. Though she'd inherited him as a boss and he'd been stuck with her as a deputy, she did appreciate his love of the limelight—just as he appreciated her willingness to work behind the scenes with little to no recognition.

"No idea." He nodded, his expression thoughtful. "No idea."

"No," she said. "Why?"

"Forgive me, Mariette, but I find it curious that you've made your second trip to New York in three weeks, and suddenly the new secretary-general of the UN thinks you're capable of structuring a major international relief program."

She gritted her teeth to keep from telling him that she *was* capable, or, for that matter, that she was far more capable than he, who had never even bothered to learn the structure or key missions of the agency.

"To be perfectly honest, so do I," she said. "I've never met the secretary-general, and, to my knowledge, no one in this office has ever spoken to his people—at least not at my request." She let that hang in the air for a moment. David had already told her that Bernie had put the staff to work on tracking down Carpathia's schedule for the Washington trip. "I haven't got a clue why he'd request my assistance or how he'd even know who I am."

Bernie studied her a minute, his eyes narrow and full of malice. With a dark oath, he surged out of his chair and stalked to the window. "I expected better than this from you." He pulled back the curtain and stared out at the city. "I expected loyalty."

"I don't see how—"

He turned from the window, his expression angry and resentful. "Since the day I got here, I've left you alone, haven't I?"

"Yes."

"I could have fired you, you know. I could have replaced you with someone I trusted. The president would have supported me if I'd done that."

"I'm aware of that."

"But I didn't. I let you keep your—" his swept an arm toward the outer office—"your fiefdom. And the only thing I demanded of you was that you let me make major policy decisions and present those decisions to the media."

"And I have complied," she pointed out.

He grabbed the letter from his desk in his fist and waved it at her. "You've complied? You've complied? Do you even know what this memo means?"

It meant the what-ifs of last night had begun to come true and that soon she'd have to put her faith into practice. "I'm not sure," she hedged.

His laugh was humorless. "No? You haven't been out of politics that long, have you? Didn't you learn anything about this game when you were married to Max Arnold?"

"I learned enough to know I don't like it, and I have no intention of getting involved in it again."

"Well, you're up to your neck in it now," he told her. "Because what this says is that Nicolae Carpathia is getting ready to create a new and powerful arm of the UN patterned after this office, and he wants you to run it."

"Bernie—"

"And I've been around too long to believe you had nothing to do with that. You jerked the rug out from under me, didn't you?"

"No, I—"

His eyes glittered. "You knew I'd jump at the chance for this and you couldn't stand it. You've resented me from the day I walked in this building. You think I'm ineffective and disinterested. And while you enjoyed having free reign of the budget, you couldn't stand that I was poised to get something you wanted."

"That isn't true."

"Sorry, Mariette. I think it is."

"It's not. First of all, that letter doesn't say anything about a new agency or a new director."

He propped one hip against his desk. "Rumors have been floating for the past several days. Everyone knew this was coming, and the memo says it. You just don't know Charley Swelder as well as I do."

For which she was immensely grateful. "And it also doesn't say that the president or the secretary-general are considering me for the position—just that they want my input. It makes sense, Bernie," she said. "I've been with the agency for ten years. I have more experience—"

"So you think you're cut out for something of this scale? Are you really that naive?"

"I don't even want that job," she insisted.

"Do you know how many politicians insist they aren't going to run again but already have a campaign manager on their staff?"

"I'm not a politician."

"No, you aren't. Which is why you are in way over your head. You couldn't begin to handle something like this."

"And I don't want to."

"I'm not buying it. Nobody would turn this job down."

She drew a calming breath. "Look. I'm sorry you think I did something to bring this about. I didn't. If you want to see them, I can show you my TDY logs for both trips to New York."

He studied her a minute, his gaze speculative. "And you've never met with Carpathia or his people?"

"Never."

For a moment, she thought he was going to launch into

a second tirade, but finally, he leaned closer to her, the memo still clasped in his fist, his eyes still narrow and angry. "Then here's what you're going to do. When you get the call to sit on this panel, you're going to explain to the secretary-general's staff why you think I'm more qualified."

Ringing in her ears was the conversation with her friends that, loathsome as the thought might be, she'd be in a position to provide outstanding support and information to their mission if she were to work in Carpathia's organization. "Bernie—"

"If you don't want the job," he said, his tone menacing, "then I don't see how that's a problem."

She took a steadying breath. "It's a problem because I am not going to tell the president or the secretary-general of the UN or anyone else for that matter that you're qualified to handle something which you clearly aren't."

Momentarily, he looked stunned, but too soon the shocked expression turned to glittering rage. "How dare you—"

Mariette stood, tired of being at the disadvantage. "It's true, Bernie, and you know it. Tell me how you go about determining the per capita rations needed in a general relief situation. What about transportation and relief workers? Where do we keep the records of the reserve workers? How do we mobilize them? How many square miles can a search-and-rescue team cover in a day? What kind of equipment and hardware do you have to have when you're cleaning up after an earthquake? What if it's a bomb? Are the needs different? What do you do for floods? How much food, water, and basic necessities does a relief team need on an average day in summer weather? What about winter?"

She crossed her arms and gave him a hard look. "Can you answer any of those questions?"

"You don't get it, do you? I don't need to answer those

questions because people like me always find people like you who will do the work for them."

"Not this time, Bernie," she said. "I'm sorry."

He took a step toward her. "Are you out of your mind? Do you have any idea what I could do to your career?"

She shot a glance at the paper that he'd now crumpled into a tight ball. "Evidently not as much as you think."

"I'll have your job. Don't think I won't do it."

"I don't," she said. "But I also know that while you've been running around talking to the press and making sure your face was on every news station and in every paper in the country, I'm the one who's been taking calls from congressmen and senators and mayors and governors and solving their problems. When they need something, they call me. When Daniel Berger needed advice, he called me. When the governor of California needed assistance yesterday, he called me. So before you start throwing around threats you can't back up, you'd better take a long hard look at the mess you've created. Because at the end of the day, the people on Capitol Hill you think you can control are going to side with me."

"You little—"

"And that's where you lost the game, Bernie. You forgot that the White House doesn't make all the decisions in this town. The president only has as much rope as Congress allows him. And if you push me on this—so help me—I will make you such a major liability to the Fitzhugh White House that you and your $20,000 campaign contributions will be on the next plane back to Wisconsin."

His face had turned red. "If you think," he said, his voice lethally quiet, "that you were humiliated after your divorce from Max Arnold, then you can't even imagine what your life is going to be like when I'm through with you."

"I wasn't the one who was humiliated. Max was. And he

was humiliated because the whole world found out that he was a fake and a liar and a cheat. I don't think you want the whole world finding that out about you, so I'd reconsider that threat if I were you." She turned to leave.

"Don't you dare walk out on me."

"Sorry, Bernie. I've got a job to do. And, evidently, I have a suitcase to pack if I'm supposed to be in New York on Thursday." She glanced at the clock. "There's no more room for you in my day."

★   ★   ★

Randal double-checked the address before switching off the ignition and heading up the sidewalk to Emma's condominium in Loudon, Virginia. Brad had sent him on this errand with a note for Emma and a message that he'd make it out to see her as soon as possible. Officially, he couldn't make the trip because Carpathia's visit at the White House for a second day of meetings had him tied up most of the day.

Unofficially, he was concerned that he might put Emma in danger if he were followed to her home.

Emma's sister, who had been at the hospital, opened the door.

"Um . . . hi," he said. "I'm Randal Arnold. I met you at the hospital."

"You work for Brad Benton," the woman said with a slight nod. "Come in."

Randal stepped into the tiny foyer and looked around. "Is Ms. Pettit here? Is she feeling all right?"

"Who is it?" Emma called from the living room.

"She's improving," the woman assured Randal as she closed the door. "It's that young man who works at the White House," she announced as she led the way past the kitchen toward the living room, where Emma sat propped against some pillows on the sofa.

When she saw Randal, Emma noticeably brightened. "Mr. Arnold, how are you?"

"Fine," he told her, crossing the room quickly. "Brad wanted to come, but he's tied up today."

"We've been watching reports of the president's meetings on the news," Emma said. "I'm sure Brad's got all he can handle."

The other woman, Randal noted, didn't look as benevolent. Randal gave Emma a smile. "He does. He misses you." He handed her the note from Brad. "He asked me to bring this. It's something that needs your attention."

Emma's sister made a scoffing noise, then said, "She's not even back at work yet."

"I don't think it'll take long," Randal said. "Just something Brad can't find."

That made Emma laugh. "If I know Brad, he hasn't been able to find his own shoes since I've been out." She glanced at her sister. "Pearl," she said gently, "I'm hurting a bit. Would you mind bringing me my medication?"

"Not at all," Pearl said, then gave Randal a hard look. "She's not supposed to be overexcited."

Emma laughed as she waved Brad's note at her sister. "I'm sure this is nothing more exciting than a lost phone number, Pearl. Don't fret like that."

Pearl looked unconvinced but hurried out of the room in search of the medicine.

The moment she was out of sight, Emma's expression turned serious. She leaned toward Randal. "Is he all right?"

Randal sat on the chair by the sofa. "Yes, ma'am. He's doing okay."

"And what about Rudd?" she asked in a low voice. "What's he got on Rudd?"

Randal shot a glance at the hallway where Pearl had disappeared. "Rudd is definitely involved. It's got something to do with South Range. That's what I'm here about. Brad needs some information from you."

Emma quickly scanned the note, her eyebrows knit together in concentration. Pearl reentered the room with the requested medication and a glass of water. Randal's palms had begun to sweat, but he avoided the urge to wipe them on his trousers.

"Here you are," Pearl announced. "And it's time for you to rest, Emma. You know what the doctor said."

Emma carefully folded the note and handed it back to Randal. "Poor Brad," she said lightly. "The man's never been able to make sense of my handwriting or my filing system." Her sister set the glass of water on the coffee table and dropped a pill into Emma's hand. "Thank you," Emma told her as she slipped the pill into her mouth.

Randal hurried to hand her the glass of water. The outside of the glass was cold and wet and he had to cradle it with one hand under the base. Emma took it, swallowed her pill, then returned the glass to him. "Thank you, Randal. And you can tell Brad that the file he needs is in the third drawer of my desk behind the divider. It's marked 'collection.'"

Randal exhaled a long breath, put the glass down on the table, and grinned. "Everything he says about you is true, Mrs. Pettit," he assured her as he stood. "You really are amazing."

She leaned back against the pillows. "And tell him I said he'd better keep his head down. I love the man, but I'm not going to take another bullet for him."

"Emma!" Pearl admonished, shocked.

"I'm kidding, Pearl." Emma laughed lightly, but Randal saw the gravity in her expression.

"He'll come see you as soon as he can," Randal said. "He promised."

"I'm eager to talk to him. I've got so many questions—" she tipped her head to one side—"about him, about what he found in California. About the Lord."

Randal didn't miss the slightly sour look that crossed Pearl's face. He suspected that Emma had not found her new faith easy in the slightly overbearing and decidedly cynical presence of her sister. Suddenly, he was struck with an idea. He wiped the dampness off his fingers and turned toward the door. "Hang on just a minute," he said as he hurried through the living room. "I have something in the car I'd like you to have."

Randal pulled open the door and sprinted down the front steps. Digging his keys from his pocket, he punched the security button on the key tag to unlock the trunk.

He ducked his head inside and grabbed his gym bag. That morning, for reasons he only just now understood, he'd slipped one of his thin New Covenant Bibles into the bag with his gym clothes. When he'd noticed the stack of Bibles in Marcus's office, he'd commented on them. Evidently, the ministry had used them for years as thank-you gifts to donors. With only his grandmother's Bible to study and read, Randal had hesitated to write on the fragile worn pages. Marcus had handed him a stack of the Bibles and encouraged him to keep them wherever he thought he might need one.

Now he rezipped the bag and slammed the trunk shut to hurry back to the house. Maybe Emma had a Bible already. She might even think him naive and silly for offering it to her, but something in Emma's expression had told him she was starving for the Bread of Life. He knew the feeling. In the days immediately following the Rapture, he'd been unable to read or study enough to assuage the biting hunger for knowledge.

Pearl had followed him to the door and held it open, giving him a wary look. He shot her a brief smile before he hurried back into the living room to Emma. "I had this in the car," he explained, handing her the Bible. "It's an extra. I thought you could use it."

Emma looked at it curiously for a second until she recognized what it was. With a warm smile, she cradled it to her chest with both hands and beamed at him. "Tell Brad he's in my prayers."

"I will." He tilted his head toward the Bible. "Start in John. And the Psalms, maybe. Then just see where it takes you."

I have the information you requested. I think we should meet.—GW

Brad frowned while he deleted the deliberately vague and uncharacteristically terse e-mail message from Colonel Grayson Wells. Whatever Wells had learned about Brad's ill-fated flight from California, he didn't want to put it in writing.

The president was set to resume his discussions with Carpathia at 10:30. They'd met long into the night, and according to his morning briefing papers, they'd made some headway. Fitzhugh and Carpathia had agreed to make a joint announcement at noon about the disarmament treaty.

Wells's office was about as far from Brad's as it could be and still be technically in the House, but Brad decided he'd rather risk taking the two flights of stairs to see if the colonel was in than try using his phone, which was probably as unreliable—and as public—as his e-mail.

★　★　★

Randal curiously read the telephone number on his cell phone display, keeping one eye on the Dulles Airport

Road. He didn't recognize the area code or the number. He forced aside a twinge of anxiety and punched the receive button. "Hello?"

"Is this Randal Arnold?" a woman's voice asked.

"Yes."

"My name is Liza Cannley. Brad Benton gave me your number."

Randal recognized the reporter's name. "Oh, sure."

"I just tried to reach him on his cell phone, but I can't get through."

"That doesn't surprise me," Randal told her. "Security's really tight at the White House today. They're patrolling in fighter jets and it always screws up the cell phone reception."

"Then where are you? Isn't this your mobile line?"

"I'm on my way in now," he explained.

"So you'll see Brad this morning?"

"Yes. Is something wrong?"

"I found something," she said. "It took a while, but I think I finally found the link Brad wanted between Rudd and Kostankis."

Randal's fingers tightened on the phone. "You have proof?"

"I'm on my way to pick it up from my source at the customs office. That's why I tried to reach Brad. I need to know what he wants me to do with it."

"Don't use his e-mail," Randal said quickly. "Personal or business. It's not secure."

"He told me about the diskette."

"I can ask him what he wants to do."

"Just tell him this," Liza said. "I was digging up what I could on Kostankis when I had a hunch about his shipping enterprise. Since I had a source at customs, I decided to check the records on shipments Kostankis had going in and out of the U.S. during the last two years. In the thirteen months before the South Range story first broke, Kostankis—or his affiliated companies—had seven rail freight shipments that left New York in sea containers and were transferred to ships at the port of Los Angeles."

"What's that got to do with Rudd?"

"When the shipments left New York, they were logged with the Interstate Commerce Commission. The manifest says all seven shipments were carrying benevolence supplies donated by Rudd's company to the International Fund for Freedom and Relief."

Randal recognized the name of the nonprofit organization from his research at the Federal Election Commission. Kostankis was the primary bankroller of the organization. The fund's stated mission was public education and awareness of international democracy movements, but their rhetoric was sharply political and had twice come under IRS investigation for violating their nonprofit status.

Rudd, on the other hand, was a maxed-out donor to the loosely affiliated International Freedom political action committee. Randal and Brad had discussed the link. By law, PACs and candidates could only accept donations from American citizens, and maximum contributions were limited during primary and general elections. The Greek Kostankis was not eligible to give to the PAC, but he could pour unlimited funding into the nonprofit arm of the organization. On their own, the FEC records had given only circumstantial evidence linking Kostankis and Rudd.

Now Randal recognized the significance of Liza's discovery. "You're kidding."

"No. And here's the other thing. Because those shipments were tagged as benevolence supplies, they weren't subject to interstate taxes—which means they didn't have to go through inspection when they were transferred to the ships in L.A."

"Which would explain," Randal mused, "how Rudd was able to move international gold reserves out of South Range without detection. But the inspectors never turned up discrepancies—"

"Because during the same period, Kostankis's ships delivered nine shipments to the port of Miami. All nine were registered under the Liberian flag and were supposed to contain raw materials for one of Rudd's manufacturing plants."

"Let me guess—they never actually went to the plant?"

"Technically, they did, but here's the strange part. Those containers were transferred to trucks and driven to Rudd's Birmingham facility. On the same nine occasions, Kostankis had other shipments of durable goods bound for New England. One of his largest clients is a Hong Kong small appliance manufacturer who routinely exports to the U.S. Kostankis usually routes those shipments through Miami. So there's nothing odd about it except that the dates coincide with Rudd's shipments."

"There's a *but,* isn't there?"

"Yeah. The coincidence was a little too compelling for my taste, so I checked the Interstate Commerce Commission's logs. During that period, two of the nine trucks supposedly headed for the northeast were logged at weigh stations as being more than seven hundred pounds overweight. In the fifteen years he's been carrying cargo for that manufacturer, he's never had a truck exceed ICC weight limits."

"So he could have been moving South Range gold in the appliance trucks—"

"And a load full of toasters is in the landfill in Birmingham."

Randal exhaled a long breath. He sped past the Iwo Jima Memorial as he headed for the Constitution Bridge. "I'm almost to the White House. It's going to be tough for me to get to Brad before noon, but I'll try."

"Just tell him I'm waiting for his call."

★   ★   ★

Brad knocked a second time on Wells's door. No response. A young Air Force lieutenant rounded one of the cubicles in the central area and gave him a surprised look. Brad recognized her as a member of Wells's small staff. Her eyes were red with recently shed tears. "Oh, Mr. Benton. I-I didn't expect you so soon."

"Soon?" he asked.

She wiped her eyes with her fingers. "I sent word upstairs, but I know how busy things are today. I didn't mean for you to rush down."

"I got an e-mail—," he began.

She cut him off. "E-mail? I told Marcy to make sure she told you in person—or at least your assistant." She shook her head. "I don't think I'll ever get used to working with interns."

"My assistant is out."

She looked momentarily confused; then her face crumpled. "Emma Pettit. Yes, of course. I was just so shocked about Colonel Wells, I guess I wasn't thinking clearly." She began fumbling with the key ring in her pocket. "I guess you're here to check his secure files. I have a key to his office—"

The blood had started to roar in Brad's ears as his blood pressure kicked up several notches. He held out a hand. "Lieutenant, I have no idea what you're talking about."

She looked up sharply. "You don't? Oh. Oh, I'm sorry. I just assumed—"

"What about the colonel?" he asked quietly.

Fresh tears welled in her eyes. "Mr. Benton, I'm so sorry. The colonel was killed this morning on his way to work."

The news knocked the breath out of Brad. He sagged slightly against the doorjamb for support. "How?"

"He . . . a truck hit him on the interstate. He died before they could get him to the hospital."

Brad shook his head as he considered the ramifications. He'd pulled Gray Wells into his circle and now he was dead. He scrubbed his face with a hand. "His family . . ."

"The Pentagon will take care of notifying them," she assured him, "so arrangements can be made." She wiped her eyes with the back of her hand. "I just can't believe it."

"I understand," Brad said. "He was a good man."

She nodded. "The best boss I ever had. Sir, I don't want to be insensitive. I know you're busy, but the reason I sent word upstairs is because I need someone from your office to secure the colonel's sensitive files before I can go in his office. I'd like to call his sister myself, but I need the number from his index." She held up the ring of keys. "I hate to ask—with everything going on today. But do you think—?"

Suddenly, the diskette in his breast pocket felt warm against his skin. "I can take care of it right now, Lieutenant."

★   ★   ★

Randal pulled into an empty space in the White House parking garage and hurried from the car.

"Hey, Arnold," one of the dispatchers yelled, "you gotta sign the log sheet."

Dead ahead, the elevator arrived. "Uh, later. I promise."

"Oh, come on, man. You know I'll take heat."

Randal signaled the woman entering the elevator. "Could you hold that please?" She gave him a disgruntled look but held one hand on the heavy door. He glanced at the dispatcher again as he started to jog toward the lift. "Look, I swear. I've got to get upstairs. Fifteen minutes. Thirty, tops."

"Your boss giving you heat?"

Someone was giving him heat, Randal thought. Enough heat to burn his skin off his bones and them some. "Yeah, something like that." He jammed a hand into the elevator.

"This morning," the dispatcher said with a note of warning. "Or I'm writing you up."

"Deal." Randal slipped into the elevator and punched the button. "Sorry," he muttered to the visibly irritated passenger as he slumped against the wall, anxiously watching the numbers. There were two elevators that led from the garage level to the offices in the White House. One was reserved for upper-level staff only. The drivers, nonexecutive staff, and permanent White House employees all used the other. That had always seemed a little skewed to Randal, who knew that any member of the senior level staff in a big enough hurry to use the dedicated elevator would simply have a driver pick him or her up at the portico.

But he'd never minded the rule—until now as he watched the painfully slow progress of the ancient mechanism. He didn't realize he was rattling his keys against his pant leg until he caught the reflection of the woman's annoyed look in the brass door. Randal ground his teeth and stuck his hands in his pockets, keys and all, wondering if he'd still be trapped in the elevator when Victor Rudd managed to violate White House security and kill Brad.

★   ★   ★

Brad shot another look at the closed door as he waited for Gray Wells's computer to boot. He turned the brightness on the monitor all the way down. When it booted, he'd adjust it only enough to see. The lieutenant had offered to switch the lights on for him, but Brad had indicated the small window and told her he preferred the natural light. It gave him a slight advantage. Without the lights, the interior of Wells's office was dimmer than the corridor and open area where the lieutenant worked. Through the textured, frosted glass window on Wells's door, Brad could see the silhouettes of workers moving between the cubicles and along the corridors. He'd know if someone approached the office, but unless the lieutenant mentioned it, no one would know he was inside.

Shaken, he buried his hands in his face and prayed for strength. Someone had killed Gray Wells—someone, Brad suspected, who hadn't liked the questions Gray had asked about the C-5 Galaxy and its near disaster over the fields of Kansas. But what hit Brad like a bullet in the head was the fact that he had no idea where Grayson Wells's soul was today.

As the computer continued to grind in irritating deliberation, Brad drew a fortifying breath. "Lord," he whispered, "did I fail him? Did You put him in my path because I was supposed to be the one to share Your love with him?"

God was frustratingly silent. Marcus would tell him, Brad knew, that God delegated His work to men for *their* benefit, not because God was incapable of getting His work done without help. If Brad had missed an opportunity to witness to Gray, then God would have brought someone else across his path. In the end, the choice was Gray's.

A wave of sorrow washed over him and he desperately

missed Christine. She would have understood his grief. She would have known what to say. She'd have taken his hand and sat in silence while he mourned.

"Soon, Lord," he said. "Please let this be over soon."

At the loud buzz of the intercom, he jerked his head up, heart still pounding. It rang four times before it finally stopped. Again, he looked at the clock. Seconds dragged into minutes. Brad pulled himself together and took a yellow piece of paper from his pocket where he'd scrawled the access code he'd found in Emma's file. "Thank you, Randal," he said quietly. Randal had sent a text message with the information Emma had given him.

11:07. Time was running out. Soon, Swelder would have someone looking for him, demanding to know why he wasn't in the meeting with Carpathia. Wells's computer continued to grind. Typical White House policy: Put the oldest computer in the newest guy's office. Never mind that the guy is responsible for informing the Pentagon whether or not the president has his finger on the button.

Brad fumbled with the keys the lieutenant had given him and found the one that unlocked the colonel's desk. He opened the bottom file drawer and quickly located Wells's classified accordion folder. The thick folder had the familiar eyes-only warning on the front and was sealed with what looked like a fresh label. Policy required that employees with security clearance reseal any classified information each time they accessed it. With his military training, Wells was precise and diligent about following policy.

When he set the heavy folder on the desk, Wells's desk calendar caught his eye. Brad flipped through the pages while he waited for the computer. The colonel had several appointments down for today, but yesterday's page of the calendar was torn out. A quick search through the book indicated that no other pages had been removed.

Behind him, the computer pinged, indicating that it had finally booted. The dialog box asked for his log-in and pass code. Brad entered the information from the yellow sticky note.

When he hit enter, the computer monitor flashed once, then displayed the familiar network settings box. He breathed a sigh of relief as the network loaded and let him onto the server.

11:09. He probably had less than ten minutes before Swelder's office started scouring the building. He popped George Ramiro's diskette into the floppy drive and clicked on the icon to scan the contents.

There were two text files and a data file. He selected the first text file and pressed enter.

> If you're reading this—something has probably happened to me. If you don't know who "ME" is, then you don't need to. The second text file on this diskette has installation instructions for a program you will find on the White House main server in a hidden file named "solo." When you install the program, it will decipher the contents of the data file.

Brad located the hidden folder and opened it. The executable file began to process when he double clicked it. Through the frosted glass of the colonel's door, he saw someone approaching. He leaned back in the chair, holding his breath as the stranger neared the office. The figure was three steps from the door when he stopped abruptly, pulled a cell phone from his pocket, then turned and headed back in the direction from which he'd come.

Brad's pulse pounded a little harder.

The program finished installing. He opened it, then located the data file and told it to load. In seconds, he was staring at a set of three access codes. A string of six numbers followed by three letters. The letters, he knew, were alpha indicators for the category of the archive. PEM—Personal Executive Meetings. Those were meetings the president conducted in the Oval and asked to have designated as personal business. CAM—White House Council Advisory Memos.

But the last was unfamiliar. SRI. Brad frowned for a moment; then comprehension dawned. South Range Investigation. His heart pounding, he grabbed a pen and scribbled the access code on his sticky note.

★   ★   ★

"What do you mean he's not here?" Randal demanded.

Charley Swelder's assistant gave him a cool look. "I mean he's not here. Your boss hasn't shown."

"He's in the White House."

"According to Security, yes. But he hasn't been seen since ten. He didn't show up for the meeting."

"Where is he?"

"Security is checking. Mr. Drake isn't happy—" She cut off the sentence when her phone buzzed. Holding up a hand to Randal, she picked up the receiver. "This is Patricia." Randal turned to go, but Patricia grabbed his arm. "Yes. Are you sure? That doesn't seem . . . Very well, thank you." She hung up. "Mr. Benton's in Colonel Wells's office. He must be securing his files." She glanced at her watch. "I realize he thought that was pressing, but you'd think it could have waited in light of today's meeting."

Randal forced himself to remain nonchalant. Securing Wells's files. That meant only one thing: Colonel Grayson

Wells no longer worked at the White House. "Mr. Benton likes to take care of those kinds of things as soon as possible." Randal knew Brad had asked Wells to look into the C-5 Galaxy and the Pentagon's apparent lockdown on the incident. Knowing that Brad had George Ramiro's diskette with him and the information Randal had called in from Emma that morning, he suspected Brad was doing more in Wells' office than merely gathering a few classified files for clearance.

Patricia punched a number on her intercom.

"Yes?" came the voice on the other end.

"Colonel Wells's office. He's securing some files."

"Now? Why?"

"You heard Wells was killed this morning?"

A chill made Randal's skin tingle, and his breathing turned shallow.

"No," the voice said, sounding shocked.

"Car crash," Patricia explained. "I guess Benton thought he needed to take care of the files right away, but Mr. Swelder wants him in this meeting. Can you send one of the interns to get him?"

"Sure. I'll take care of it."

"Thanks," Patricia said. Randal was already halfway out of the office when she called after him. "I've sent someone for him. If you just wait a minute—"

Randal waved his hand in dismissal. "Can't. Gotta file a dispatch log." He exited the outer office, pulled the door deliberately shut, then took off at a run.

★   ★   ★

11:14. Brad hit the command key and watched as a stream of files began downloading to the hard drive. "Come on. Come on," he urged the groaning computer. Another shad-

owy figure passed by the office. Brad quickly closed the
download window and opened Wells's e-mail browser.
Somewhere there had to be a clue about the missing page
of the calendar. A clue, he was willing to bet, that would
lead him to the cause of Wells's mysterious accident that
morning.

He was skimming the third message when he heard the
sound of rapidly approaching footsteps.

★   ★   ★

At 11:16 Randal pushed open the heavy door of the stair-
well and emerged into the corridor that led to Gray Wells's
office. The intern Swelder's assistant had sent after Brad was
at the end of the hall, headed his way. Struggling to catch
his breath, he wiped a hand through his hair as he made his
way in long strides toward the lieutenant who appeared to
be the gatekeeper to Wells's office.

From the corner of his eye, he saw the intern closing in.
"Excuse me," Randal said to the lieutenant.

She looked up from her computer terminal, visibly startled. Her eyes betrayed that she'd been crying. "Oh. I'm
sorry." She reached for a tissue. "Can I do something for
you?"

He fought the urge to glance at the intern who was now
less than forty yards away. "I work for Brad Benton. I understand he's here."

"Oh yes. Of course. You were here the other day. The library."

"Yes." Brad had asked her to get a copy of *Jane's Military
Report* from the small research library around the corner
from Wells's office.

"I know Mr. Benton's here—"

"He's securing Colonel Wells's files."

Chilled, Randal swallowed hard and fought for his composure. "I . . . um . . . was hoping you could let me in the library again." The door had a coded security lock. "That information Mr. Benton needs is pressing."

"Of course." She touched the tissue to her eyes. "The colonel mentioned he was helping Mr. Benton with some research." She got up from the desk and started toward the library. "He actually—" Her voice broke on a sob. "He was supposed to meet with Major Nuñez today."

From the corner of his eye, Randal saw the intern pass the last bank of cubicles. The young man held out a hand. "Excuse me," he called. "Excuse me, ma'am—"

Randal held his breath. The lieutenant glanced at the intern. "I'll be right with you. Why don't you have a seat?" Relief washed over Randal as she turned back to him. "It's one of Mr. Swelder's interns," she said under her breath. "They drive me crazy."

Randal nodded when they rounded the corner toward the library.

Please, he prayed silently, *let Brad be almost done in that office.*

★   ★   ★

Brad exhaled a long breath as he watched Randal and the lieutenant pass by the door of Wells's office and head toward the library. The files in Ramiro's hidden folders were two-thirds done downloading. He'd heard Randal's conversation with the lieutenant and realized the young man was buying him some time. He could make out the intern's outline seated next to the lieutenant's desk. As Randal and the lieutenant had passed Wells's door, Brad heard her tell him that the intern was from Swelder's office—

which meant Brad had mere minutes before his presence in Wells's office aroused suspicion.

He reached for a pen and wrote *Major Nuñez* on the yellow sticky note. There, he suspected, was the source of information that had gotten Grayson Wells killed.

★   ★   ★

Randal thanked the lieutenant for helping him locate the copy of the large reference book. He'd bought Brad all the time he could. He glanced at his watch. 11:19. *Please, God, let it be enough.*

The intern was already on his feet when they returned to the lieutenant's desk. "Mr. Swelder sent me," he said impatiently. "I'm supposed to get Mr. Benton from Colonel Wells's office. Mr. Swelder wants—"

"—me at the meeting," Brad said as he emerged from Wells's office and shut the door behind him.

"Sir—"

"No problem," Brad told him. "I'm on my way."

Randal searched Brad's face but found nothing to indicate whether or not he'd finished his task in the colonel's office. He had a security-sealed accordion folder under one arm, but his expression was impassive.

"I . . . um . . . got that book you wanted," Randal said to Brad.

"Good. Thanks." Brad tucked a yellow piece of paper into his pocket as he looked at the lieutenant. He tapped the accordion folder. "I'm just about done. I'll send someone later to handle a few more details, but you can go ahead and get what you need from there."

"Thank you, sir."

Brad indicated the corridor to the intern. "All right. Let's get to the meeting before Mr. Swelder gets anxious."

15

Randal glanced over his shoulder before he slipped into the phone booth near the press room in the White House. In the elevator, Brad had pressed the yellow paper into his hand with Major Nuñez's name on it. Randal had understood the unspoken communication. Nuñez must hold the key to Wells's death, which meant he might also know who was after Brad. Hands shaking, Randal dropped a dollar in change into the phone. He hadn't dared use an inside line or his cell phone for this call.

In the corridor outside the press room, he saw the steady stream of White House press corps reporters who were heading to the motorcade outside. Because the president was making a joint statement with Carpathia at noon, the decision had been made to hold the conference at the National Press Club, where the larger room would more easily accommodate the overwhelming number of correspondents. Soon Carpathia, the president, and whatever staff was to attend the announcement would head downstairs from the Oval Office to the secured limousines waiting in the south drive. Most of the regular press corps would ride in the vanguard of the president's motorcade.

The phone rang twice before it connected. "Senate Armed Services Committee. May I help you?"

"This is Randal Arnold," he said. "I need to talk to my father, Senator Arnold."

★   ★   ★

"Well," Fitzhugh said as he stood and extended a hand to Carpathia. "Then we're agreed."

Nicolae Carpathia nodded and rose gracefully from his chair along with the rest of the staff in the room. "We are. Thank you, President Fitzhugh." Brad watched as the Romanian clasped the president's hand in both of his. "I know we will look back on this historic moment as one of history's greatest advances for peace."

"Save it for the press, Nicolae," the president said dismissively.

Carpathia laughed. The sound chilled Brad's blood. "I am afraid I am not as experienced with the media as you are. I only say what I mean. Nothing else."

Fitzhugh was noticeably agitated, and Brad wasn't surprised. Though Carpathia might feel he wrested a few major concessions from Fitzhugh, Brad knew what had chafed the president was the way the secretary-general had trapped him into offering the new *Air Force One* for his trip to Israel that weekend. The president had finally given in to the request when it became apparent that Carpathia was not going to budge on the disarmament issue.

The president shot a look at Swelder. "Is everything ready over at the press club?"

"Yes, sir. The motorcade is waiting."

"All right, then." He looked at Carpathia. "Anyone told you how this is going to work?"

"I have watched enough of your press conferences to know that we will enter the briefing room from the back. Your representative will introduce us. I am sure you wish to speak first."

Fitzhugh's face twisted in frustration. "Yeah, I generally like to speak first to my own press corps. It's the way we do things around here."

"Of course. Of course." Nicolae held up his hands. "Forgive me. This is all very new to me."

Brad inwardly shuddered as he considered that Carpathia himself might be a relatively young man, but the forces of evil directing him had been destroying the earth since the serpent had entered the Garden.

★　★　★

"I can't explain it," Randal told his father. "Not now. This is urgent." He'd decided after a moment of prayer that the fastest way to find out about Major Nuñez was to call his father. As Chairman of the Senate Armed Services Committee, Max Arnold would have expansive inside information and access to anything and everything that went on at the Pentagon.

"Helen's checking," Max assured him. "Does this have anything to do with that briefcase I retrieved for your mother?"

"Yes." Impatient, Randal rubbed at the tension in the back of his neck. Calling his father for help had not been an easy choice, but he was convinced it was the right one. Despite the strain in their relationship, he knew he could trust Max's patriotism implicitly. His father might have lacked moral integrity in his marriage, but he'd be as sickened and appalled as Brad that someone at the Pentagon might be involved in covering up whatever had happened at South Range. "Someone's still after Brad." He quickly told his father about the Galaxy.

"Are you sure?" Max demanded in the tone that had always irritated Randal.

"I'm sure," he snapped. "This isn't a game."

Max swore. "I didn't mean . . . We'd normally have something on an incident like that. That's all I'm saying."

"It may not have been an on-the-books operation," Randal said. "That's why I need to know if you have anything on this Nuñez guy. Colonel Grayson Wells was looking into this for Brad, and he used Nuñez as a contact. This morning, Wells was killed."

"Killed?"

"Probably murdered," Randal said, checking his watch. "The press conference is in twenty minutes. I've got to get this to Brad before he leaves for the—"

"Hold on," Max said. "It's Helen." Randal heard Helen's voice in the background. "What have you got?" Max asked her. Randal strained to hear but couldn't make out what she said. "You're sure?" Max asked, then said to Randal, "Where are you?"

★ ★ ★

Brad checked his watch as he headed down the hall toward the motorcade. 11:42. The president and Carpathia, surrounded by a ring of Secret Service, walked at the front of the large group. Brad and Swelder brought up the rear.

"Where were you this morning?" Charley asked Brad. "You knew we were starting at 10:30."

"Colonel Wells was killed this morning. I was securing his files."

"I don't get you, Benton. We're in the middle of one of the most historic moments ever and you're doing some bureaucratic hoop jumping with classified files." He shook his head. "I don't mind telling you, Fitzhugh was furious you weren't there."

"I'll apologize later. I felt it was important."

The group descended the wide, carpeted stairs that led to the south entrance. "When we get to the press club," Swelder said, "just stand to the side and wait until the president invites you to the platform. We've already given the press a prebriefing that you're going to head the disarmament committee. Depending on how things go, you may or may not have to make a short statement."

"I understand."

"Just make sure you toe the party line."

"Don't I always?"

The exit loomed ahead. Brad saw the green canopy that stretched over the narrow walkway to the driveway. He glanced over his shoulder, looking for Randal.

★ ★ ★

Randal slammed down the phone and jerked open the door of the phone booth. He raced down the hall, his mind spinning as he prayed desperately for a solution. There was a chance his father's information could be wrong—a chance he was about to embarrass himself and Brad, but he couldn't risk it.

Ahead he saw the president, Carpathia, and the entourage were nearing the exit. Brad and Charley Swelder were at the back of the line. Randal knew he didn't have time to relay to Brad what his father had told him. Their only hope fell squarely to him.

The president and the staff would use the double glass

doors that led to the drive, Randal knew, so he ducked
quickly to the left and pushed past a security guard.
"Sorry," he muttered as he raced out the side door. At the
head of the line of sleek black limousines, sedans, and security vehicles, Randal spotted the president's mobile security detail. The president and Carpathia had emerged from
the White House and were making their way along the red-
carpeted walkway beneath the green canopy. A Secret Service agent held open the door of the front limousine.

Randal realized with a sense of horror that the president
and Carpathia were going to share the lead car. He'd
known Fitzhugh would take the lead car to the press club,
but it simply hadn't occurred to him that Carpathia would
ride with him. Randal's heart pounded as he dashed into
the driveway and ran along the line of cars. In a million
years, he couldn't have pictured himself facing this dilemma, but his heart told him what he had to do.

A cluster of photographers was gathered on the grass opposite the driveway. They called to the president and
Carpathia as they emerged beneath the green canopy. The
pair stopped to pause for a picture.

Randal ran directly to the Secret Service agent at the
head of the president's detail. Gasping for breath, he thrust
his badge at the man. "I'm Randal Arnold. I'm one of the
drivers."

"You're not on this detail, son. What are you doing
here?" the man asked.

"This car," Randal said between broken breaths. He put
his hand on the lead limousine. "It's not secure."

"What are you talking about?"

"Not secure," he said again. In the motor pool, there
were six limousines that were cleared for presidential transport. Each underwent a complete security inspection before and after every use. His interchange with the agent was

beginning to draw attention. "Wasn't inspected this morning," he continued. "I didn't file my dispatch report."

The agent frowned. "You used this car this morning?"

"I didn't file my dispatch report yet," Randal said again. "You can check with the dispatcher. He'll verify it."

The agent hesitated a moment longer. The president and Carpathia were through with the photographers and were now approaching the car. The agent held up a hand. "Just a minute, Mr. President," he said. "This vehicle may have been compromised."

Fitzhugh gave him a startled look. "What?"

"We're not sure." The agent motioned the driver to pull the limousine up and to the side. "We'll verify it," he told the president, giving Randal a glacial look. "But I'm going to send you in the next car until I'm sure."

The president shook his head. "What's the matter with it? Someone forget to vacuum the floor mats?"

"We're not sure, sir," the agent repeated. To Randal, he said, "Wait over there. I'll deal with you after we've cleared the motorcade."

Randal nodded and hurried toward the sidewalk on legs that felt suddenly weak.

"Mr. President," the agent said, "we'll have to double up one of the cars in the motorcade. We're one vehicle short."

"Fine, fine," Fitzhugh grumbled. He motioned to Swelder. "Charley, you and Benton come up here and ride with us, will you? I don't want to stand around here bickering about protocol."

When Randal slumped against one of the concrete security pilings, he caught Brad's eye. He gave him a nod and looked skyward. The president and Carpathia entered the limousine. Charley Swelder and Brad emerged from the back of the crowd, ducked their heads, and climbed into the car.

Randal sighed. *God, please let this be the right thing.* He checked his watch. If his father's information was correct, he'd know in a matter of minutes. Randal saw the driver of the now-abandoned limousine approaching him. The car sat a hundred feet up the drive in a paved pull-off area.

"What's up, kid?" the man asked when he reached him.

"It's that car," Randal said. "I think there's a problem with it." He wasn't willing to tip his hand until he knew for certain. He dug into his pocket and pulled out four of the quarters he had left from the pay phone. "I'm sorry I pulled your duty."

The man shrugged. "No problem. To be perfectly honest, I'm glad to be out of it. Those roads over by the press club are a mess, and the president always complains about them."

From the corner of his eye, he saw the Secret Service agent continue to load the cars in the motorcade. Randal handed the man the quarters. "Just the same, why don't you go get a soda on me? I'll stay here and explain to the Service."

The man thought about it a minute, then nodded as he pocketed the quarters. "Okay, but I don't envy you." He motioned toward the head agent. "That's Agent Bowles. If you've done anything to screw up this motorcade, he'll have your job. That's if he doesn't get your head."

Randal nodded. "I know." When this day was over, he was going to be either a hero with a lot of questions to answer, or an out-of-work college student who'd managed to embarrass himself, his boss, and the president of the United States. The driver took off down the sidewalk. Only Randal, Agent Bowles, and a couple of photographers remained in the south drive.

Finally, the motorcade was loaded. The Secret Service agents slammed the doors of the limousines and hurried toward their security vehicles. The two motorcycle cops at the head of the procession started down the drive with the president's limousine following close behind.

Randal checked his watch again. The president's limousine was going through the gates toward 14th Street.

Agent Bowles turned to Randal. "All right, Arnold. You'd better be able to explain this, or I'll have your job."

"Yes, sir. I know that." Randal glanced at the limousine. "But it's like I told you. I didn't have time to file a dispatch report this morning. That car wasn't secure."

"But you don't have clearance to drive presidential transport," the agent said. "Whatever dispatch report you had, it couldn't have involved that car."

"I know, but—"

An earsplitting explosion ripped through the still air as the inside of the limousine suddenly exploded into a ball of fire. The armored car contained the blast, but the force of it lifted the vehicle two feet off the ground. The bulletproof windows blew out, shooting glass into the sky in a rain of razorlike shards. Both Randal and Agent Bowles covered their heads to avoid the debris.

The scent of burning metal and leather filled the air. Security was now racing toward the scene. From the rear of the White House, a small emergency vehicle emerged, and security guards brought fire extinguishers.

Agent Bowles threw an arm around Randal's shoulders and shoved him toward the canopied entrance. "You've got a lot of explaining to do, kid," he yelled above the din.

He certainly did, Randal thought with a shudder, knowing this was only going to make matters worse for Brad. Not only had Max Arnold's information been correct, but whoever was after Brad was evidently willing to assassinate the president of the United States. Now Brad would have to explain why his driver had been the one to expose the plot.

Randal shot a final glance at the burning vehicle. God had not allowed Nicolae Carpathia to be in that car when it exploded. Yes, God had protected Brad and the president, but He had also extended the shadow of His wing to the man who was a servant of His enemy.

Randal would probably never understand that. But one thing he knew: The future was more uncertain now than ever. And he'd never been more thankful that he could rely on the hand of God to guide him through it.

IN ONE CATACLYSMIC MOMENT
MILLIONS AROUND THE WORLD DISAPPEAR

Experience the suspense of the end times for yourself. The best-selling Left Behind series is now available in hardcover, softcover, and large-print editions.

1
LEFT BEHIND®
A novel of
the earth's last
days . . .

2
**TRIBULATION
FORCE**
The continuing
drama of those
left behind . . .

3
NICOLAE
The rise of
Antichrist . . .

4
**SOUL
HARVEST**
The world
takes sides . . .

5
APOLLYON
The Destroyer is
unleashed . . .

6
ASSASSINS
Assignment:
Jerusalem,
Target: Antichrist

7
**THE
INDWELLING**
The Beast takes
possession . . .

8
THE MARK
The Beast rules
the world . . .

9
DESECRATION
Antichrist takes
the throne . . .

10
**THE
REMNANT**
On the brink of
Armageddon . . .

11
ARMAGEDDON
The cosmic battle
of the ages . . .

12
**GLORIOUS
APPEARING**
The end of
days . . .

FOR THE MOST ACCURATE INFORMATION VISIT

www.leftbehind.com

UBRIDGED AUDIO Available on three CDs or two cassettes for each title. (Books 1–9 read by Frank Muller, one of the most talented readers of audio books today.)

AN EXPERIENCE IN SOUND AND DRAMA Dramatic broadcast performances of the best-selling Left Behind series. Twelve half-hour episodes on four CDs or three cassettes for each title.

GRAPHIC NOVELS Created by a leader in the graphic novel market, the series is now available in this exciting new format.

LEFT BEHIND®: THE KIDS Four teens are left behind after the Rapture and band together to fight Satan's forces in this series for ten- to fourteen-year-olds.

LEFT BEHIND® > THE KIDS < LIVE-ACTION AUDIO Feel the reality, listen as the drama unfolds. . . . Twelve action-packed episodes available on four CDs or three cassettes.

CALENDARS, DEVOTIONALS, GIFT BOOKS . . .

FOR THE LATEST INFORMATION ON INDIVIDUAL PRODUCTS, RELEASE DATES, AND FUTURE PROJECTS, VISIT

www.leftbehind.com

Sign up and receive free e-mail updates!